By

Luke Walker

Luke Walker

A HellBound Books LLC Publication

Printed in the United States of America

Ascent

Also by Luke Walker

BOOKS:

Die Laughing: January 2015.
Hometown: July 2016.
Dead Sun: June 2018.
The Unredeemed: July 2018.
The Mirror Of The Nameless: August 2018.

SELECTED SHORT STORIES:

Serial Killers Tres Tria: Contains 'Bear':
September 2013.
Postscripts To Darkness Vol 4: Contains
'Echidna': November 2013.
Wicked Words Quarterly: Contains '6/13':
September 2014.
9Tales At the World's End 3: Contains 'Rapture':
June 2016.
Creepy Campfire Quarterly #4: Contains 'All The
Time In The World': October 2016.
9Chews (9Tales Dark): Contains 'Hungry':
October 2016.
9Tales Told in the Dark #20: Contains 'The
Sisters In The Green': December 2016.

WeirdBook Magazine: Contains 'The Mouth At
The Edge Of The World': November 2018.

Luke Walker

ACKNOWLEDGEMENTS

Firstly, thanks to James and the rest of the team at HellBound. For all their recommendations, opinions and help during various drafts of *Ascent*, I owe a huge debt to the writers (and my friends) Laura Mauro and Julia Knight. A big thank you to Adam Millard. And once more, all the love in the world to my wife Rebecca, without whom, there would be no words.

Ascent

This one is for my parents.

Luke Walker

ASCENT

Luke Walker

Chapter One

Kelly Brown crashed to the polished floor. The impact shoved all the breath from her lungs and turned her vision into a white noise of pain for a moment. Unable to cry out, she slid to a stop against a stone pillar. Directly above, the open space of the stairwell glared down. A great stream of sunlight shining through the wall of windows at the building's front made the reception of Greenham Place feel like a sauna. Kelly lay utterly still, staring at the lift doors, breathing no more than tiny puffs of air, praying she hadn't broken any bones.

A voice inside that could have spoken from an old memory said: *the bomb went off.*

At once, denial gave a furious argument back. If the bomb *had* detonated, she wouldn't be here.

The building wouldn't be here. The whole city of Willington and the surrounding countryside would be nothing but a burned hole in the earth along with the open spaces and towns of the entire county. She was on solid ground; she could see the lift doors and she was all too aware of the hurt from the impact on the rock-hard floor. Therefore, the bomb hadn't exploded, and she wasn't dead.

Kelly took a shuddering breath, and a weak laugh fell out of her mouth. When you struggled to convince yourself you really were still alive, things couldn't get any more messed up.

If the bomb didn't go off, then what the hell was that light and what sent you flying through the air?

Ignoring the questions, Kelly eased herself into a sitting position. While her body, from feet to forehead, was nothing but aches, she was pretty sure no bones had broken or been sprained. Biting back a groan, she stood and turned in a slow circle. The foyer of Greenham Place was deserted. Silence crushed her ears—the silence of an empty building sleeping in the middle of the night, even though darkness was yet to arrive.

She craned her neck. Although plenty of sunlight lit the ground floor, a subtle gloom lurked in the corners and around the massive reception desk to the side of the entrance. The murk couldn't be called shadows. Not yet. But *something* wasn't right; something—

"No lights," Kelly whispered as she scanned the ceiling that opened for the stairwell. All the lights were off. So was the heating. The constant soft breath of the warm air circulating back and forth should have been audible, since there were no voices or the tap of heels to cover it. Listening harder didn't help because there was simply nothing to hear.

What pushed you through the air? The voice asked it again, and again, Kelly blanked the question. She rested a hand on the pillar, doing all she could to breathe slowly. Sweat worked its way down her back; she'd been wearing her fleece while at work in the library a few minutes' walk from Greenham Place—the building cool thanks to the October afternoon and an old heating system. Now, in the unbroken stream of sunlight cooking the floor and entrance, Kelly's body temperature had risen to uncomfortable levels. She told herself it came from the trapped heat, and not from any fear or panic over what had happened only moments ago—the fire alarm braying into life and the panicked shouts from her colleagues all standing around a computer to watch the video uploaded to Facebook seconds before. On screen, the lone Korean man stood by a van out in the countryside while he ran towards a high fence, topped with barbed wire in the distance. The man's tearful, ranting confession in broken English of the horrendous events he and several others had set into motion.

I sorry, so sorry. Not meant this, I not meant this. Clear your army. Run your city. The bomb goes off. Run. Run. Please run.

Then the man shrieked, terrified as another van sped towards him, bearing down as he ran. The view spun, dancing as his arms waved madly. Immediately after, a hollow pop of small explosions chased him before the view spun over and over to offer a quick shot of the lifeless miles of fields and woodland around the base.

RAF Lakenheath: the road encircling it, the huge grey sky, trees beginning to bloom, hedgerows full of spiky bushes, and all the green and brown of the land caught in the view of the phone in the seconds before the screaming man had somehow managed to upload the clip while he sprinted from the approaching van and what could only be gunshots.

Remembering, Kelly wiped her damp face and crossed towards the automatic doors that opened to the pavement. Whatever had been going on near Lakenheath had either been some joke or stunt aimed at going viral, or the police and army had dealt with it. No way had it actually happened. No way.

No way. This isn't what happened in Los Angeles.

This isn't last June.

Last June on the other side of the world, Kelly shivered. Thoughts of the previous summer similar in feel to the memory of being at school and seeing the images of New York that seemed dated to her childish eye, the impact of the second plane and the explosion like something out of a film. The memory and those images were taken to new, impossible levels last summer.

6/13, they'd called it. The end of the world by any other name. Except four months later, the world didn't realise it had ended and was still shuffling along while a global stalemate and the frantic efforts of the diplomats and an American President with her finger hovering over the button (and not hammering on it) were the only reason everyone in the world remained alive.

Most of these thoughts lost in the immediacy of her confusion and fear, Kelly reached the doors. Her foot, still moving, struck the glass. The doors remained closed.

"What?"

She tapped the entrance before waving a hand—still sore from the crash to the hard floor—at the sensor above the doors. It stared back, black and blind.

Faraway, but coming closer fast, realisation bore down on Kelly. At the last second, her mind tried to shove up a wall, blocking it. The awareness landed and came with only a dull fear.

Not one single person walked on the pavement outside Greenham Place, and not one vehicle drove along the main road that cut through the centre of Willington. Separated by the thick glass and the motionless doors, Kelly gazed at the road she'd sprinted over minutes before while the world was filled with screams and the thunder of people fleeing from the shops and businesses as if the buildings were on fire or had already been claimed by the bomb. And hadn't she wondered, in a broken, confused manner, about the lack of sirens? Hadn't she legged it from the back of the library, dashed down the alley between the old building and restaurant at its side, hit a great throng of milling people, and wondered why there was no terrible wail of a siren as there always was in films featuring nuclear attacks? Had she done that or had it all been outside her head? Had—

Kelly realised she'd been tapping on the window for at least a minute without hearing or feeling the warm glass on her too hot hand. And still, Greenham Road was completely empty of people or traffic. Four thirty on a Friday afternoon and this section of Willington, filled with shops, takeaways, *a fucking Tesco fifty feet away,* looked like Christmas Night when even the pubs had closed, turning Willington's centre into a sleeping animal.

Kelly's fear, blanketed by confusion since she'd felt the massive shove at her back a second after she'd sprinted to the entrance, pushed its way back to full life. It claimed her body as the pain from crashing to the floor had. From toes to skull, she grew as cold as stepping from her warm car to the bright but frozen sun of a January morning.

It wasn't right. Nothing was right.

A gentle ding brushed the air.

Already naming the cause of the sound, Kelly turned to face the now open lift. The mirrors around its sides, the wall of buttons marking each of the ten floors, and the gleam of the metal railing encircling the lift's interior were all invisible. Black swallowed them and looking into the lift was like staring into a hole in the earth, peering straight down into a secret space where daylight never reached.

Kelly told herself to not say a word, to not move or make a sound. The heat of the glass warmed her back, head, and neck. It took another second for her to realise she'd backed up, stepping as far from the mouth of the lift as she could.

A faint whisper of anger brushed by and Kelly seized on it. What the hell was this shit? Scared of an open lift and the lack of light inside it? There were no lights on *anywhere,* so why the hell would the lift be any different?

Before she could stop herself, Kelly pushed away from the glass of the main doors, took three quick steps forwards, and spoke as loudly as she dared.

"Hello?"

At once, the lift doors slammed closed. They didn't glide shut. Impossibly, they snapped together as if weighted down.

Her body a spinning wave of hot and cold, Kelly threw herself back to the doors, smashed her head on the glass, and did not register the impact because of the noise right behind her.

Kelly spun to see the main road through Willington's centre no longer empty but as full of life as it should be on a normal day. And her sprinting thoughts couldn't come close to making sense of the outside being deserted one moment and populated the next.

Afterwards, she'd play it all back and see and hear more than she would have thought her mind had any chance of taking in over those few seconds. She'd see the glint of sunlight as it fell upon the side window of a passing white van, the long shadow cast by four businesses—a jewellers, a recruitment office, a travel agent and an empty unit last used as a takeaway— staining the centre of Greenham Road. The sun shone from exactly the right angle to cast that shadow. The group of school kids, still in their red blazers, walked close together towards the bus stop outside the Tesco. The cast to the late afternoon light that came only in the few weeks before the clocks changed, and the days were abruptly much shorter.

All that took over no more than two seconds. All that and the growl of an approaching bus and the steady throb of traffic stuck at the lights further down Greenham Road where it met Park Road; the occasional gust of cool wind skittered along the streets, dancing through litter and over all the walking bodies.

All that and the man, barely five feet from the doors to Willington's main Council offices, stood there on the pavement with a mobile to his ear. His face, kind of good- looking in an older guy way and the spinning black shape rained towards him, *screaming* like a missile towards the man's head.

The falling office chair struck his skull. Blood exploded, turning the window red in his falling, crushed his body, and showered Kelly with chunks and lumps of head.

That's his brain, oh Jesus, oh my God!

Hand over her mouth, Kelly sprinted without thought from the entrance to the left of the lifts. She passed through a set of open doors and another reception desk; she fumbled for the smooth surface and dropped to the soft carpet.

A few moments later, a door to the right of the lift eased open. Beyond the door, a short corridor led to stairs and a curving wall of windows, letting clear sunlight inside which turned the steps into smooth, white stone.

Unseen and unheard, a man crept out into Greenham Place's silent reception.

Chapter Two

At the foot of the stairs, the non-stop pounding and thuds crashed out. Standing immobile, Simon Law stared behind. The empty set of steps, leading to the sixth floor and beyond, mocked him. No safety there, and the only other way was straight down to whoever was kicking the hell out of the door. He'd heard him—a man—shouting for the last minute. The words more or less lost, but the fear and mad panic totally clear. And now here he stood, no way past the noise and nowhere to hide.

On the next floor, the attack on the double doors increased in pace and ferocity. Wood splintered; the little glass panel in the door's centre shattered and a man's voice broke through to the sun-lit air.

"Yang. Where are you?"

No way past, Simon thought. *And definitely no way back.*

At the battered doors, a few small pieces of glass rained down, the sound of their impact on the hard floor lost beneath the man's frantic yells. Another yell of a name—*Yang*—and one half of the doors broke free. At the same time, Simon lunged for the small table sitting between a large sofa and a fake pot plant. He booted the table over; its glass top shattered. Grabbing a wickedly sharp chunk, he held it as carefully as he could and ran halfway down to the next landing. A man dashed across the corridor and jerked to a stop. Their eyes met. It took all of Simon's strength to remain where he stood. The man below was not physically intimidating. Too thin and his face tired and strained, his desperation and raw panic wafted off his skin in a stench. He'd been made dangerous by both, and Simon knew he had to tread carefully. *Even more carefully*, his mind amended. Whatever the hell had happened to everyone upstairs would have to wait while he dealt with this new man.

"Hi," he said. "I'm Simon."

The bloke stared up and spoke in a voice that sounded like his throat hurt. With all the yelling, that was probably the case. In one limp hand, he held the remnants of a shattered chair, the furniture destroyed from his attack on the door.

"I'm Dao. My son." He stumbled backwards, hit a wall, and quite clearly came within seconds of sliding down. He let go of the chair, which broke into more pieces at his feet. "My son's here. Have you seen him?"

"No." Something more was needed. All Simon found was a simple apology. "Sorry."

"You *must* have seen him. He was right here. I heard him. You're up there." Dao laughed, the sound pregnant with tears. "You must have seen him."

Dao rubbed his hands together, palms and wrists red and bleeding from his assault on the doors. "Please," he whispered.

Walking with exaggerated care, Simon descended. He glanced at his hand and the shard of glass as he reached level ground. "Dao. Listen. Do I need this? I mean, there's some weird stuff going on, but are you. . ."

Silence slid between the men, a quiet full of a threat neither could identify. Swallowing, Simon gave a slight wave of the glass. Dao stared at the shard, seemingly unable to find any concern for it as a weapon or much concern for anything at all. The effort of doing so seemed ridiculous when put against what he'd heard.

"Suppose not." Simon dropped the makeshift blade and nudged it away from his feet.

Blowing from several floors above, a whisper of a breeze rolled down, coating empty corridors, tracing its way over fake plants and expensive leather sofas sitting in the corridors with equal disinterest. That is, until the moving air reached the turning of corridor to the steps dropping to the fifth floor. There, the faint breath slid over each stair without a sound, flowing further down to end at Simon's feet. Its fading stink reached his mouth, and he closed his eyes for what felt to be long seconds but was only a brief moment. The wind died away, leaving the suggestion of its aroma and the memory of what happened up on the ninth floor.

"Dao." Simon opened his eyes as he spoke. The other man wept silently, then jabbed a trembling finger towards the doors he'd bashed in.

"My son. My boy. He was there. I heard him." Dao's throat worked, and it seemed impossible that the shout he let out came from his narrow chest. *I heard him screaming. He's only six and I heard him screaming.*

There was nobody there, Dao. I stood up on the next floor, shitting myself while you kicked the crap out of that door and I didn't see anyone.

The thought refused to come to Simon's mouth. Given Dao's state, that could only be a good thing.

Dao wept. His fingers shook as he wiped at his eyes and nose. The tears smeared over his cheeks, and fresh ones fell. "Yang," he muttered.

He staggered to the railing separating the landing from the high wall of windows and leaned on the pole. Outside, the afternoon sun streamed directly into the stairway, and Simon had to marvel at the warmth. Probably no more than ten degrees today, but the design of this place turned exposed areas into a sun-trap.

Have to tell them that back home.

He caught the thought and wanted to laugh at

himself. Until he found out what was going on and where the people on the ninth floor—not to mention the rest of the building—had gone, telling his office in Oxford about Greenham Place and Willington wasn't even close to being an issue.

Discomfort poked at his chest and throat.

Simon undid the top button of his shirt, loosened his tie, and welcomed what little air there was as it circulated inside his clothing. At the railing, Dao lowered his head, no longer crying.

"Nobody out there," he said, more to himself than Simon. After breaking through the door to see this stranger and not his boy, he was apparently close to dismissing Simon as utterly unimportant.

Unsure if he'd caught Dao's words properly, Simon inched closer. "What?"

Dao nodded to the glass. "There's nobody out there. No traffic. No people. Nothing."

Simon again inhaled the slightly stale remnants of the wind from above. It was like the last breath of a huge beast, pieces of flesh from its most recent meals already rotting in its hundreds of teeth. And that's what he breathed in along with his fear, sweat, and Dao's panic over his son.

He walked towards where Dao stood, both men freezing when a woman called out: "Neither of you move."

Dao tried to turn. His centre of balance spun; sunlight smacked his eyes and he clung to a surety—a *welcome* surety—that all this was the result of a fever.

"I said, don't move!" the woman screamed, and Dao came back to himself.

She stood at the bottom of the next flight of stairs: the points of a set of keys jutting from one hand, and her eyes huge and staring. Sweat marked her white blouse, turning it grey in places. Tiny droplets of perspiration coated her upper lip; she licked at it repeatedly. The lanyard around her neck swung as her hand wavered, and the tremor worked its way up her arm.

"It's okay," Simon said, keeping his voice low. "We're not dangerous. Just put the keys down." He tried a smile that felt thick and greasy. But then, it usually did. "Or just away. Either's good for me."

"Who are you?" The keys remained a dull silver and gold in the smooth black of the woman's hand.

"My name's Simon. This is Dao." Whatever came after his introduction, he had no idea. Confused? In trouble? Totally fucking clueless about what was going on?

All of the above.

"Where is everyone?" She lowered her hand slightly.

"I don't know. You two are the only people I've seen since… since all the panic and that."

He wanted to laugh. Summing up a melee of dozens of people all running for the lift and stairs because a nuclear bomb was set to detonate within minutes as a *panic* had to be one of the weakest things he'd ever said.

"Alex," the woman said. "My name's Alex Herron."

Dao left the railing beside the window and eyed her. "Have you seen anyone else?" he asked, doing all he could to keep calm.

She shook her head. Dao swore, the word almost lost under his breath.

"No boy? No kid? Six years old? Small? My son?"

"No. Sorry."

"Fuck," Dao said with no energy or anger, only resignation. He sat on the top step, hands limp between his knees. Simon saw the question form on Alex's face.

"He heard his son. Somewhere round here while I was coming down the stairs. But I didn't see anyone."

"He can't be here." Dao spoke to the floor, and the square of sunlight stretched out there. With each passing moment, he grew more convinced Simon and Alex were no help to him. "My sister-in-law would have picked him up from school an hour ago. They're in her house. My wife's here. She works here and there's no way Yang is here."

"I work here, too. What's your wife's name?" Alex asked.

"Lin. Qian. She works in the council tax department." Dao looked at Alex, hoping his thought about the two strangers from a moment before would prove false. "Do you know her?"

"No. Sorry. I'm in Children's Services. It's a big place, though. A lot of people here."

"Yeah."

Silence, heavier than the quiet between Dao and Simon, landed on all sides. Some of the tension between the three eased, although enough remained for Alex to keep a firm hold of her keys and for the men to keep their distance from her. She eyed them without making a sound and did all she could to get a hold on the mad race of her thoughts. Nothing of the last few moments was under her control, and that was as terrible as it was new.

The constant warmth coating the stairs and corridors lessened a degree although nobody felt the slight change, yet. Dusk was closing in; sunset would turn the sky blood-red, and the night would be as fresh as any from recent weeks. With the clocks changing the next day, summer seemed to belong to a long-ago past, although 6/13 was never more than a moment away from anyone's thoughts. For now, the two men and the woman stood or sat in the greenhouse effect of Greenham Place, smelling the sharp tang of their fear and confusion.

"What's your story?" Alex asked, making Simon jump.

"Not a lot." He shrugged. "I'm from an insurance company in Oxford. Here to talk to your Council about maybe moving our head office this way. I was upstairs on the ninth floor when it, whatever it was, happened. The panic and everyone legging it. Then… " He shrugged again, the movement awkward and not buying him anywhere near enough time to think of a way to explain what he'd seen, or heard.

"They vanished," he said simply.

"What?" Dao whispered.

"They vanished. I was in a room with five people and loads out in the other offices. Someone started screaming; they were online. The news or Facebook or something. They'd seen a clip of a guy out there." Simon pointed to the bright squares of the windows. "You've got an RAF base what—forty odd miles away, yeah? Turns out the guy was out that way, crying and saying he was sorry. He said they'd got a bomb, and he didn't want it to go off, but he couldn't stop it. He said his group bombed LA last June and they were going for London today, but he managed to get the bomb from the others. And there he was, eighty miles from blowing up London and he couldn't stop it. He was screaming like a kid by then. Said to get out of the city." Simon tried not to shiver. "That's when everyone ran. I got shoved out the door of the main offices and everything flashed white, really quickly. Like that." He clicked his fingers. "And something shoved at my back, knocking me over. And all the people, they vanished right in front of me."

"That's bullshit," Dao said. For a few moments during the man's story, his attention had managed to shift away from the raw panic of not knowing where Yang was. With his brief judgement of what Simon told him and the woman, Dao's focus fell back on to Yang. Inside, he heard the boy crying out for his father again and again, and it was all Dao could do to stop his terror from boiling over.

"No." Simon shivered. He couldn't tell them what else had happened after those horrible few seconds. He couldn't think of it.

"I was by myself. If anyone vanished, I didn't see it," Alex muttered.

Anger needled Simon. While Alex didn't sound as if she disbelieved him, he heard the doubt in the woman's voice. It made her sound like she was addressing a naughty kid.

"If they didn't all disappear, then where are they?" he asked her. Sliding his iPhone free, he waved it in the air. "And why isn't my phone working?"

"Neither's mine," Dao muttered.

"I have no idea about either. And to be honest, I'm not thinking about it. I'm thinking about going downstairs, getting outside, and calling my husband." Alex finally lowered the keys to her leg. "Anything else isn't my concern."

She turned to walk to the next flight of stairs and Simon called after her.

"There's someone else here."

At once, Alex froze. For no good reason, a nameless fear with many legs crept up and down her back.

"Who?" Dao shouted. "Yang?"

"I don't know about your son, okay?" Simon told him and Alex turned.

"Who?"

"I don't know, but I saw what they did." Simon glanced at the windows, unable to stop the horrible moment from replaying in his head. In the same way, he couldn't stop the memory of what happened on the ninth floor from creeping in. The sensation was like smoke sliding under a door, black and choking. It swallowed the scene outside the window and the man on the pavement, chewing that image with eager teeth.

"I saw them throw a chair out of a window," he told Alex and Dao, and instead of that falling chair, he saw the ninth floor.

He saw everyone disappearing.

Chapter Three

The scream is in Simon's mouth, and if he parts his lips, it'll come out. He doesn't think it'll ever stop. He'll shriek like a little kid because this isn't just mad, it's wrong. It's nothing that makes any sense, and that doesn't change a thing.

He's still the only person in the office; a breath after dozens of running, terrified people filled the space. They knocked chairs over, barrelling for the doors, shouting into their phones for their husbands and wives and children to get out of Willington, to get away before it was too late.

All that gone in the time it took a flash of white light to burn behind his eyes like someone taking a photo up close in the dark. All that turned into crushing silence while a wall of wind kicked him in the back and sent him crashing over a table and knocking the keyboard to the floor.

On his feet, Simon keeps perfectly still. Maybe he's gone deaf. That would explain the silence. Groaning, he tries to think and can't manage it. Disorientation turns his senses into a wave and all he can seize upon is the sensation of time having passed in a jump rather than a smooth motion. Nauseated, he runs for the windows, the city laid out in a carpet of roads and streets towards green in the distance, the view from up here on the ninth floor impressive. Willington is exposed, clear on a sunny day, and that sun is a hot ball of white so many miles above. Below, people pass by Greenham Place, not one paying the building any attention; people going about their business as the day winds down and the weekend comes closer and closer. A bus, two taxis behind it, and then a Transit van were coming from the junction of Greenham Road and Allen

Way. The van slowed to let a couple of old gents cross from outside a pub, and moving directly under his line of sight.

There's time to see it all in exquisite detail: shards of broken glass booming from the hole in the side of the building, each piece spinning, turning over and over as they rain towards the pavement. The air takes them just as it takes the office chair, and that chair is a falling boulder cutting the daylight in half as it speeds down, dropping with an impossibly increasing weight each second, passing window after window, spinning, turning, wheels pointing straight up, then dropping to the side, then bearing down on the pavement, and the shattered pieces of window fall with the chair that has become a blur and he doesn't have time to even think of a warning let alone yell one before the chair collides with the guy outside, turning his head and chest into a crushed mess of flying gore and snapping bone.

Nine floors above, he watches the remains of the man fall into a destroyed pile that is not even close to human. The chair grows from the mid-section as if it has sprouted legs from its wheels, and the sprays of blood paint the pavement red in a wide circle. What might be an arm reaches from the crushed body. Nine floors distance is too much to see the wrist and hand turning completely around from the rest of the arm, too far to see the split in the skin that exposes blood-smeared bone from forearm to bicep. Or the small bubbles of white light slipping free from miniscule cracks in the ground to play over the exposed bone and meat of the man's body and form small heat bubbles in the blood.

High above the mess, Simon staggers away from the window, eyes closed until he feels that he has at least a modicum of self-control. And in the darkness of his sealed vision, he asks himself why no cars stopped, why nobody ran to the accident, why everyone on their way home from work or to the Tesco or going for an evening pint didn't go fucking nuts after a man was hit by a falling fucking chair?

Every single phone in the office—from the landlines to mobiles still sitting on tables beside monitors—comes to life. The noise, a mad mix of ringtones, snatches of songs and noises, hammers at his ears, banishing all coherent thought. He runs for the nearest desk and grabs the phone, yelling hello before it's at his ear.

The phones fall silent as if they've all been answered. From the one he holds, a faint but steady breath can be heard. It's a breeze on a summer day, too weak to dispel the heat, and too faint to do more than touch sweat on his face, let alone dry it.

He says hello again although, for some reason, his throat and mouth are abruptly dry and the word falls out as a croak. In reply, the gentle breeze grows stronger, becoming a wind, and the wind is full of a terrible, ancient stink: the breath of a monster, the dying exhalation of a huge animal brought down by a disease that rotted its insides centuries ago. And it is centuries since the breath came to the air. He's listening to the sound of countless years in the past, countless millennia. This is the wind pre-dating anything the world knows now as normal and everyday. He could travel back in time to before dinosaurs, before the earth was a boiling rock floating through a new galaxy, and he'd still be nowhere near reaching the epoch of the dead thing blowing the wind of its last breath to him. His tie flaps, then dances over his shoulder. Sweat on his forehead turns cold, and the wind gusts out of the phone he's dropped to the table, doesn't remember dropping. He still hears it, though. It's right beside his head; it's all over this empty office, scattering loose sheets of paper beside the printer, knocking over a bin, then bashing into monitors. One slides over a desk, reaches the edge and drops with a mighty thud of snapping plastic and cracking glass. He can't do a thing while the air shakes. Running is out of the question; he's lucky to still be standing thanks to his now useless legs. All he can do is grip the back of a chair, sink his fingers into its spongy support and try not to take in the rotten stench of a monster's breath.

It's gone as quickly as it came. The fluttering papers and bits of debris from the bin fall still. Overturned mugs roll to a stop, and chairs are sent spinning by the gale creak as they slow. From the phone he answered, the exhausted murmur of a single word reaches him, even though there's no way he can possibly hear it.

Simon.

And that's when Simon is finally able to run from the empty office and the view of Willington, from the horror of the squashed man down on the pavement and from the dead wind gusting his name again and again.

Chapter Four

"**R**od? Are you here?"

Rod Moore's useless mobile fell from his fingers and bounced off his shoe. The sensation of the impact and the soft thud didn't register.

"Rod? I can't find you."

For a terrible few seconds, a conviction he was about to wet himself gripped Rod. His bladder had become a bursting balloon, even though he'd drunk no more than normal at lunch with his brother. Fire burned at his groin and piss was going to spray like a fountain down the front of his trousers.

He would wet himself like the little boy he had been fifty years ago.

He squatted and crawled for the nearest desk, the horrible sensation inside his middle easing a fraction. As he reached the underside of the desk and tried to squeeze his bulk into its comforting closeness, the voice coming from the corridor of the fourth floor raged.

"Rod, where the fuck are you, you little bastard? Don't make me hurt you. Little fucker. Little shit. You fucking shit. Where are you?"

Rod covered his mouth and nose, inhaling tiny snatches of hot air from his palm while the echo of the last yell rang around, bouncing from the floor of the landing to the high ceiling and back again, living out in the corridor and unheard by anyone. In the daylight unmarked by shadow, nothing moved or breathed.

Help me, Joan. Get me out of here.

If his wife could offer any help, it was no good to him here, more than two hundred miles from their home in Cardiff. All he could do was hold on to the image of her face, so kind and smooth compared to the deep lines around his mouth and eyes.

"Where are you? Little shitting bastard. I'll find you, Rod. Don't think I won't. I know you're here somewhere. Give me time and I'll track you down if I have to kick in every door."

It was no good; the scream would escape, and he'd go mad because surely nobody could take this level of fear without losing their head over it. Surely not.

Wedged into the underside of the desk, Rod rocked back and forth. The pressure of his body eased and flexed on the carpet, creating a tiny whisper that seemed too loud. Even so, he couldn't stop. If the man out in the corridor, yelling threats and obscenities, tracked him down because of the little sound, then that's what would happen. He could not stop the movement. Not without going insane.

Something laughed, the sound as soft as a strand of spider web on his face.

"We've got time. Don't worry about that."

Abrupt silence closed in, the sudden absence of sound pregnant with dark possibilities. Rod focused all of his energy on listening for the slightest noise, the smallest breath, beyond the office door.

He was alone. The man who in no way on God's green earth could have shouted such horrible things had gone.

Rod told himself if he really believed that, then all he had to do was stand up and try the door handle. Do that and take a look to the stairs he'd run up, fighting for every breath. Sure, the unfamiliar exertion would give him a heart attack long before he tracked down his brother, Clive. That hadn't happened, and maybe he should be grateful for it. He wasn't quite sure. Being stuck in what felt like a totally empty building minutes after a nuclear bomb might or might not have gone off. Hearing the voice of a man dead for forty decades had done things to his head.

The sick taste of nervous laughter bubbled up; a giggle escaped before he silenced himself. Rod kept his gaze on the patch of purely blue sky visible through the clear windows and let his self-defence systems take over, not quite aware of it on any conscious level and happy as much as he could be to be so oblivious.

No way I actually heard the man, Rod's mind whispered in a soft, calming voice. It was the sort of tone a policeman might use to calm an aggressive drunk before resorting to force. *Something* mad had happened here, that was for sure. It was possible he'd had a heart attack and all this was a dream, a bad dream taking place while paramedics fought to save the life of a man who should have taken better care of himself. For all he knew, the real world was just beyond this dream and would come crashing back down once his overworked heart got its bloody act together.

The thought was almost comforting, and more than welcome. It was essential for Rod to eventually slide from under the desk twenty minutes, which felt more like an hour, after the last of the terrible yells ceased. He rose too quickly and had to steady himself as the blood rushed to his head. The dizziness eased, and he spoke in a mutter.

"What's going on, Joan?"

If Joan knew, she wasn't saying.

"Where the hell is everyone, Clive?"

Clive was keeping quiet, too.

All right. Think. You're walking through the town and everything's normal. You've got an hour or so by yourself while Clive comes into the office to do some work; he says go for another pint and he'll meet you by four. Only at ten to four, he calls to say make it half past and you knew that would happen, but you don't fancy another pint on your tod, right? So, you take a walk through this town and you think about it in comparison to Cardiff and you think, actually, Willington is a nice place, as it goes. Clive's all right here with Julie and the kids. The boy's happy enough. You're thinking that, and you see people stopped right on the pavements, not giving a monkey's about others who want to get past them. They're looking at their phones, staring at them and you reach for them when the screaming starts and, before you know it, you're running like a kid to this place and you're shouting Clive's name as soon as you're through the doors. That's what happened and let's face it, man. You're not in good shape. All that running, all that stress and then all the running up the stairs instead of taking the lift. What was it? Four floors? Five? Bloody hell, you're lucky to have made it past the second set of stairs. So, keep yourself together here. You're in an ambulance; you're breathing from one of those tanks and you'll come to when they wheel you into the hospital. Sounds fair, right? Makes sense?

It all made perfect sense. Even without the cool, slow manner in which his head spoke to him, it made sense. Problem was, it didn't really help. That was why he grabbed for the nearest phone as soon as the interior voice fell quiet.

Before he put the phone to his ear, he knew it would be no good. Nothing on the display. While Rod's experience with new handsets didn't go much beyond the basic one Joan bought from Argos a couple years ago he knew a piece of useless machinery when he saw it.

The lack of dial tone confirmed it.

"Shit."

Rod placed the phone down, took his mobile from the inside pocket of his jacket, and pressed on the screen. Nothing happened.

"Shit," he said again, sweating freely. Panic, held in check for a few moments, was coming closer. Soon, he'd be buried in it, and what would happen then? More shouts from the corridors? More memories given voice here? The air seemed to drop ten degrees at the thought, pushing his exposed skin ahead into winter instead of autumn.

"Get it together," he said too loudly while cringing, eyes on the doors at the far end of the office. He'd bashed through those as they swung shut from a man running it to the pavement and road. Coming from the stairs like a big, fat boulder, Rod didn't have enough breath to speak his brother's name, so he'd just pounded past the silly fake plants and knocked his shoulders into the milling, panicked storm of office workers.

Through the doors to a pulse of white light, a shove in his back and complete silence, apart from his own struggling gasps.

The landing and stairs were out there. Out where a dead man had screamed his hateful abuse.

Hand almost too damp to hold the phone, Rod grabbed hold of another one. It was as useless as the first, as obsolete as his mobile. Same with the next. And the next. He ran through the office, only managing to get every other phone to his ear, the others spilling from his sweaty fingers.

Running out of desks, he came to a stop by a wall plastered with statistics and figures that meant nothing to him, then slammed an open palm on the nearest keyboard. The screen fluttered as if a connection had come loose. It flared into life in a brilliant white flash. The image lasted no longer than a couple of seconds, but that was still long enough. Plenty long enough.

Rod backed away, fist against his mouth as the screen eased to a soft black. Staring at nothing, he saw the memory of the display—the window at his back showing not the sky a few floors above the streets of the city centre, but instead giving him flames streaking down from the top of the world in colossal fingers of red, bearing down on the building, ready to turn it into boiling ash.

Didn't see that. Did not. I'm in a hospital bed right now and Clive's with me. He's called Joan and she's with the neighbours. Clive's with me and that's good; that's all I can ask for right now, even if he's his own man with his own family that's not really anything to do with me. He's got his life here that's miles away from Wales, the past, and the farm you think of sometimes in the middle of the night when Joan's asleep. You can't because your head's full of too much beer, you watch the moonlight against the curtains, and you think of being nine again. You think of that, don't you, Rod? Don't you? Don't you, you little shit, you—

Rod whirled, reaching at the same time and digging his fingers into the soft padding of an office chair. It lifted from the floor as if it weighed no more than a kitten; the long muscles in his arms flexed in a way they'd had no call to in years, and the strain in his back and chest belonged to someone else.

"Shut up."

He let the chair go at the same time as his bellow. It flew much further than it had any right to, passing over desks and chairs and no people because there were no people here, nobody but him and the voice that wormed its way into his head like a disease.

The chair smashed into one of the wide windows. Glass coughed outwards; a wheel came free and hit the carpet with a thud as the chair passed through the jagged hole it created. It dropped.

His heart pounded as it had during his mad dash through Willington's streets and into the building where he'd yelled for his brother. Rod sped towards the window, reaching it at exactly the right moment to see the thrown chair collide with a figure standing directly outside the main entrance to Greenham Place.

A breath later, that figure was a fountain spraying silent waves of red.

With nothing but white noise inside his head, Rod ran.

***

A huge crash as the running, crying man struck the double doors connecting the fourth-floor landing with the offices for Adult Social

Care; he thuds as one of the doors hit the wall, chipping the smooth white of the paint; a stain on the ground as the shadow of the door met the dark cast by the man's bulk, and lastly, the man himself bent almost double as he raced for the stairs, finding the railing by accident rather than judgement and descending as fast he could.

Unfelt and unnoticed, something watched the man race down to the ground floor where he would meet the first woman.

Something saw it all. Something pleased.

Chapter Five

Once again, Simon spoke in the tone that was already beginning to irritate Dao, despite the argument barely registering.

"We need to find the other people."

"No." That was Alex. Dao tuned her out a second too late to miss her next words. "We need to get *out.*"

Dao had walked away from them moments before. He stood now as close to the windows as possible, back to them, doing his best to think through the noise filling his mind. Finding Yang: everything came down to that. While Dao knew there was no good reason for his boy to be here, that didn't change what he'd heard in those horrible, *awful* moments after all the sounds of the terror-struck people had vanished.

For a few moments, he was powerless to stop his mind playing back the time on the other side of the doors. The evidence of his panicked, terrified assault on them still clear in the throbbing of his fingers and in the chipped paint of the wall where the handles had impacted.

He'd been running through the open-plan offices on the fifth floor, checking as many faces as he could for a sign of Lin. Her door came up on his left, closed and no sign of movement beyond the frosted glass. The second he'd reached for it, the entire building seemed to shake, dropping him to his knees. Up again a second later, he'd registered the sudden lack of noise and still moved for Lin's office before the dreamlike realisation of everyone having vanished hit him.

Not a soul in sight. Not a sound left in the air.

Moving on a sort of auto-pilot, Dao eased the office door open, exposing the room, empty apart from his wife's desk, chair, and other pieces of furniture. In memory, it seemed there'd been no gap between the surreal lack of anything and what came after it, but he knew that wasn't true. He'd had a good few minutes of calling Lin's name, trying the dead phones and tapping at her keyboard in a pointless attempt to get online. Then a brief moment of wandering around the open office, listening for anyone else on the same floor if not in the same room, and finally standing at the windows overlooking the left side of the building. Below, everything appeared normal. Cars, people, buses, and the day wound down before sunset. He could even see the top of Willow Lane in the distance, the narrow side-street where his restaurant did good business every night of the week. The horrible dash from there to Greenham Place, usually a walk of no more than five minutes, came back as he surveyed Willington from the fifth floor. It seemed everyone in the city had been trying to run from the city. He'd knocked more than a few to the pavement and road without looking back as he ran for the Council offices. Dao knew he was not a big man; he'd never been muscly, but that no longer mattered when the panic about a bomb just down the road began.

That's probably when the screaming—the *other* screaming—started, coming as if cued by his thoughts of the fright outside. From the landing and blocked from him by doors that no longer opened, his son cried for help, then squealed wordless noises of pain and terror. Unable to stop the sounds echoing around his head while Simon and Alex argued about what was best to do, Dao wondered if he'd gone a bit mad while Yang sobbed and shrieked. Either he had actually lost it, or his surroundings really had vanished, leaving him with a void filled with nothing but the awful noise that went on and on no matter how hard he beat and kicked on the doors. Suddenly, something snapped in the handles, and then there was no sign or sound of Yang, and all Dao had was a confused looking guy frozen in mid-move up the next flight of stairs.

That, and the question coming fast, coming like an out of control train; he managed to jump out of its path in time to not have to answer it.

You sure that was Yang?

Almost drowning in the awful possibilities, the question threw up, he'd yelled at the guy on the stairs and he knew even as he spoke that Yang being here made zero sense. Pretty much as there was zero chance of him joining any hunt for others; not when he had his boy to find.

"Do what you like," Dao said, and he crossed to the stairs heading up.

"What?" Simon replied, wanting to reach for Dao and not daring to. "Where are you going?"

"To find my son."

"Wait." Keeping her voice deliberately low and calm, Alex drew closer. She had the air of a loving mother, come to cheer up a child. An image, disconcerting in its suddenness, hit Dao: Alex in a church, surrounded by people all hot, sweaty, and dressed in their best while they sang gospel songs. Alex clapped, but she wasn't smiling as she praised the Lord. And in the distance, a soft murmur of a lone bell, ringing to bring mourners, not the joyful, to the church.

Dao's vision greyed for a moment. He reached blindly, found the stair rail and held tight until his eyes cleared.

"You can't go alone," Alex said.

"Are you coming with me?" he asked, honestly
curious.

She glanced at Simon, who in turn studied the floor. Even though the *no* lived and breathed between them, they were spared the embarrassment of answering Dao by the careful approach of someone coming up from the floors below.

"Hello?" A bloke. Older than Dao or Simon by the sound of it. And not English. He had a slight accent Dao couldn't place from single word.

"You up there? We need help."

Welsh, Dao thought.

"We're in trouble. The doors are locked."

However, many people were down there, they were still coming. Despite the almost overwhelming urge to begin his search for Yang at the top of the quiet building, Dao joined Alex and Simon. Alex held her keys high again, and Simon's fists hung by his thighs, the pose unconscious.

"We need help," a woman called. She sounded younger than the Welsh guy. "You have to help us."

Frowning, Alex took a step closer to the stairs that led down. Confusion merged with the background fear, non- stop since the first of the disbelieving murmurs about the bomb rose. It couldn't be *her*. It couldn't be Kelly.

"Something's happened; we can't get the doors open downstairs and—"

"Kelly?" Alex said weakly.

Two people came into view at the curve of the floor below. They met a big man, easily in his sixties, dressed in smart blue jeans and a light jacket. Beside him, a woman who wasn't much more than a girl. Dao's quick eye took in their clothing and appearance in a glance; the big guy's gut; the girl's small stature, her face pretty, her skin black like Alex's.

"Alex?"

Both women ran at the same time, Alex dropped her keys and descended as the girl called Kelly dashed up the stairs. They collided, both talking over each other, babbling, and Alex wiping at her eyes.

The other one's not crying, is she?

Dao looked behind as if someone had spoken the thought. Above, not a thing moved. Even the dust motes—visible in the sunshine if you looked hard enough—were still.

"You know each other?" Simon asked.

"This is Kelly, my little sister," Alex said. On the stairs, the women parted, and the Welshman ascended, keeping his distance from Alex and offering a smile.

"Hello. I'm Rod."

"Alex." She finished wiping her eyes and spoke to Kelly. "Are you okay? Are you hurt?"

"No. I fell over earlier, but it's all right. I—"

Kelly broke off. Dao sensed Simon looking at him, as if to ask what was happening. Ignoring the other man, Dao took a few steps down.

"Something's happened outside. Or in here. I don't know. There's nobody anywhere. I ran in here, looking for you when it all went off outside, but I only just made it inside when. . .something happened." Kelly looked as if she wanted to say more but fell silent.

"I know. The phones don't work, and the computers are off."

Simon interrupted Alex. "So are the lights. And the heating." He raised a hand in a shy wave. "I'm Simon." Dao glanced above, noting for the first time the dark bulbs. In the dazzling sunshine, the lack of fake light hadn't registered. With the trapped warmth, neither had the failure of the building's heating.

"Did you see anyone else?" Alex asked.

"I… " Kelly glanced at Rod.

"I think I killed someone," he said quietly. "I panicked when everyone vanished and when I… Jesus." He turned away, shoulders jerking. "I panicked, okay? I lost it and threw a chair. It went through a window and killed someone outside."

Alex placed her hand softly on Rod's shoulder and his sobbing, close to inaudible, eased.

"Nobody came, Ali," Kelly whispered. "Out there when the guy and the chair, nobody came. They just walked by."

Like they didn't see him. The voice spoke again from behind Dao. He resisted the urge to turn.

They don't look that happy to see each other, do they?

The slightly snide tone was unlike his usual thoughts but, even so, there was some truth to it. Kelly and Alex now stood a few steps from each other, their embrace seemingly forgotten.

"Okay." Alex sounded as if she'd taken charge without considering it. The same thought occurred to Kelly as Dao. "We go downstairs, and we get out."

"I tried the doors." Kelly pointed to Rod. "We both did when Rod got down there. They're locked."

"Then we find other doors or a window. I don't care what. We smash it if we have to."

There was no need for any thought or voice to point out the undercurrent of something not quite in control floating below Alex's words. They all heard it clearly.

As Simon passed Dao, nodding a greeting to Rod and offering the man his hand, Dao backed up. He'd meant to move without making a sound; his trainer squeaked on the polished floor and the others turned.

"I'm going upstairs." He kept moving. "Got to find my son."

"What?" Rod asked while frowning. He searched the others' faces for clarification.

"He's heard his son here somewhere," Simon explained in a mutter.

"You get out; call the police or whoever. I don't care, but I'm not leaving here without Yang."

Dao's heels connected with the first step. He pictured the landings, corridors, and offices of the floors above. They all were presumably empty as the rest of Greenham Place, all one big hiding place for his terrified boy.

"Listen, Dao." Simon raised his hands in a calming gesture. Probably the same movement he made in business meetings when things got heated.

"You get out and get help. I'm finding Yang."

Dao didn't give Simon or the others chance to speak or try to stop him. He whirled and ran for the next floor, aware of their eyes on his retreating back, hearing them cry his name, and unaware of the sound as entreaties to stop and come back.

Above, the empty floors waited for him.

Chapter Six

Despite the majority of Willington's population viewing Greenham Place as familiar as the cathedral half a mile away, it was not an old building.

Growth through the late nineties and beyond, and rapid expansion of the population, meant the town hall, now seen as a quaint throwback rather than useful, wasn't up to the job of operating the city council's services. The city needed a new base of operations, somewhere to direct the working processes of a city embracing the twenty-first century—or so said the council when they had to demolish a long row of shops that, in turn, had once been Victorian houses, as well as destroying a small woodland forming the city centre's perimeter and the first of Willington's suburbs. The protests, the letters to the local paper, the complaints from nearby businesses that they'd suffer with all the noise—not to mention the roadworks as a result of putting in a new system—didn't make a bit of difference. Willington was growing. People needed to have the service they expected of a developing city and the elected officials were the people to give them that service.

So, the shops were purchased, closed, and demolished. The woodland was cleared; the trees hacked down and the grass, at least two hundred years old, was crushed by the heavy weight of concrete as the land became a smooth, flat canvas. Then the builders and their machinery moved in.

The complaints died away because they were doing no good for the people unhappy with the work; the building grew into a hulking mass of brick, glass, and steel with scaffolding encircling it. The dozens of men in their hard hats and hi-vis jackets came and went while the sun shone, the wind grew stronger as autumn closed in and the clocks changed, and the council kept the name of the new development under wraps. The construction grew beyond the tallest buildings in Willington's centre: its wall of windows and its roof seeing the backstreets, the snaking roads, and the people passing by on foot and by car. They gazed on all while the sun turned the glass into white pools and the rain dribbled down its new gutters to sink into the pipes below the foundations and into the dark under the city.

All the while, the structure saw the city and came to know its people.

Days and months passed while the people of Willington grew used to the noise of the work. It seemed to most of them that the building had always been there. The memory of the pretty wooded area and the relative peace of walking through it, while the takeaways and pubs were still nearby, became an image they might have been told about years ago. It belonged to their parents; it was as dated as the seventies and eighties and didn't have much place well into the second decade of a new century.

Progress, they thought. Times were changing, so they'd change, too.

And as the building developed, third floor growing into the fourth, then the fifth, and the land under its base slept and dreamed. But its dreams were not restful.

In the pitch-black vacuum below the earth, where even the storm of machinery moving tons of bricks couldn't reach, a tiny light shone, its illumination cold and sharp.

It dreamed. It waited.

When the last of the machinery was removed and the mayor gave Greenham Place its name in an opening ceremony, the icy radiance like that of a tiny star gazed upwards to its sky and saw the realm above. It saw where people walked; it saw through the eyes of the building to the country and beyond. It heard anger and fear and savoured both.

Men and women filled Greenham Place. They worked, they laughed, and they argued. They left in the fierce red sunsets of the winters. They came in the dampness of spring mornings, and they ate their lunches in July when the air-conditioning battled the summer.

Below, the light listened. Watched.

Waited.

When, far from the city fewer than two hundred thousand people called home, another city was turned into fire, the light in the dark earth began to make its slow way to the surface.

And while the majority of the people trapped in Greenham Place descended the silent flights of stairs and the one who'd gone in desperate search for his child heard only the hollow tap of his own shoes on the floor, the light broke through the pavement directly outside the building's main entrance.

Nobody saw it. Nobody commented. Willington had again become the shell Kelly saw from the foyer. Even the wind had deserted the roads, streets and parks.

The light spread in a small pool, too hot for human flesh to take without burning, and closed in on the remains of the ruined body.

With one smooth motion, the legs of the crushed man slid around, bone and torn sinew making no sound as they turned in an impossible manner. The remnants of a shattered hand pushed at the ground, slipping through the wide circle of blood, smearing it into the knuckles and nails.

The light drew closer to the moving body.

While the exposed bone of a kneecap glowed in the new light, the body rose to a standing position. Above the waist, the stomach and chest were not recognisable as human. They'd become a cave-in, a mid-section smeared with ruptured organs while relatively whole innards attempted to squeeze their way through the giant gash running the width of what had been the man's ribs. On a dangling piece of flesh, loose skull still contained one unseeing eye. The other eye had landed on the window and stuck there.

The boiling light crossed the gap between it and the pool of blood. Its touch on the red liquid acted as a scour, wiping the blood clean and turning the slight grey of the paving slab a bright white. A moment later, it fell upon the body's feet, then streaked higher, swallowing torn skin, bone and muscle, catching the remains of the man's shape as it dropped. The last to be burned into nothing more than ash was the open eye. As the roasting white took it, the eye closed in a slow wink.

The body was removed, and the pavement became a smooth, unmarked surface. The illumination raced to the great smears of blood coating the windows.

They were wiped from existence in less than five seconds.

The scorching light eased back to the ground and vanished as silently as it had come. On all sides and further out to the streets and roads not visible from Greenham Place, Willington was as hushed as the deep pocket of earth living underneath the building's feet.

A moment later, the same doors Rod had eased open before encountering Kelly parted with slow, frightened care.

Chapter Seven

After Dao raced up the stairs and the noise of his sprint faded, there didn't seem to be any point in hanging around. The old guy who'd come up with Kelly (Alex remembered his name was Rod) said they should go after the lad, but Alex wasn't having that. Letting the guy go and not making more of an effort than shouting after him surprised her. Alex considered herself caring and decent, without going overboard. A few quid to the homeless man, who always sat between her branch of HSBC and Starbucks; calling on Mrs. Jenkins who lived next door alone since her husband died last year. There was more to do, always more to do, but she had to focus her energy on what *really* mattered and that was her family: Carl, and more importantly, her twin daughters. Alex wanted to be a mother Charlotte and Louisa looked up to and maybe, if they'd been there, she'd have gone after Dao, told him they had to stick together.

But they weren't, and she hadn't because getting out of this strange, frightening building, with its disappeared workers and weighty silence, was her sole purpose.

Alex was the first to speak after Dao's departure.

"We go straight down, and we get out through any door we can," she said.

Simon trotted past her, turning back as if to ask what she was waiting for. Alex eyed him until he glanced at his feet. Kelly behind her, Alex passed Simon and started down. Bringing up the rear, Rod offered Simon a smile that did not feel genuine, and the men followed the women.

The hush of the landings took them, as did the non- stop light and warmth raining through the windows. Whoever designed the place had known what they were doing by using sunlight, Alex often thought. The open-plan offices and wall of windows on the east and west sides caught the morning and afternoon sun, turning the stairwell into a brightly exposed space. She usually found it welcoming, but now, with the stress of not knowing what was going on and the potential of a nuclear bomb less than fifty miles away, fine beads of sweat oozed down Alex's neck and collected under the collar of her blouse, dampening her breasts.

After a hot shower and a drink later (maybe a few drinks), she would have chance to focus on everything else that was happening here. The old guy apparently killing someone with his thrown chair, the stress of not one bloody phone working which meant no way of contacting Carl, and not forgetting what might be some Korean nutcase with a bomb out near RAF Lakenheath. Alex didn't believe the mad events of LA the previous June were coming to her city, not in Willington. No way. But even so, there'd been a terrifying few minutes when she *had* believed it. Now, all she could think of was home, with the girls and Carl cooking something in the kitchen. Once the mystery had been explained. Once she'd had time to call the hospital.

They reached the top of the second-floor stairs before she voiced the niggling fear of the last twenty minutes to check on her dad.

"Have you spoken to Anthony today?" she asked Kelly, glancing behind and not missing how her sister's eyes darted from side to side. Also catching the shifty glance, Rod found it easy to dismiss. The terrible moments before he'd found Kelly were a loop in the background of his thoughts. Same with knowing what he'd done to the man outside.

Kelly replied to her sister. "No. Called him last night. He said there was no change."

Alex knew her dad's condition. She'd called her cousin at lunchtime to be told Dad slept his forced sleep and the nurses said he was comfortable, exactly as they said he had been for the last six weeks. And really, why was she asking Kelly? The girl wasn't anywhere near as fussed as Alex might have expected. Not like she would have been with her own father.

"Everything okay, love?" Rod asked, bringing Alex back to herself.

She nodded and faced ahead again. Concentrating on each step, she spoke over her shoulder. "Our dad's in hospital. He had a car accident recently, so we take it in turns being with him. Our cousin Anthony was there last night and this morning."

"Sorry to hear that," Rod said. "I hope he's all right."

"Yeah." That was the other guy, skinny white boy Simon and his weak offering.

Alex stumbled and slapped her hand down hard on the railing, then righted her pace without comment.

Skinny white boy? What was that? She didn't think of people in terms like that. Never had. Her parents— especially her mother—believed there was good in all people, despite their own experiences of racism when they arrived in England back in the sixties.

Treat people well, her mother said, and it didn't matter that she'd been dead for four years. The woman could have spoken right beside Alex, the soft smell of her perfume as welcome as her lovely smile. *Treat them nice and let them go if they don't do the same.*

Alex shook off the strange, slightly alien thought about Simon, as well as letting go of her mother's voice and the phantom aroma of perfume.

"Thanks," she said. "He's in a coma, our dad, but they're hoping he'll come out of it soon."

"*Your* dad."

"What?"

Alex stopped without registering it and faced Kelly without feeling her body turn. Inside, the need to keep going down and get out was as strong as ever; she saw herself doing exactly that and stepping into the slight chill of five o'clock, but her body and head had other plans, it seemed.

"What was that, Kel?"

Kelly frowned. "I didn't say anything."

"Yes, you did."

"No. I didn't," Kelly replied in a tone Alex hadn't heard from her in a few years; not since Kelly was about fifteen and had become, frankly, a bit of bitch since their mother passed away. The tone a mocking, superior reply that implied Alex was closer to seventy than thirty and should stay out of matters involving young people.

Quickly, Alex studied the men's faces, searching for a giveaway. She saw only a slight confusion.

So, what? I'm hearing things? I'm making them up?

That was bullshit. Kelly had muttered her negation, her rejection of them as full blood sisters the way she'd always felt. It didn't matter that they'd grown up together or that they shared a mother. Different dads meant, to Kelly, they weren't blood in the way most sisters were. She'd made that pretty clear quickly back when all that business with Dean went on the year before last.

"Let's just get out of here." Inwardly, Alex berated herself. It wasn't as if anyone but her had stopped their descent. None of the others were hearing stuff that slowed them down.

I didn't hear that.

Mouth set firmly, Alex turned back to the stairs and started down again, Kelly and the men following. At the end of the line, Simon peered back the way they'd come, wondering if he had heard a whisper or just imagined it. Nothing moved behind them. Trotting to keep up, he stayed close to Rod. They reached the last step, crossed into a wide beam of sunlight, and Alex's body temperature dropped. Their surroundings of building, stairs, glass and heat vanished in a breath. A savage chill of mid-winter had come, exposing her to the wind and air as they sank deep claws into her naked flesh. On all sides, unbroken, open land spread in dead fields. The lonely cry of a solitary bird echoed across the acres; the high-pitched whistle of the wind answered it and carried it at the same time, and Alex turned on the spot, horror keeping her in place.

A churchyard was close by, grown from the lifeless ground in a second even though there'd been nothing but stunted grass and the freeze of the day in its place a moment before. Twisted trees poked their branches towards the grass. Old trunks and rotting foliage spread over the yard, meeting thick bundles of bramble bushes. The green of the shrubberies should have gleamed in the cold sunlight. Instead, they were faded, sickly.

This was a dead place, somewhere to do nothing but live in the awful weight of fresh grief and be stuck there forever.

And the church, *oh my god the church. The church. No.*

Jutting from the earth where there'd been only more brown grass and ancient trees all twisted together, the church loomed as large as a cathedral, impossibly bigger than it was fifteen years after Alex last visited it. The grey stone was bleached white in places, bricks and mortar cracked and crumbed, and the windows all with jagged holes and flaking glass. The building didn't simply exist on the grass, it ate the space it filled, chewing it, mashing it into a gooey paste, and then swallowing what was left where it would be dissolved in the icy world of its stomach — broken down into nothing as if it had never been.

Alex's darting eyes took in more and more of the old building, even as she screamed inside that it couldn't be here because it was a good place, a happy place of light and worship and decent people. It didn't belong on a dead day in a dead place with dead wind caressing its exterior, then blowing in through the holes and pitted scars of its frame.

Or through the doors creaking open, the old wood buckling and crumbling as the hinges gave way, snapping before the rusting metal clattered to the ice-cold stone of the steps.

One half of the doors broke free from the frame. It split into several pieces on impact with the ground; the other half hung loose, and the pitch-black night living inside the church swirled, danced, *beckoned* her.

A skinny arm, unclothed so she could see what the disease had done to the flesh and muscle, jutted out of the doorway. More and more of it exposed as the figure slightly beyond the opening came closer. A finger uncurled, the bone no thicker than a twig, and the skin as thin as tissue. It curled, uncurled, curled again, and the woman's voice barely a croak didn't live in the air and earth as hard as rock. *Nothing* lived here. The voice was the air and earth; it was every part of this dead place and dead day.

Alex. Come inside. It's time for church.

A lone bell rang once from somewhere inside the building, the sound not for welcoming the worshippers or to praise God on a Sunday morning but to bring them in for a funeral, to mourn and ache with their loss. They would file inside, weeping, broken with their hurts, and there'd be no comfort from God or faith here. There'd be nothing but the lonely wind blowing over the open land and through the gnarled branches while the sunlight faded, and the sky burned with the bloody red of a winter twilight.

And the heat.

The heat was back, closing in on all sides, come to burn her to ash and turn the universe into a blank canvas.

"Alex?"

She muttered a reply that was lost to her, reached blindly, and found a hand. Kelly's hand.

Alex landed back in herself. She remained in the large square of sunlight painting the floor of the landing into a smooth white. Behind Kelly, the men stared at her, neither looking as if they dared speak.

High above, a church bell gave a muted ring, the sound echoing as if falling down a deep tunnel. It faded into nothing and Alex thought:

I did not *hear that.*

"You okay?" Kelly asked.

"Yeah." She had to whisper it. Anything else felt like it would take way more effort and strength than she had. Alex cleared her throat. "Just had a moment." She waved an arm that felt like it might fall off, encompassing the warm air. "It's hot in here."

Rod shifted a fraction on the spot. In his wide, pleasant face, Alex saw an emotion she named immediately.

Recognition.

"What?" she said, slightly too close to a shout.

"Nothing, love."

Whatever just happened, it's happened to him, too.

She didn't care. She *wouldn't* care while her girls were outside, and she was inside this strange, empty building.

Alex set out again, fingers trailing on the railing. With every step, leaving the mad sights and sounds of the church out in the middle of nowhere became marginally easier. She held hard to that idea as they took the last flight of stairs and approached the doors opening to the foyer. Believing it was easy.

Or so she told herself.

***

Dark pools stained the pavement of Greenham Road, sliding together to form flat puddles. Although the daily temperature had yet to reach any higher than thirteen degrees, the small section of land turning black was rapidly becoming its own atmosphere. In the silent heat, the puddles flowed upwards like tar. With no human eyes to witness, the first of the tar-shapes grew legs.

Chapter Eight

*T**his is like being in a church.*

For some reason, Dao found that thought unpleasant. It was like turning over a rock and watching the woodlice and centipedes scurry for darkness. While he'd been in a church only a handful of times for friends' weddings and a couple of funerals, he knew the quiet of old buildings. It was a specific sort of hush as people gathered and sat, studying their feet on the stone floor, waiting for serious business to begin.

Up here on the tenth floor of Greenham Place, that same expectation wouldn't leave him. In the same way, the idea of speaking at any volume higher than a whisper seemed as if it would invite stern looks and silent admonishments from other people.

What other people?

He stood at the entrance to the main corridor of the tenth floor. Unlike the others, this floor was not comprised of open-plan offices. The tenth was the money floor, the executives and the decision-makers. Up here, the big choices for the running of the city were made. Spacious offices, the doors all closed, lined the left-hand side while several meeting rooms, with chairs tucked tidily under the round tables, took up the other side. Leather sofas, presumably only for decoration rather than actually sitting on, were pressed against the magnolia walls with healthy-looking plants placed between them. Dao guessed they were as fake as any of the others he'd seen on the lower floors. The corridor became a two-way junction beyond the last sofa, leading to more offices down the right hand turning. The left was nothing but plain walls that ended at a solid door with an alarm bar covering its centre. None of the executives walked to the left turning; they had no reason to. The door was always locked. The maintenance staff had the keys, and even they rarely had reason to disengage the alarm and open the doors. Occasionally, a contractor required access through to the air-conditioning units or heating systems. Otherwise, the entrance to the small room below the roof was kept locked and the hatch that opened the way was bolted shut.

As Dao crept along the corridor, fingers trailing on the smooth wall, the air inside the roof access listened to the man's slow, careful steps. Underneath the hatch, a ladder jutted from the wall, bolts as large as a man's fist holding it to the wall. Each of the ten rungs was cold enough to stick to skin and tear it from fingers and thumbs. Above the ladder, the hatch was a wide rectangle, smooth and sealed by three chunky bolts and a padlock hanging like a growth. The metal of the hatch was as cold to the touch as the ladder and the room. No breath fogged the air; no exhalation sent steam from a mouth or nose. Even so, the air listened.

Unaware of anything but his own barely controlled fear, Dao walked on and kept Yang's name in his mouth instead of screaming it into the silence. The others had to be out by now, he thought. They'd get a signal or get a working phone and call for help and the police would come; ambulances, too, and they'd make sense of this strange place and this mad situation.

He reached a door, a small plaque in its centre proclaiming: **Alan Letts. Head of Service.**

"What do you service, Mr Letts?" Dao asked nothing and closed his mouth to keep a mad giggle inside.

Not believing the door would move, Dao pushed on the handle. The door opened, sliding over the plush carpet and revealing a desk almost the width of the room, along with polished white walls and a sofa deep and thick enough to sleep on. A few filing cabinets sat against walls, their drawers firmly closed, and clear windows overlooked the desk and computer. Even from the other side of the room, the view of blue sky and the tips of the surrounding buildings told Dao this was the room of someone important, someone from the upper echelons of management. Not that it mattered. If his son was anywhere near here, it wasn't important if the office belonged to the Grand High Chief of the Council or a cleaner.

"Yang," Dao whispered and crossed towards the window.

In the stillness of the corridors, the door to the roof access stood wide open. A wall of frozen air crept towards the junction. At the same time and several floors below, Simon was peering behind the small group and dismissing the tiny noise as imagination.

"Yang, where are you?" Dao spoke as loudly as he dared to his faint reflection in the window. It was only after asking his question that Dao realised he was just as scared of no answer as he was of hearing his boy begging for help again.

At that, Lin spoke to him, and Dao stood still, listening to his wife's soft voice.

You didn't hear a thing. I don't know what's happening where you are, but I do know Yang isn't with you. All you have to do is accept that and leave. We're out here. We want you home, my love.

Hot tears threatened. Dao closed his eyes, almost managing to keep the weeping trapped. A few tears fell; he inhaled a shaking breath, then another, before opening his eyes.

Lin—or whatever part of him spoke for his wife—was right. Whether or not the bomb had gone off, there was no reason that made any sense for Yang to be in Greenham Place. Of course, if the bomb had gone off, then he and the other people presumably heading for the exit were dead, so what did it matter?

"Funny," Dao whispered. He didn't believe the bomb had detonated. The normality of this office building and the little visible chaos beyond its walls was proof of that. He didn't stand in the middle of a torn apart structure; its windows nothing but blackened holes and its innards of metal cooking in the fire of a nuclear attack. Willington was not a hole in the earth, and the sky was not aflame. Whatever had happened to him and to Simon, Rod and the two sisters, it was *not* the terrorists' bomb blowing an RAF base, the hundreds of square miles of green around it, and this city into hell as they'd done to Los Angeles last June.

You sure about that?

"Yes."

Refusing to ask himself any more questions, Dao took the last few steps to the window and gazed straight down to the road and pavements.

Several seconds passed before his brain registered the problem. Later, Dao would ask himself if the delay was deliberate. Perhaps his mind simply couldn't take it, and so he refused to do so immediately.

Ten floors above the centre of the largest city in the county, Dao watched precisely nothing. No cars took Greenham Road to either of its ends. Nobody crossed at the lights. No buses dropped off their passengers outside Tesco, nor has any anyone collected shoppers laden with heavy bags. Dao's eyes darted from the shop frontages to the three pubs visible from his vantage point. No smokers near the entrances, no guys selling the Big Issue, no traffic, no bodies, no movement, no shadows, no winding down of the late afternoon, and no approaching evening bringing sunset an hour earlier than Sunday's would after the clocks changed.

Nothing.

Willington had become a painting. Dao stared at a flat, lifeless landscape created by someone with enough talent to produce the idea of a city centre, but neither the skill nor time to develop the image into a living, breathing canvas. The city he'd known since moving here as a child twenty years ago was an idea of a city; it needed blood and breath to turn it into a real place. It needed light and dark in contrast. As it was, it had neither. When his mind insisted, there were no shadows on the pavements, that the takeaways, pubs, and bus shelters outside and opposite the supermarket sent no shade over the cracks and lines in the paving slabs. It had been exactly right. The high sun, still strong even if it wasn't summer light, might as well have been hidden behind cloud.

And what about the guy? What about the dead man, crushed by Rod's falling chair?

Dao trotted to the end of the window and stretched to get a better view. While he faced more of the right-hand side of Greenham Place than its front and the entrance, he had enough of a view to tell the squashed man wasn't there. Neither was any mess of sprayed blood.

The sun.

"What?"

The thought muttered again.

The sun.

Dao's mind stuttered back a few seconds to his realisation the sun cast no shadows. What about the sun? What was the problem?

It turned the blue of the sky into a dazzling white, almost directly opposite from Dao's position. The illumination was strong enough to make him squint and that…

That was wrong.

Dao backed away, doing all he could to take a firm hold of his racing thoughts. Unable to stop the images forming, he saw the house he and Lin bought together five years ago along with their pretty garden, so well-tended by Lin. He saw the high fence bordering its end from beyond the small woodland, and the sunrise each morning turning the green of their grass and the brown of the large oak near the fence into a shining carpet.

The sun rose in the east. Their garden faced east.

And from where he stood inside this horrible, dead building, their house was east.

So why was the sun setting in the east?

The bitter chill in the corridor a few feet from the door of the office of Alan Letts, Head of Service, caressed the floor and wall. It reached for the door.

Still backing away from the window, Dao whispered: "Yang."

A mammoth shriek answered him, and surely no child's lungs could power such a noise.

Daddy.

Dao whirled around. The door he'd left open slammed shut, the noise a crash of thunder blowing everything else out of the office. A crack raced along the door and the handle exploded loose.

"Yang." Dao lunged forward.

It was like racing headfirst into a wall.

He bounced off nothing, head and chest feeling as if they'd been hit with a hammer, and collapsed. Barely able to breathe, Dao squirmed on the carpet, and tried to say his son's name. He managed a hiss, which sent lightning bolts shooting from his stomach to his face. And outside, Yang screamed and screamed. The sheer agony in his yells swallowed them. Dao could do nothing but inch his way over the carpet and rage inside at whatever was hurting his boy.

Above his head, a shape in the air reached.

Claws sank into the skin of Dao's forehead. Blood flowed from fine cuts. He still didn't have the breath to make a noise, despite the pain rapidly becoming agony. His head was turned; he had no choice but to go with it while Yang's wails rang out, non-stop, beyond awful.

Whatever held Dao's head pushed him back towards the window, the glass looming closer as he dragged useless fingers over the carpet and wept. The forced movement took him to the window and kept going. His nose pressed into the glass, then his forehead. And still, the claws in his head wouldn't let go. Dao's first coherent thought in seconds was:

It's going to crush me.

Dao's vision rippled. For a tiny moment, even the terrible sensation in his skull lessened. Then the glass of the window parted like oily water, its surface shimmering and dancing on all sides as Dao's head oozed through it. He couldn't close his eyes even when the window—or whatever the window had become—pressed its cold into his pupils for a moment, then flowed to the sides, then up and below.

Air found Dao's face.

He'd been pushed *through* the surface of the glass as if it were fresh mud. His knees and hands remained on the carpet while his head and neck jutted from the side of the building, offering him a God's-eye view of Willington's centre and its new lifeless surface.

But it wasn't totally lifeless.

The claws forced Dao to bend his neck and see what moved on the pavement ten floors below.

Skittering, black pools sliding together, growing and forming wider circles; those circles slowly began to jut from the ground and form the unmistakable shape of bodies, while the same fierce white light that shone in the east rose from the pavement. The faint whiff of something meaty rose. Something burning reached Dao's nose.

The stink and the shapes too awful to be called human were not the worst. Neither was the impossible horror of his head pushed through a window without any glass breaking.

The claws gripping his skull, piercing skin to send tiny lines of blood streaming down his face, had changed.

They had become the soft weight of a hand.

A child's hand holding his skull and forcing his neck back, so his staring eyes couldn't help but see the silver of the sun shining from the wrong direction.

Chapter Nine

The memory of the people in his meeting simply winking out of sight had left Simon alone since he'd found the others. For no good reason, it returned in clear, exquisite detail as they walked into the foyer of Greenham Place, filling his head to the point of shoving aside their immediate surroundings.

Alan Letts and Patricia Macmillan stand close to the window on the other side of the meeting room. Their backs are to him as they gaze outside, Alan on the phone to his wife and telling her to get the kids into the house, to get them down into the wine cellar. Behind Simon, a barrage of panic and fear arrives, and none of it makes any sense. This doesn't happen, not in real life. It's film stuff; it's as pretend as a book he might have read once. Even as he throws this denial at himself, the noise of panic grows louder. More people run for the tenth-floor corridor; the clatter of their high heels and the hollow snap of their smart shoes is a rat-a-tat of machine gun fire, and that mad image makes him want to laugh and cry out at the same time.

The others who sat around the circular table— Heather Aldridge, Steve Roe, Joanna Carter and Rachel Wilkinson—sprinted for the corridor a moment ago. As Simon takes a step towards Alan and Patricia, trying to think through the noise inside and outside his head, Steve dashes back into the meeting room.

"It's happening. Just saw it on Facebook," he screeches like an injured bird. Before Simon or the others can reply, he dashes back to the clean white walls of the hallway, fleeing to join the throng of escaping people. And all at once, the air is a baking ball of heat; the light is a pulse of white that should swallow Simon's sight but leaves him able to see Patricia and Alan turning towards him a fraction of time before they simply wink out of existence. The barrage of howling voices at his back is cut off with smooth precision.

Silence falls down around Simon and the stifling burst of heat is gone, leaving the room cool and still. And—

The pain in Simon's hand brought him back. He'd dug his nails into his palm; relaxing his fist took a fair degree of effort. Flexing his fingers, he told himself to forget for now what had happened ten floors above and focus on the present.

That'll be easy, he thought. *Of course, it will.*

Out of nowhere, Simon shivered. He'd left his coat in the meeting room and wished for it in the bright light illuminating the floor. Although the high windows forming the building's front acted as a greenhouse, sunset was not far away. The cold of the evening was already creeping down with the last of the sun.

"I tried the doors." Kelly stood in the centre of the foyer, framed by two huge pillars. Another four grew from the floor and reached long arms through the open stairwell above. The glass of the lift enclosure shone; the lift itself was a glowing square, its sides unmarked.

"No joy with them?" Rod asked, far too lightly. Simon understood. No way the old fart would want to pass the remains of the man he killed by accident. No way—

"It's gone." Kelly ran for the exit. Before she reached it, Simon understood.

The squashed body and whatever might be left of Rod's chair were nowhere in sight. Same with what Simon could only imagine was a huge patch of drying blood. The pavement, clear and clean, gleamed white.

The others joined Kelly, all treading slowly as if afraid they might make too much noise. While no pedestrians passed by, the occasional car did so. People were visible on the opposite pavement, most heading away from the city centre. A few entered Edwards, the pub standing on the corner of Greenham Road and Banks Lane. Early evening drinkers were seated beside the windows, and the simple human sight made Simon want to cry out with longing.

"Where… " Rod could barely get his voice louder than a mutter. He had to hold his stomach, convinced he would soon vomit. "Where is it?"

No need to ask what *it* was. Rod had killed someone; now, that action had been impossibly undone.

"Did I do it?" Rod's wide eyes sought each of the others out in turn, beseeching them. Simon had no answer. Even as Rod lowered his head, the Welshman crying, Simon had nothing.

Alex held Rod, letting the big man weep on her shoulder. Unsure if he should move but still desperate to get out, Simon counted to ten. He then joined Kelly at the doors. She pushed on them as Simon reached her and there was no give. While they should have opened automatically if anyone came within a few feet, they refused to yield.

"There's no power," Simon said.

"No shit. You think I didn't think of that?"

He raised a placatory hand to Kelly. "I'm not saying that. It's just that's why they're not opening."

For a moment, Kelly wanted to argue the point, if only to have something real to focus upon. Outside, a couple laden with shopping from Tesco passed directly by the doors.

"Hey." Kelly struck the doors. They shook, the impact jarring her wrists. The couple walked on.

Simon ran to the right, hammering on the windows while keeping pace with the couple. Even though all that separated him from them was glass and a few feet, they gave no reaction and walked out of sight.

"What the fuck is going on?" he whispered.

Kelly kicked at the doors, small boot connecting squarely and the thud making her toes throb. The glass trembled. On the pavement, an old woman waiting to cross gave no reaction. A taxi slowed to a stop. The driver waved to the woman, who returned the gesture and crossed the road.

Cold in a way that was not purely to do with the incoming evening, Simon fumbled for his iPhone. It was as useless as it had been on the floors above.

"Shit." The shout escaped before he had chance to swallow it back. He hit the door again, so he didn't have to look at the others.

At the main reception desk, Kelly tried one of the phones with little hope.

"Dead," she said to the others without turning.

The answering silence lived with a collective wince. *Dead,* it said. *Dead like the man Rod killed and oh and by the way, where the hell is that man?*

Kelly fumbled with the next phone before throwing it down in disgust. It knocked a cup of pens over; the pens scattered to the floor, one rolling towards Rod's foot. Letting go of Alex and wiping away the last of his tears, Rod kicked idly at the pen.

"Well, I tell you what. No bloody way I'm staying here any longer. Either we smash those doors down or we go out another way."

Rod strode past the pillars, moving towards the cash office.

"Rod?" Alex moved to follow. "Where are you going?"

"I broke one sodding window with a chair. I'll break another."

Rod made it another five steps before he, Kelly and Alex heard the voice bellow from the air.

COME AND SIT DOWN WITH ME, ROD.

Still standing at the useless doors, Simon jerked back as Kelly let out a whispered scream and Alex ducked.

What the hell's going on?

The women looked in all directions, searching thin air. Simon walked closer to Alex, utterly unsure of what to do or say. This wasn't like his usual lack of skill in any situation outside work. This was things slipping over to the wrong side of sanity.

"What is it?" he hissed.

Then he saw Rod.

The man looked like he was about to faint. Rod's cheeks, forehead, and nose had gone beyond white to an almost blue. His lips were one faint red slash. His hands were fists; he swayed as if blown by a strong wind. Some intuitive part of Simon's senses, something the twenty-first century had no use for, caught the wild aroma of an animal's terror. *Death was here*, the smell said while Simon's rational, human awareness knew nothing of it. *Death on all sides and all that could be done was to face it.*

Simon's panic broke the surface. *"What is it?"*

The reply in the air was again for all of them apart from Simon.

WANT A CUP OF TEA, ROD? COME AND HAVE A SIT DOWN IN MY SHED AND WE'LL HAVE A CUP OF TEA.

Rod's answering scream was a wordless negation of his horror.

Behind Simon, something thumped against the glass of the exit.

He turned.

Standing on the pavement, *filling* the pavement, dozens of bodies stood upright.

Before his backing away from the window became a mad sprint, Simon had time to take in the terrible injuries and ruined frames. Skin had been stripped away, layer by layer, to reveal the rich red of the flesh underneath. Weeping scars curved cheeks and lips into nothing more than lines. Melted flesh from foreheads rained over eyes, leaving them as tiny holes through which black balls, all blind, stared out. Clothing was reduced to tattered remnants. Shirts, jackets, jeans and skirts, now scorched material, flapped in the breeze. Somehow breaking through the windows, the reek of the burned skin and cooked flesh filled

Simon's nose and oozed across the foyer. He tried to gag and failed. All he could do was *see*.

More people joined the crowd, pushing those at the front a step closer to the doors, making the damage to their faces even clearer. Features became pooling strands of dangling skin, noses melted into mouths, and mouths slipped down over chins. And all the skin, the red and orange of a healthy bonfire, and all the exposed sinew and muscle cooked like overdone steak.

Mouths opened as Simon stared. Skin tore, dropping blood and small pieces of roasted meat to patter on the floor. A chorus of agonised voices sang as one.

We're burning.

Chapter Ten

For Kelly, thinking coherently was out of the question. So, she ran.

Alex reached for her sister; the women collided, both trying to yell at the other. Alex's greater weight propelled Kelly towards the doors leading back to the stairs. Something Kelly would later think of as a hand shoved her head and turned her around.

More of the burned people stood at the windows, lining the pavement and jostling to get closer to the glass. The distance made no difference. Their injures were as clear to see as they'd been when Kelly stood at the reception desk, watching Simon smack his hands on the glass. The mental picture was an invitation: a middle-aged woman splayed her hand on the glass, smearing blood, the hand moving back and forth as if she was waving.

"Run," Alex shouted, but Kelly remained seemingly glued to the spot. Even Alex's powerful shove did no good. A rhythmic pounding sounded as dozens of people beat on the windows in unison; red coated the glass, turning the outside into a blurred montage of people who couldn't be alive let alone stand upright. Backing away from the exit, Simon tripped and went down hard. He turned as he fell, landed on his elbow, and cried out. Someone outside echoed the sound with precise, terrible skill before every single burned body took the cry and let it fly from their lungs, which then turned black. The vocal cords are now little more than baked string. Simon skittered over the floor, flailing through huge pools of sunshine and his legs kicking as if he'd lost the ability to walk. He crawled, moaning, crying, and one limp hand reached towards Kelly. She saw him and took a tiny step backwards.

Let him go. That's what she had to do. Get away from the people outside.

They're dead, dead, they're all fucking dead and they're going to make me burn like they burned.

Kelly's mind blocked away all consideration, leaving her with a lone imperative—to get away.

The sight of Rod made her freeze.

The big man stood between two of the stone pillars back to the exit. He faced the lift, and although Kelly only had a profile view of the lift, she knew what Rod was staring at.

The doors were open.

ROD YOU LITTLE FUCKING BASTARD COME AND HAVE A SIT DOWN IN MY SHED.

The rage rained from above as it broke free from the floor. It was everywhere, and it was all the mad anger in the world.

ROD I'M GOING TO FUCKING KILL YOU IF YOU DON'T COME INTO MY SHED RIGHT FUCKING NOW.

Rod let out a tiny gasp, the sound swallowed by the barrage of mocking yells still chorusing from the pavement. Kelly saw his mouth open wide; she saw his barrel chest expanding and she saw despair eclipse every light of hope in Rod's eyes.

He stepped towards the lift.

"Rod."

He stumbled at Alex's shriek, glancing towards the women as if not believing they'd still be there. A distant voice mocked Kelly, telling her if she'd listened to herself, she and Alex would be nowhere near either of the men. Holding Kelly's wrist in a rock-hard grip, Alex ran for Rod, and Kelly had no choice but to also run. Simon finally made it to his feet, and the sisters came within a few inches of running into him. Bundled into a tight group, they all saw the pitch-black inside the lift. Although the afternoon light shone into all corners of the ground floor, it couldn't penetrate the darkness inside the lift.

The lift doors smacked together, snapping shut with a tremendous crash as they had when Kelly stood alone, sure she was being watched.

A lone finger touched the back of her neck with a lover's care and a name came close to spilling from her mouth. She bit it back at the last second.

"Move," Alex shouted.

The women in the lead, the group sprinted for the doors and the stairs. Alex hit them first, one arm raised to send them bursting open. Kelly let go of her sister, took the lead and the first of the stairs. She raced up two at a time, not aware of the thunder of her heart or the thick layer of perspiration coating her from her feet to the top of her head. She didn't give a shit about anything other than the need to get away from whatever the hell was going on behind them.

She reached the first landing; Simon dashed by, taking the lead. Kelly turned back, waving Alex on.

"Fucking move it."

Parting, Alex reached the landing, leaving Rod not yet halfway up. He'd turned a nasty shade of red and fumbled for the railing, crying out as his sweat-soaked hand missed it. Dismissing the man without registering doing so, Kelly pushed Alex on and moved to race behind her sister. Simon was already at the next flight of stairs. His long shadow became a stain on the white of the floor, and the world was the building and the building was beyond hot; it was a scorching wall of desert air, and all Kelly could smell was the rotten stink of her sweat and terror.

"Wait for me."

Rod had made it halfway up the first flight of stairs. A foot in front of Kelly, Alex was turning around, and Kelly *knew* the stupid bitch would. She couldn't help herself when it came to other people, even if those other people would fuck everything up.

Still running but now slowing, turning even before she came to a stop, Alex looked over Kelly's shoulder to the top of the first flight of stairs.

Convinced she was turning around to see the Welshman have a heart attack, Kelly moved to follow her sister's gaze.

Alex spoke before Kelly completed the movement. "Dad?"

The figure stood on the top step, facing them. A man. As the people outside had been charred to the point of surely being unable to move, the man not ten feet from Kelly and her sister was never getting out of his hospital bed again. He'd be lucky to even wake up. That's what Anthony said, even if the doctors and nurses weren't saying it. The car driven by the drunken idiot had sent the man now standing at the top of the stairs flying from the pavement to the hard road, where it had welcomed his skull and his brain. The road had welcomed them both to the point of drinking his blood and sending him into a sleep next door to death.

Alex. Help me, baby. I hurt.

Kelly groaned and tried to back away. The words weren't quite a voice or a thought from outside her head. They'd come in the hot air. They swam into her ears.

My head hurts, baby. You have to help me.

Bandages wrapped around the man's skull bloomed red. Streams of blood ran from underneath them, down his cheeks, and into the curls of his thin beard. From there, they dripped to the faint green of his hospital gown, staining it, soaking it to his scrawny body before forming a widening puddle at his feet.

Rounding the corner that turned to the stairs, Simon crept forward with eyes on the sisters' backs. There was no sign of Rod and no sound following Alex's lone word. And had she said *dad,* or had he misheard? Simon drew closer, saw the empty air the women stared at and drew breath to shout at them or for Rod. At the last moment, instinct commanded Simon to keep quiet. Fighting to control his breathing, he wiped sweat from his mouth and said nothing.

Still at the halfway point of the stairs, Rod stared at the back of the black man who'd come out of nowhere to block the route ahead. With grim fascination, Rod watched the puddle of blood drip from the top step to the one below, the thick red shining like oil.

I have to get past him. Perhaps surprisingly, Rod felt no fear. It seemed he'd used it all during the terrible few seconds that could have been hours while the featureless space inside the lift howled at him in the voice of a dead man. Presented with the image of someone who clearly should be attached to machinery keeping him alive, Rod felt only an animal need to escape. Fear would keep him rooted to the spot; he had no use for fear.

Alex's father. That's what she said. In hospital. He can't be here.

Argument changed nothing. The black man was here in the same way the voice from the lift had been there.

I knock him down. I get past him. He's only a little fella. He'll go down easily.

Convinced he could deck the bleeding man as easily as he'd beaten men in pub fights years before, Rod readied himself to run the last few steps. The sharp sting of the stitch in his side and the lack of breath went away. He could do this, could get to the girls and get them away.

The black man's upper half turned. Bones cracked with a ghastly snapping sound and split his skin. The movement stopped, leaving his legs and feet facing the landing. Everything above the waist turned a hundred and eighty degrees. Rod shrieked. He couldn't help it.

They are mine. He is yours.

If the twisted shape spoke with a voice, it was lost to Rod. Although the words came as clearly as speech, so did realisation.

Alex's father wasn't speaking to him.

Without turning, Rod knew who was breathing against his neck.

Chapter Eleven

Hello, Rod. Nice to see you. You've grown, but I suppose it's been a long time, hasn't it?

Among those remaining in Greenham Place, only Simon couldn't hear the voice. He stood at Kelly and Alex's backs, hands twisting uselessly together, too scared to run from the others.

"Alex, we need to move," Kelly whispered and Simon's mind roared agreement. His voice remained frozen in his mouth. All he could do was stare at nothing and listen to a faint wind blowing from the floors above, refusing to turn and see what might be behind him.

Still on the stairs, Rod faced the man at his back. And while he knew exactly where he was, and the names of the people behind, he knew those things as if they were fading memories from his childhood. Here and now? No, not even a little bit. They belonged to the wide-open land of his parents' farmland. They lived below the massive Welsh sky that dwarfed the boy he'd been fifty years ago. They were as long-ago and forgotten as the child who'd laughed at the man now standing on the stairs in front of him, when that man snapped his false teeth together, then tried to scream when he saw the pink worm of that man's tongue coming closer.

They're right here, Rod. They haven't gone anywhere, but they will if you come with me. Come and sit next to me. We'll talk about the old days. Would you like that?

"No," Rod breathed. The fact he had any voice at all was a miracle. Arguing against the image of this man with his smooth, black hair; his easy smile; and the chunky gold of his watch bouncing the sunshine back and forth was beyond anything Rod knew.

"You are not here," he whispered.

Of course, I am. You can see me, can't you? That means I'm here and I can see you. I see how fat you've got. Mind you, you always were a big boy, but look at you now. Big, fat, slow, and old. Too much food? Too many good meals from Joan? Too many beers? Stuffing your fat fucking face and drinking all those pints down the pub with the boys after you retired? Before that, wasn't it? Careful not to drink when you had a shift coming up, but happy to spend a weekend afternoon with your mouth in a pint, isn't that the truth, Rod? Shoving it all into your gob like a fucking animal? My God, how revolting you are these days. Not like before. Not like when you were a boy. My, how lovely you were, Rod. How perfectly fucking lovely. How—

"*Shut up,*" Rod bellowed. A snatch of white-hot pain stabbed him directly in the centre of his chest; a curiousness that felt as if it belonged in the same dead past of his childhood. He wondered if he was about to have a heart attack, and another part of him welcomed that. Maybe, with a bit of luck, he'd be dead before he hit the floor.

Let's talk, son. We can talk about how fat you are now. Like the food, do you? The beers? The hearty meals? The man let out an ugly noise that might have been a laugh in another world. *Burying yourself in fat, Rod? Doesn't surprise me. People like you always do. Better to eat and drink and eat and drink than face anything, eh?* That same mock-laugh echoed up and down the stairs, and Rod wondered if he was going to throw up or soil himself.

Better overdoing it all than facing a truth, right? Better that than admit what you might end up being even now.

The man snapped his teeth together with a shocking, sudden movement. Rod cringed.

Joan, the kids, the grandkids, the buses, and your life. A cover, Rod. Let's talk about that. Let's talk about you hiding things behind stuffing your face and going to the pub and thinking you might be like—

Another voice interrupted the man's raving.

It hurts, Alex. Please help me. Get the doctors.

It was the other man, the chap Rod had almost forgotten about. Rod twisted, searching for an escape past either of the horrors above and below.

"Dad?" Alex sobbed, shaking Kelly off and advancing upon the shape of her father, dressed in his blood-soaked bandages. The oxygen mask was supposed to be covering his mouth, and now his nose is a torn, stained piece of useless plastic. It dangled against his chest like a necklace.

Turn the machines off and let me die. I'm never going to wake up. The man's voice abruptly shifted from a whining, pained mutter to a shrill shriek that made Alex cry out and fall backwards. Simon caught her, his face betraying his confusion.

A sound muted but still recognisable reached Alex's ears and she understood at once that none of the others heard the ringing bell. For whom the bell tolls. Oh yes. For *her* and her alone. That was it. That was her freezing death in a fresh grave. Hers and hers alone.

And then her father's shrill voice broke the noise of the ringing bell in half.

Let me fucking die, Alex. For once in your life, do something for someone else, and let me die. I'm dead already, so just switch the fucking machine off before I get out of my bed and come find you. Fuck you and fuck you and fuck you and—

Alex's howl raced from the landing to the soundless floors above, crashing over stairs and closed doors, racing higher and higher to the tenth floor where a listening shape welcomed it.

Five steps from Alex's dad, Rod's overflowing terror met an outraged disgust. Stomach churning, bowels hot, he lunged up the rest of the stairs. His fists were already swinging. As the injured man continued to shriek his vile threats, Rod punched him in the back of the head.

It was like punching hot mud.

Rod's fist slid wrist-deep into the heat. Disgust at what the man was saying became revulsion at the sensation against his skin. Rod yanked his fist free and stepped back as the man tried to turn. His head and neck fell into his narrow chest; muck oozed downwards, forming a spilling goo, and Rod could only think:

He's melting, Jesus Christ, he's melting.

Alex cried out in horror, unable to do a thing as her father decayed into a mess of ruined flesh. What might have been his face slipping into his stomach twisted around, and the two pits were unmistakably his eyes, staring, marking her.

Alex fell to the side. Simon and Kelly caught her but couldn't take her impetus or weight. They lowered her to the ground as she wept.

"It's not real, Alex," Kelly said. "That isn't him."

"What the fuck is happening?" None of the others heard Simon's mutter.

The last remnants of Alex's father sank into an oily patch, staining the stair. Panting hard, Rod stared at the man further down and spoke as deliberately as he could.

"I killed him, and I will kill you." The next two words took everything Rod had. "Martin Williams."

Naming the monster was a form of magic. It had to be that rather than the threat. Williams winked out of existence, leaving the stairs clear save for the dripping mess that had been a man moments before.

With no warning, Rod's stomach rebelled. He vomited thin strands of his lunch, keeping his eyes shut as the mess splattered at his feet. Retching the last away, he straightened and wiped his mouth with the cuff of his shirt.

Whatever the man had been made of, it was already flowing to the next step. On legs that felt like they would spill him at any second. Rod skirted the mess and walked to Alex. She gazed at him with a child's frightened eyes.

"Alex—" Rod began.

His legs shook, and all he could do was hold the woman as she sobbed against his shoulder.

Lost outside horrors he didn't share, Simon stared at the empty stairs and again heard the soft whisper of a distant wind. When Alex jerked back from Rod, mouth open in shock, Simon stepped away.

I don't want to know what's going on here. No thanks. Not for me.

"What was that?" Kelly whispered. "What the fuck was that?"

On the floor, Alex heard it again. The cold clang of a tolling church bell.

Chapter Twelve

For a tiny moment, it seemed to Dao that the hand gripping his head would let go. Instead, it lifted him from the carpet while he cried his agony. It then flung him across the room.

Although no more than a second passed between being yanked up and thrown, Dao still had time to see the dazzling blue of the sky spread across the windows on the other side of the room, the clean white of the carpet, obviously kept pristine and shampooed by cleaners, and the nothing in the air that could possibly have touched him.

He hit the wall beside the office door five feet above the floor. Fire replaced the breath in his lungs. Crashing to the floor, Dao tried to gasp and inhale at the same time. Fire turned his back and chest into a conflagration, and rational thought belonged in another universe.

The sky had changed from a sheer blue to the burning red of fire. The flames licked over the tops of buildings and streamed through the air, all converging on the windows of the office for Mr. Alan Letts, all coming soundlessly as they turned the space over Willington's streets into an oven.

Dao crawled for the door now open, unaware of the blood dribbling down his forehead from several gashes and cuts. If anything watched him, it watched with curiosity and amusement. Dao reached the door, dug his fingertips into the plush carpet, and pulled. Convinced the door would slam shut on his arm at any second, he pushed himself on and finally registered how much he bled when the salty tang of his own blood reached his mouth. Spitting red flecks, he swung his feet around.

The pain living and breathing through his body didn't matter.

He was out of the office.

Dao rolled over in time to see the noiseless fire in the sky blow against the windows. The door crashed shut hard enough to shake in its frame. There was no pause between the mighty thud and the wailing from its other side.

Daddy, he's here. Make him stop hurting me.

"Yang." Dao made it to his knees, pitched forward and tried to rise again. "Yang, let me in."

Dao reached for the handle and, by some white magic, his damp fingers found the metal. It refused to move. Pulling, Dao managed to stand. Right by his ear, Lin said:

Get away from the door, Dao. Our boy isn't here and he never was. Get away.

With a savage increase in pain and volume, Yang answered her. *He* is *here, Mummy. You said he was dead, but he's here.*

With numb lips and a numb tongue, Dao said a name he hadn't spoken in two years, only thinking of it in memories that stung with loss and grief. And at the same instant, Yang howled it on the other side of the sealed door, and all Dao had was his pain dancing with his son's agony.

Huan. Leave me alone. You're my brother. You have to leave me alone.

Chapter Thirteen

The ground floor.

The lift.

The sunlight beginning to ease as half past five approached and dusk closed in.

The trapped warmth leeching out of the air as the shadows spread from the corners and the edges of the pillars.

All still. All without a single breath to disturb the silence.

Ding.

Nothing again except for a slight disturbance outside the open lift doors, a movement close to imperceptible making its way across the floor towards the automatic doors motionless for almost two hours.

The faint outline of a human hand waved in front of the sensor over the doors. They slid open.

The same movement brushed the sensor over the outer doors.

Whatever walked from the lift returned to the dark space of its innards. A moment later, the lift doors eased shut.

Silence, again.

The outer doors parted. Then the inner.

Fingers, the flesh, sinew and muscle burned down to the bone, pressed on the override button unnoticed by Kelly and Simon during their pounding and kicks on the glass doors. The entrance to Greenham Place sealed itself.

A voice, low and musing, addressed the dozens of charred figures grouped across the floor.

Wait.

Chapter Fourteen

Out of breath, hurting, and unable to think clearly, the group halted on the landing of the sixth floor, although Alex had to ask herself if she was sure about this being the sixth. Every floor looked the same; every landing had the same features, and every set of double doors opened to the same fucking open-plan offices. Why the fuck was she thinking about this shit when there was her dad, her dad, *her fucking dad.*

Alex closed her eyes, counted to five and opened them again. Taking a mental breath helped a tiny degree, if only because she no longer wanted to scream until her lungs exploded.

"Can someone tell me what the hell is going on?" Simon asked nobody in particular. He collapsed on a chunky sofa between two of the fake plants and gazed at each of the others in turn. "Anyone?"

"It was my dad." Alex focused on the facing sunlight, registering it for the first time. "My dad."

"Where?"

She stared at Simon. "What do you mean *where?*"

"I mean, what are you talking about? Your dad? Where?"

Confused silence filled the space of the landing and the stairs. Rod broke it.

"You're saying you didn't see anyone?"

"I'm saying I don't know what the fuck is going on and nobody's making any sense," Simon yelled.

Alex opened her mouth to say something—she had no idea what—and Rod raised a hand to calm the situation.

"Hold on a second. Let's get this straight." He addressed Simon. "You didn't see anyone on the stairs? No men?"

"No." Because something else seemed required, Simon added: "Sorry, but I didn't."

Kelly stood at the railing beside the window, back to the others. "He can't have been there, Alex. No way." She faced her sister. "Those things he said... no way."

Alex laughed, although it was without humour. "He was and he did, Kel. We all heard him." She jabbed a finger at Simon. "Apart from you." It came like an accusation and he flinched. Wanting to take back the snide tone, Alex dismissed the man by turning away.

"Who was the other man?" Kelly asked Rod.

"Nobody."

"Bullshit."

"I'm telling you, he was nobody. Just… a family friend from when I was younger."

"He was more than that."

"He was nobody."

Kelly cringed at Rod's yell and he stepped forward to take her hand. "I'm sorry, love. It's just been… it's been a bad day."

While Simon took a seat apart from them, the others barked shrill, mad laughter, their pressure escaping a fraction. Rod wiped his eyes, still giggling, while Alex turned away, crying again but still laughing. Eventually, the strained humour faded, leaving only growing shadows and a new chill in the air. As insane as it seemed, evening was coming in quickly. At the windows, Kelly studied the roofs of buildings, not daring to move closer and see if the streets were normal or devoid of life.

Did it go off? The bomb? Did it go off and we're all… what? Dead? Is that it? I'm dead?

Nothing approaching an answer replied.

"I think it's safe to say something unnatural is happening here." Rod's face had regained some of its healthy colour and he'd stopped breathing so heavily. "We can call it whatever we like. Supernatural or whatever. I'm not fussed. It probably doesn't matter too much what we call it or what's happening. *Why* might be more important."

Simon stood. "I'm not part of this, whatever the hell is going on, so if you'll excuse me." He moved to pass Rod and descend. Surprising herself, Alex stopped him.

"You can't go back down there." He met her eyes.

"Why?"

Alex's mouth worked for a few seconds before she managed to speak. "Because you might bring them back."

The fine hairs on Alex's arms danced as a wave of cold swooped down from the floors above. In her mind, she saw her bleeding father, heard the terrible things he yelled, listened to the *squelch* of his body dribbling into so much mess after Rod's punch.

"Who?" Simon whispered.

Alex's mouth opened, closed, and opened again. All she could offer him was a soft exhalation.

"Dead people," Kelly muttered, and Alex whirled around.

"Don't say that. Don't you say that."

"Why not? They were dead. They were fucking dead, Alex—"

With fingers like claws, Alex ran for her sister. Dumbstruck, Simon could only watch as Rod shoved himself between the women, his body taking Alex's and saving Kelly's face from her sister's nails. Raging, Alex pushed and pummelled at Rod; he grabbed her wrists and shoved them away while telling her to calm down. Kelly ran to the next flight of stairs, stopping on the third floor. She sat, holding her knees while

Alex dropped into a sobbing mess and Rod held her and murmured comfort.

Moments passed while Simon could do nothing but stand and feel useless. More of the day's light faded. The pooling shadows on the stairs that fell away to the next floor were terrible; all the worst things in the world lived down there, and Simon could only wonder why he didn't share those things with the others.

When the group heard the hesitant steps from above, gradually descending, Alex eased away from Rod and stood, waiting for her father to reappear and voice his terrible threats.

The footsteps came closer.

Chapter Fifteen

D ao?"

Alex managed a few trembling steps towards the stairs, and stopped before collapsing again. The surety that her father was coming back, the knowledge of it had been as real as knowing her own name. He was coming back with those awful threats, bleeding through his bandages, and begging for her to kill him. She wouldn't be able to do a thing to stop any of it. But that hadn't happened, and wasn't there something just out of sight, something in the gathering gloom that capered and laughed at her? And if she turned fully, she'd see it and then it would be her turn to scream and scream.

Pretending no such thoughts whispered to her, Alex said Dao's name again as Kelly backed away from the stairs, and Rod joined the sisters. Even Simon rose, staring up to the shuffling shape of a man, bloody and bruised.

Gripping the railing, Dao descended. Trickles of blood ran down his forehead and his cheeks from nasty gashes in his forehead. Sweat stains discoloured his shirt. A sleeve had ridden up to reveal a bruise filling his forearm. He moved like an old man, or as if he was drunk. His gaze couldn't or wouldn't land on any one of them for longer than a second.

"Fuck." Simon reached for the other man and Dao stumbled the last few steps. Simon caught him. "What the hell happened to you?"

Dao spoke words too soft for anyone to hear. Even so, Alex thought she understood and she heard Rod's words from a few minutes ago.

Something unnatural is happening here.

"My son," Dao muttered.

Unnatural? This is a nightmare.

They took Dao to the sofa and eased him down. He spoke without looking at anyone. It seemed easier that way.

"Up there. I was in an office. The door closed by itself and something put me through the window. It put me through it like it was water. I saw the streets and roads. There's nothing outside. Nobody. It's like a drawing out there. And the sky was on fire. The sky burned. It pulled me back in and threw me against the wall. I got out. The door closed and—" He lifted his head and saw none of them. He was back up on the tenth floor, and the terrible shrieks echoed between his ears. "My son was in the office. He screamed for me. He screamed for Huan to leave him alone."

Simon met Rod's eyes. The older man gave a tiny shrug. Sitting beside Dao, Kelly took his hand and couldn't ask the obvious question. Alex crouched, banished her fear for a moment and said:

"Who's Huan, Dao?"

He let out a shaking breath. "My other son. Yang's brother. He died two years ago."

In a shocked whisper, Rod said: "Jesus Christ."

He placed the solid weight of his palm on Dao's shoulder, offering silent comfort and wishing he had any helpful words. Alex lowered her head to stare at the smooth floor and try to make any sense of what was going on. She couldn't even come close.

"We need to get into one of the offices," Rod said. "This one will do."

The meaning behind what the man said broke through. Alex stared up at him. "You mean stay here? With all this? Stay here?"

"We can't get out, Alex," Kelly said. "Not now, anyway."

"No fucking way I'm staying here." Alex stood, a distant voice asking if she'd ever sworn as much before today.

"We can't get out," Kelly said again.

Desperately, Alex tried to come up with a third option: another exit from the ground floor. While there might have been one at the back of the building, she had no idea how to find it. Her four years working in Greenham Place had only ever involved the fourth floor, with occasional meetings on the sixth. The ground floor was simply the entrance. She hadn't given the reception or the lift any thought since her first week.

"I'll get out through a window if I have to. I'll jump from the first floor. I'm getting out and I'm getting back to Charlotte and Louisa."

She strode to the top of the stairs, stared down, and then hesitated. While she knew the shadows were simply due to the fading light, the faint shape of something human growing from a corner on the next landing made her stop.

It's a trick of the light, like seeing a shape in a cloud or in a tree. It's nothing.

Nothing or not, she wasn't going down there.

Kill me, Alex. Kill me or I'll fuck you.

Baring her teeth at the shadows, Alex backed away.

"In there." She pointed to the doors that opened to the offices of the sixth floor.

Simon helped Dao to his feet. Rod took the lead, and Alex and Kelly came behind him. At the entrance, Rod drew a breath and pulled his foot back to boot the doors open. Faint but definitely there, a bell rang once from somewhere above. If any of the others heard it, they gave no reaction. It seemed it was for Alex alone, and her head was filled with visions of the abandoned church, standing cold and lonely in the winter sunset.

Rod kicked the doors open. They flew apart and the group entered without speaking.

Shadows slid further in from the windows.

Chapter Sixteen

Expecting no result, Simon flicked the switch for the main set of lights in the staffroom. As with the other three he'd tried, they did nothing. A quick look to the windows told him they probably had half an hour before full dark and what the hell they were supposed to do then. Still, he had no idea. Sitting on one of the three sofas, he shook and tried to ignore the growing cold. His coat remained up on the ninth floor and no way was he going for it by himself or in the dark. Simon didn't believe anything was happening in Greenham Place that couldn't be explained, but that didn't mean he relished the idea of wandering around the empty building when he couldn't see more than a foot in front.

Dao sat beside him, the guy as close to catatonic as someone could be while still able to move. Alex took a bundle of coats from a rack in the corner and handed them around. Marginally warmer wearing someone else's coat, Simon dug his hands into the pockets and didn't want to think about what had happened to the people who owned the clothing.

In the small kitchen, Rod searched cupboards for food. Eating seemed like a mad idea, but as they had no way of knowing how long they'd be stuck in the building, they had to fill their bellies. There was little in the cupboards. He found a packet of bourbons, jars of coffee and packets of tea. Holding the biscuits, he let the cupboard close and wished for enough power to boil the kettle. Going through this was bad enough. Without a brew, it was hellish.

Trying to smile, he opened the tall fridge and spied a few unopened sandwiches and pots of pasta. Unclaimed lunches, presumably. He took them to the others sitting on the sofas and chairs.

"Not a lot, but it's the best we've got. And the taps are still working if anyone's thirsty."

Wordlessly, Kelly crossed to the sink and filled a mug with water. She drank it with her back to the rest, then filled the mug again.

"Come and eat, Kel."

Kelly turned when her sister spoke. Her face gave nothing away, and Simon wondered what festered between the two women. Something, obviously, and that something was ugly. Still not speaking, Kelly filled another three mugs and carried them awkwardly to the round table at the middle of the seating area. Water slopped over the rims as she placed them down. Staring up at the darkening sky, Simon ate without tasting the chicken sandwich. For a moment, everything but the sound of chewing and swallowing faded. It was only after a minute passed that Dao's lack of movement became obvious.

"You going to eat, Dao?" Simon asked.

Dao remained silent, face flecked with drying blood.

"Dao?"

Simon might as well have addressed a statue.

"Dao, mate, you need to—"

"Fuck off and leave me alone."

Simon recoiled from the yell; Alex shook, spilling water onto her leg. Rod remained still. He'd seen the anger coming and knew the fear that powered it; he knew it was directed at all of them rather than only Simon. The boy was cracking under the unimaginable stress of his boy, somewhere here and being tortured by what could only be described as a ghost.

"It's okay, Dao," he said as quietly as he could. "It's okay, son."

Dao let out a breath that sounded as if it hurt.

"Sorry. I'm sorry."

"Don't worry about it." Simon knew he didn't sound at all genuine.

Dao put his uneaten pot of pasta back on the table and walked to the windows, where the last of the sunset was fading. He peered downwards.

"There are people out there. Cars and people." Dao smacked on the glass as Kelly ran to him. *"Hey. Hey, we're up here."*

Dao turned as Kelly reached him, his thoughts racing. They needed to break a window. It no longer mattered what had happened when Rod did just that, because that body was gone, was gone, was—

"Where?" Kelly asked.

Outside, the dark streets were as empty as they'd been when the invisible hand shoved Dao's head through the window to show him the painting of Willington's centre. One by one, the streetlights began to go out, letting the night fill the spaces they'd illuminated.

"No," Dao whispered.

The others crowded round, watching each light wink into nothing. The same was happening with the glow from the interior of the Tesco and the three pubs. And the same in the takeaways. The same in the little shops, the travel agents.

Willington was becoming a void. Kelly fumbled in her back pocket for her mobile and thumbed the screen. The little illumination shone white on the window and turned their faces into slightly more distinct shapes than they had been a second before. Like a tiny miracle, the cloud passed over the moon. That shine and the gleam from Kelly's mobile were all they had.

"Everyone, keep calm," Rod said. "No screaming, no shouting, no shitting ourselves, okay?"

Simon let out a laugh he didn't know he had in him.

"How are you keeping it together?" he asked Rod.

"I barely am." Rod sat again. Simon took the space next to the bigger man and placed his iPhone on the table. He turned the light on the screen. Kelly and Alex placed their phones beside his. Without comment, Dao did the same. The collective glow of their displays became a welcome beacon in the new dark.

"We need to talk," Rod said. "We need to get everything we know out in the open."

"What do we know? We're either all mad or someone's playing a joke on us."

"You really believe that?" Kelly asked her sister, and Simon winced at the harsh note of disbelief in the girl's question. Without saying as much, Kelly made it pretty clear she thought Alex was being an idiot.

"What the hell else is it?"

Kelly sank deeper into her chair, legs pulled up from the dark carpet. In the poor light, Simon tried to study Dao's face, but the other man was almost invisible. Was he thinking about his son? Was he hearing the boy's agony? Was he even listening to anything being said right now?

Would I be? Simon asked himself as he pictured the living room of his flat. The soft sofa, the little coffee table he only ever used to place the remotes and his cans of beer on, and the big telly and no kids or anyone else there and not one fucking thing in it that he shared with the world. He was Dao's opposite, and maybe having no kids to worry about was about as good as this shitty place could get.

"Alex, please," Rod said. "We need to talk, right?"

She clasped her knees and said nothing.

Rod took a few breaths. "So, the world's going to hell. We've got a load of idiots forty miles away with a bomb and they're going to do here what they did in America last June. They're going to bomb London, only one of them gets away with that bomb and wants to stop it, and everyone out there—" He waved at the windows. "They leg it. And *they* include us. And we have no clue if the bomb has gone off or not."

Dao spoke in a flat voice. "If it went off, then how come the buildings are still standing? How come we're still standing?"

"I don't know. Personally, I don't think it *did* go off. I think something happened out there. Otherwise, everyone else who was in here would still be with us. All I can guess at… " He paused as if considering. The others waited in silence, simply because none of them could offer any realistic scenarios. "All I can guess at is the bomb didn't go off but we're injured. Maybe in the panic. Maybe we hit our heads, and this isn't real."

Rod's last few words came quietly. He studied the floor, unwilling or unable to offer more.

"You think we're just seeing this? Like it's not real?" Kelly said. "Bullshit."

"I'm not hallucinating. I *heard* my son and something threw me across the room," Dao said.

Rod curled his hands into fists. "All I'm saying is we have to be open to possibilities."

"There *is* one possibility." Simon heard himself speaking even as an interior voice told him to shut the fuck up.

"What?" Alex said.

What the hell difference does it make? Someone's going to say it sooner or later. Probably Dao. And Rod's already thinking it. I can tell by his voice.

"What?" Alex said again.

"We're dead. The bomb went off and we're dead."

Alex barked high-pitched laughter. She crossed to the window. "Does it look like the bomb went off out there?" Anger pulsed inside Simon's chest. He could deal with fear as much as the others here, but he wouldn't take their sneering judgement. He wouldn't be reduced to nothing *(you are nothing, Simon. Just a big fat fuck all nothing waste of fucking space)*, or made to feel he had nothing to say.

"No, it doesn't, but you lot sharing a load of fucking hallucinations while the building's emptied and the doors are locked doesn't make any fucking sense, so excuse me for trying to come up with *something."*

Spit flew from his lips; the thud of his heart was a dull ache, and something at the periphery of his vision slid over the carpet—a secret thing that managed to somehow elude him.

Uncomfortable silence filled a moment between the group. Alex ran her fingertips over the smooth glass, perhaps thinking of Dao's story about an invisible hand shoving his face through the window of a tenth-floor office. Kelly caught the white circles of Rod's eyes gazing at her. Curiosity shone in that gaze. It wanted to know the score between the sisters, because Rod was beginning to look at the bigger picture, not just *what* was happening but *why,* and Kelly could handle none of that. Not any implications or Rod's slow, careful thoughts or the shit between her and Alex—shit that hadn't been cleaned up since that business with Dean, and then the mess Kelly made of everything at the party for her eighteenth last year.

Lost in his thoughts, Dao felt the throb of the small wounds in his forehead beat in time with the ache running down his right-hand side where he'd struck the wall. Dead? No way. Being dead wouldn't hurt either his body or his heart. Being dead would mean no torture of his son would reach him. As long as that had the power to turn him into a howling, raging animal, he was alive.

Without warning, words came to his mouth and letting them free was as much a relief as it was a horror.

"Two years ago, today, my son died. Huan."

It seemed, for a moment, that the others stopped breathing. Dao let his own breath out and it tasted old.

"He was four. My boy. Huan and Yang. My boys. He was… he fell off a climbing frame in the park. Hit his head."

Again, silence. Dao wept no tears or cried out. The brief story about his son came and went in seconds and left the staffroom even colder. Simon held himself much as Alex and Kelly were doing. The chill sank below his new coat *(and whose coat was this and where the hell are they now)*; he squeezed himself, resisting the need to rub his sides.

"Dao, I couldn't be more sorry, mate," Rod said.

"Thank you."

"Dao… " Alex began. A single word, but it was clear her anger, powered by fear, had faded.

"It's okay. Lin and I, we're not over it. Not close to that, but we keep busy. We have a lot to do and we focus on that and Yang. He's… a lot of work, but he's a good boy."

And he's screaming upstairs, apparently.

Dao dug his nails into the thin material of his shirt, scratching himself in an attempt to silence any further thoughts.

"Anyway, that's who I heard upstairs. No hallucination. No pretend. I heard my dead son attacking my living son."

If there was any possible comfort to be given to Dao's cold statement, Simon had no idea what it was. Neither, it seemed, did the others. They kept quiet while the small pile of phones offered their white glow against the night.

Around Simon's ears, the air shifted, the movement barely registering at first. It was only when it dropped to the collar of his shirt and whispered on his neck that he realised he felt as if he were standing outside on a late September day, the breeze not quite fresh but still far from summer warmth.

No. Leave me alone.

Gleefully, the breeze exploded into a savage gust of wind, skittering over the carpet and table and chairs, hissing as it passed across the arms of the sofas and ruffled the pages of the magazines dotted around.

"What the fuck is that?" Kelly cried.

One of the coat stands crashed as it fell to the lino bordering the main seating area; a chunk of the plastic snapped free and the last of the phantom wind blew it against the cupboards beside the sink in the little kitchen.

As quickly as it came, the wind died, leaving only a faint stink of rotting meat and old decay.

"Jesus." Rod shielded his nose and mouth. "What is that smell?"

Lie, Simon thought. *Right now, you lie.*

"I can't smell anything," he said. "What happened to the coat stand?"

He left the sofa and walked in the poor light to the other end of the seating area. Well aware he was not a good liar, and there was no way the others would believe him, Simon kept his back to them and righted the stand.

They heard it that time. They smelled that stink of old breath, and they won't believe you didn't because it was meant for you. Whatever they're seeing, whatever was on the stairs earlier, is for them. That was for you, but you shared it with them.

The thought came and went in the time it took Simon to let go of the stand and turn back to the shapes of the others, their outlines illumined by the phones.

"Must be a window open," Rod said.

"There's no wind out there. No air. Nothing." That was Dao.

"Well, maybe someone's got bad guts and let one go. How the hell would I know what it was?" Rod shouted. He quietened immediately. "Sorry, Dao."

Alex gazed at Rod and he seemed to be aware of her appraisal but said nothing. Eventually, Alex's question came and none of them missed Rod's brief flinch as if she'd yelled at him.

"Who was that man, Rod? On the stairs?"

"Nobody." He shifted. "Someone my family knew years ago. I don't know what he'd be doing here." Rod shifted again. "We're seeing and hearing things, aren't we?"

"*Most* of us are," Alex said, looking towards Simon's outline. He felt a mad sense of embarrassment. Rod went on as if she hadn't spoken.

"We're seeing and hearing things, but I don't know why I'd see that man."

"Or hear that voice when the lift opened," Kelly muttered.

"I don't know anything about that," Rod replied. They all heard the lie.

Dao's face asked the obvious question to Kelly; she shook her head. He'd have to wait to find out what had been screamed by nobody they saw down below.

Wanting to stand apart from the rest, Simon had no choice but to return to his place on the sofa. Either that or remain standing like an idiot. "We need to find out what's happening outside," he said. "The bomb. Korea. All that."

"Who cares about that? Inside here is what matters," Kelly replied.

"Kelly's right." Rod sounded calmer now. "We're in here; the world's out there, so what we have to deal with is in here with us. On that note, I say we say we sit tight in here until morning and go from there."

"A night in here?" Alex's aggression borne of fear wanted to come back, but she didn't have the strength. "You serious?"

"What else can we do?"

"Shit," she whispered. Then: "Come on, Kel." She rose, reaching for her sister as she did so.

"Where are you going?" Simon asked.

"If we're staying here, then we're blocking the doors. We'll find something heavy. Tables. Desks. Whatever."

"What about these?" Kelly kicked at the chair she'd sat on.

"We need something more solid. Some big desks should do it. Come on."

"Be careful," Rod said to the women's backs as they made their careful way across the moonlit carpet. He waited another few seconds before pitching his voice low. "Dao. I hate to ask."

"What?"

Rod sighed. "Your son."

"You mean Huan, don't you?"

Rod answered as simply as possible, aware hesitating or picking at the edges would be worse. "Yes."

"What about him?"

Rod shifted in his seat. "When you lost him. When was that?"

"I told you. Two years ago."

All at once, Simon wanted Rod to shut the fuck up because he knew what Rod was getting at. Inside, he saw his Aunt Rachel, squatting so she was at his level, opening her arms and smiling and how he'd loved her—how he'd lost his fear in that moment.

Thirty-three years ago. Simon, six years old.

Thirty-three years ago, today. His birthday.

"You mean when exactly?" Dao asked. "Yes.

Dao answered without pause. "Today. Two years ago, today."

A moment of quiet passed between the three men, broken by Dao inhaling and stilling the threat of fresh tears.

"I am sorry, Dao. I truly am," Rod said.

And all Simon could do was wonder why Rod was so curious on the date of a child's death, just as he didn't want to ever know. Knowing might also mean knowing something awful.

Chapter Seventeen

On the ground floor, the doors to the lift stood wide open. Night peered in through the dozens of windows; moonlight came with it, but did nothing to dispel the darkness coating the cold of the floor or inside the lift. The reception area of Greenham Place, only ever silent when the last of the building's staff had locked up and gone home to hope they wouldn't be called out for an alarm, had the same lonely atmosphere it held during the Christmas break or over a bank holiday weekend.

Except on those occasions, no aroma of burned flesh coated the pillars or the desk and computer monitors, both resembling unblinking eyes in the quiet. The stink remained constant and motionless in the air. Nothing of Simon's breeze disturbed it down on the ground floor; no bodies walked to waft it in the currents. The stench of cooked skin and raw muscle bubbling in fire simply existed in the same way as the night while the eyes of the open lift gazed out blandly.

From the floor of the lift, the gloom shifted, moving like a widening puddle of oil. It crept over the floor towards the doors, the few remaining in the building bashed through before sunset. They parted, and the dark reached for the first of the steps.

By the time it made it to the second floor, it had risen into a shape approximating something human, in that it had legs.

On reaching the fourth-floor landing, it also had arms. And opening hands. And claws.

Outside the double doors for the sixth floor where Rod quietly asked Dao about the date of his son's death, a motionless outline stood, hunched, listening with its head cocked and its arms the length of its deformed body, dangling by where its knees would have grown if it had any.

A harsh cold surrounded the form and brought the stink of the blackened flesh with it. That smell pressed on the doors but did not pass them. It wanted the men and women beyond to talk and wonder and fear. Let them do so without knowing it listened. It was enough. The lonely man's breath of nothing and nowhere had blown across the floor, heard and felt by them all despite his weak and pointless lies. Let him pretend. Let him not think of what breathed to him from his dead past and from the faraway corners of his life.

Let him call it nothing. That was its name after all.

Outside the double doors, the crooked thing smiled and the fires all around it were turned frigid by its glee.

Chapter Eighteen

"We need to get out of here, Kel."

Kelly froze. While the meeting room was dark for the most part, enough light from the moon streamed in to reveal the surfaces of the three rectangular desks, the silent computer screens, and Alex's pretty but stern face. She stood back from her end of the desk, arms folded over her breasts and enough visible of her face for Kelly to feel the old anger resurfacing.

Goddamn it. Why does she look at me like she's Mum?

"How the hell do we do that?" Kelly pointed to the night, pressing cold fingers on the windows. "There's nothing out. We'd be lucky to see more than two feet in front of us."

What she didn't want to say was there was no way she'd head out to the stairs and the quiet landings when she couldn't see what might be coming to meet her. Or not quite as a horrific but still bad enough, what voices might scream out of thin air as they'd screamed at Rod down on the ground floor.

"I don't give a shit," Alex said in a rapid hiss. "My girls are out there, and I'm stuck in here like I'm insane or something. I can't just stay here like nothing's happened."

"What the fuck can you do?" Kelly moved closer to her sister, smelling Alex's sweat and fear. Or maybe she'd smelled her own. By now, they all reeked of old perspiration and panic. Maybe they should bottle it and sell it. Eau De Shit Yourself.

Keeping calm suddenly felt like it was an alien concept. Too much mad stuff had happened in the short time since she'd crashed to the floor near the ground floor lift. Too much shit that couldn't be explained. And don't forget being forced to spend more time with Alex than she had in a year.

A year tonight, right? I'm surprised she hasn't picked up on that.

Kelly shoved a wall up in her mind, aware that if she let herself go down that path, there was no way of knowing what might happen.

"There's some knives in the kitchen drawers." Amazingly, Alex sounded in control. "Plates. I'll break them and use the pieces as blades if I have to. But you have to help me, Kel."

She grasped Kelly's wrists and pulled her close.

"I don't think that lot will want me to go. Especially Rod. He'll say it's too dangerous—"

"Because it *is,* Alex."

Alex dropped Kelly's arms. While the light was poor, enough ghostly white illumination fell through the window for Kelly to see the disappointment on her sister's face.

"Forget it," Alex said. "Stupid me." She tried to smile but the corners of her mouth fell. "Stupid me thinking you'd do something for someone else."

"That's not fair," Kelly cried.

"Yeah." Alex grabbed the end of the desk and yanked it hard. "It is."

Two of the monitors fell to the carpet, one screen striking the corner as it fell. Plastic snapped, a vicious, ugly sound.

Grunting with the effort, Alex dragged the table towards the door leading back to the staff area. "You going to help me with this?"

Hot tears sitting at the corners of her eyes, Kelly took her place at the other end of the table, reaching for it and any hold, no matter how weak, she could get on her spinning emotions. Again, she was a child admonished by a parent for not being good enough; again, she was a spiteful, spoiled kid refusing to see her flaws.

Her fumbling hands found the table.

Kelly.

Her name coming from behind, a sly, secret whisper. Kelly turned.

Her focus found the windows, floor to ceiling, overlooking the strange and empty night.

Except it wasn't empty.

A naked man floated in the air, his mouth forming her name and his penis stabbing at the glass.

Chapter Nineteen

Midnight.

Rod slid his sleeve back down and pocketed his phone. Although the light from the screen wasn't much, he wished he could keep it going all through the long, slow minutes of his watch. Better not, though. His battery was about half done. No sense using it all up on a piddly bit of light.

In his other hand, he held one of the three kitchen knives Alex had grabbed from a drawer after that horrible few minutes of Kelly crying. He then maintained she thought she'd seen something outside. Unconsciously, the memory of the girl's clear terror made Rod tighten his hold on the knife. At the same time, he pulled his legs up and held his knees.

How she screamed! My God. Like she'd never stop. And then to say it was just down to a quick bit of movement, like a bat or a bird… bloody hell. She must have thought they were idiots.

She'll tell when she wants to.

True, but in the meantime, any little bit of information might help them. Thinking that, Rod smiled. If that was true, why hadn't he shared his little story about Martin Williams? Why had he described the monster as an *old family friend* and left it at that? Ditto the moment before he lobbed that chair through the window; the image on the computer screen, there and gone in seconds and plenty long enough to stay imprinted on his mind and heart, now.

Simple, really. Because anything else was unthinkable. And maybe Kelly had something similar going on. Maybe they all did.

Rod hugged himself tighter in a small attempt to fight off the chilly air. Although the coats they'd borrowed were a help, any spring warmth from April or May belonged to the far future. The ache in his infrequently used muscles didn't help, either. While they'd warmed up lugging furniture about, sitting still for an hour meant the cold had had plenty of time to worm its way through the coat and lay fingers on his exposed skin.

A small whispering sounded from the seats. The soft noise of a coat moving on a chair. Either Simon or Dao—Rod's eyes weren't strong enough in the almost total black to be sure— eased off one of the sofas and crept across the carpet. He used the wall as a guide, fingertips trailing over it until he reached the space close to the main double doors, now blocked by three large desks, an armchair, and boxes of files they'd taken from a storage cupboard. Rod sat near the makeshift barricade, watching the man approach, and it was only when five or six feet separated them that he named the figure as Dao.

The younger man crouched. "Rod?" he muttered. "You okay?"

Dao rested against the wall, shoulder almost touching Rod's. He splayed his legs and kept his hands in his lap. The large pair of scissors Dao took from a desk drawer jutted from his groin.

"Not really. Can't sleep," he whispered.

"You should try, mate. Get some rest before your watch."

Dao shrugged, and his adopted coat rustled on the wall. "It doesn't matter. We need to be aware of everything, don't we?"

"I suppose."

Surprised, Dao found he could relax more beside Rod than he had on the sofa. He'd take relaxed over staring at the ceiling, hoping the suggestions of moving shapes above were simply down to his eyes playing tricks on him. Or just his imagination.

"You think we should try the doors again after
dawn?" Dao asked.

Rod kept his voice at the same whisper as Dao's. "I don't think we have a choice. Do you?"

"Not if we want to get out of here."

Dao considered his next words carefully before realising there was no way of raising his point without being point blank.

"What happens if we go down there and we see the same thing you did? The same burned people? What if nothing shouts at us like it did when you were down there?"

At first, Rod gave no reply, and Dao could only wonder what horrific thing had yelled those awful, shitty things while the people with their scorched skin and faces crowded around the entrance. While he'd been going through his own personal nightmare, while the others had theirs ten floors below, he'd heard enough to picture it and to be turned cold by the mental images.

Eventually, Rod spoke, voice still no louder than a hiss. "I honestly have no idea, mate. All I can tell you is we can't stay here. We cannot. I don't know whether we're all hallucinating or if things are real. Right now, I care more about getting out than I do what's going on."

Dao nodded, understanding the man's thinking.

"I care more about finding out if my son is really here than I do anything else," he said.

"Don't blame you. Got three myself. All grown-up now, of course, but if I thought any one of them was here and in danger… " In the dark, Rod's voice shook. "I'd tear this building apart to find them." His hand found Dao's and gave a brief squeeze. "You don't have to worry about that. No reason your boy would be here, is there?

Your wife wouldn't have brought him here and not told you, would she? No reason for that."

"No," Dao whispered. "No reason."

"There you go. It's this place." Rod fell silent.

Dao waited. There was nothing else to do.

"I've been thinking," Rod continued. "Not much else I can do sitting here on my tod. It's this place. I think there's something wrong with it. I mean, don't get me wrong. I'm not into all the spooky, horror-film stuff. Not for me, son. But I do like a bit of science-fiction, you know what I mean?"

"Yeah."

"A bit of alien cultures and that. A bit of other worlds out there in space and how they relate to us. I've been thinking and maybe we're in something like that. Maybe we're not where we're supposed to be." He paused again, although only for a second. Dao had a feeling there was no chance Rod would come out with his theory in daylight, or if the others were awake. "Maybe this is about different dimensions. Maybe we're in one and everyone else, our families and friends and all the people who should be here right now, are back in the one we know. Maybe we got pulled into another place and what we're hearing and seeing is them trying to find us."

Although Rod had clearly finished his thought, it felt to Dao that the man trailed off slightly as if there was something about the thought didn't quite work for him.

"You think so?" Dao asked. "I mean, yeah, maybe in a film. But this is real life. I can't deal with that in real life."

Rod shifted position. "I don't know. Just an idea that probably doesn't make sense. All I can tell you is what you're hearing and what the girls saw *might* be outside this and we need to get out of it, too."

"Rod?"

"Yes?"

He had to ask. It had to be now in the quiet.

"Who did you see? I heard what Alex said about the stairs and her dad. Who was it for you?"

Rod's reply was calm and gentle. Even so, Dao heard the implacable firmness living below its surface. There was no argument here.

"Not now, son. In the morning."

"Okay."

He thought Rod might stand and leave, their little conversation over. Instead, Rod voiced another thought.

"I tell you what. Downstairs. The people we saw. Whatever all that was, I don't know, but maybe it was a good thing."

"How do you work that one out?"

"Because you were up here; we were down there, and you and we were both in the shit. We needed to run. So did you."

The same thought had been needling Dao at the back of his mind for the last few hours. He'd successfully managed to focus on anything else, instead of picking at the implications of what might have happened if Rod, Simon, and the sisters had made it out, leaving him alone with whatever the hell else lived in this building. Before Dao had chance of stopping it, the thought led to another.

Had they all been forced together? Was it fate or chance or something else that had sent Rod and the others running back up the stairs to re-join him?

My son; the girls' dad and whomever Rod saw. We're all scared of something. We're all here with those fears and we're all pushed together. What is going on here?

But they weren't all with their fears. Not all of them.

"What about Simon?" Dao whispered. "Why doesn't he see anything?"

"I honestly have no clue. He's not lying. I know that much. Maybe he's not scared of anything."

"Everybody is scared of something."

Rod's laugh was almost too soft to be heard. "Yes. You could say that. Maybe he just doesn't have any imagination."

Dao didn't think that was the case but kept quiet. Rod shifted position again, readying himself to stand, and Dao asked a final question.

"Do you think it went off? The bomb?"

Rod was still. Dao listened to the man breathe and tried not to picture any part of Greenham Place outside their little corner of nothingness. No dark, only silent stairs; no moonlight shining on the floor of the foyer; no silent offices with their empty chairs and blank computer screens.

"I think something wants us to believe it has. I saw something earlier. I haven't mentioned it. Seemed like a bad idea."

"Saw what?"

"On a computer screen. When I was by myself. When I chucked that chair through the window." All at once, Rod sounded like an old man. "I hit one of the computers. It came on and the screen, it was outside. The sky. The air. Burning. Flames everywhere. It was like looking right into the sun and the flames were coming straight for me. The window behind me, they were coming for that. Something wants us to think that bomb went off and we're burned, but I don't believe it did. Not here."

Dao reached and grabbed hold of Rod's shin. "*What* wants us to think that, Rod?"

"I don't know. There's something wrong here. Maybe it's the building. Maybe it wants us to believe we're dead, and this is… well, Hell for want of a better word, but I can't believe that."

"Why not?"

In the dark, Rod smiled for the first time in hours. It felt good on his face even if nothing else came close to *good*. "Because I don't think we'd be this scared if we were dead."

The two men sat in companionable hush for long minutes while the night held fast to the windows of Greenham Place and stuck to the pavements of Willington's roads like tar. No traffic lights winked from red to green; no taxis took the late roads away from the city centre, while out in Willington's suburbs, the houses, and the tidy gardens were a black secret.

"We might not be dead," Dao said abruptly, and Rod jerked. He'd been close to nodding off. He licked the stale taste from his teeth, alert again despite the ache filling his body. Dao put a faint emphasis on his first word; seconds passed before Rod's mind registered it.

"We?" he echoed. Dao nodded.

"I don't believe in ghosts, Rod. I *don't,* but if my boy is here, if… " Dao shivered. "If Huan is here, too, then he's a ghost. He's dead. I know that. He's been dead for two years. I *know* that," he said again as if Rod had argued. "I know it like I know all I can do is try to bring it into everything else in my life. The guilt, though.

That's something else and maybe that's why his ghost is here."

"Guilt?" Rod said carefully. Inside, he walked the long fields of his childhood home, the farm his parents had owned since they were in their twenties. He saw the acres of land and smelled the nasty but still comforting aroma of cowshit.

"We were in a park. The boys were on a climbing frame." Dao could have been detailing the plot of a film that had bored him. "I was on my phone, right next to the frame. Right next to it." He made a fist and struck his leg. "Huan fell and I was on my phone."

"That wasn't your fault."

"Yeah." Dao sighed. There was no relief in verbalising the thoughts that stung and bit any time they wanted to, no comfort in telling a stranger what haunted him, and would continue to haunt him every minute of every day for the rest of his life. "It was."

Rod gave Dao's hand a rough squeeze. "We'll be fine if we stick together. Just keep your eyes open and wake Alex in two hours."

He moved away.

"Rod?" Dao said. He heard Rod turn back. "Yeah?"

"I'm glad you're here."

Rod let out a soft laugh. "I'm not, son. Good night."

Rod's slow, careful movement through the gloom of the corridor took a few moments. Dao focused on the sound of the man's footsteps, then the creak of the leather chair as he sat in it. After that, all Dao heard was gentle breathing and a few weak snores.

Chapter Twenty

Time passed as if weighted down. A single minute seemed to take at least three times as long as normal to tick by. Dao placed his scissors beside his leg. He held his mobile, resisting the urge to illuminate the screen and dispel the dark. He'd taken a quick look at the time when he rose. Barely half an hour had passed since then, making it not quite twenty to one. Dawn—if it came—was long, silent hours away. All he had to do was remain focused and rational for another two hours, then he could wake Alex to take over.

One of the women let out a moan in their sleep. Dao peered down the corridor, able to make out the suggestion of a sofa, upon which Simon slept. The other sofa where the sisters slumbered was a grey box, the white of the moonlight falling at least ten feet from it and turning the black into a murky soup.

Whoever had moaned was now silent. Dao waited another minute. He was reasonably sure Kelly had made the noise and wondered what she dreamed of. Maybe the reason why the sisters didn't get along. He'd picked up on that early on. Not that it had been hard to miss. They weren't close; something had got in the way of any natural and happy sibling relationship. Maybe that swam in Kelly's dreams now.

Satisfied she wasn't about to wake up shrieking, Dao turned back to the door.

His own shriek remained locked in his mouth.

The walls, door, and corridor beyond had vanished, as had the makeshift barrier to keep out any visions or ghosts. In their place, white stretched back into featureless miles. It was like looking down into a massive hole in the earth and seeing not mud or rock or layers but a nothing-space. Dao's stomach turned, and dizziness raced behind his eyes. He managed to blink, pupils shielded from the dazzling white for a tiny second.

The void was no longer empty. Where the door should have opened onto the corridor, Yang stood on nothing. The boy's arms were outstretched; his head hung towards his little chest, and Dao tried to block the word *crucifixion* from forming in his head. He failed.

Yang. Oh God, my Yang.

Yang lifted his head. His eyes, exhausted and almost lifeless, found his father's. His mouth trembled as it creaked opened.

DADDY.

The shout blasted into Dao's skull, not as words but as an impact. He rocked back on his knees, managing to stay upright through simple luck rather than intent. He tried to say Yang's name even as he tried to rise. Neither action would work. It was as if he had been glued to the floor.

Yang began to scream. He didn't draw a breath or pause; he screamed in one non-stop, terrible sound. Around him, a dark mass darted through the white, never stopping and never slowing enough for Dao to get a decent look at it. All he took in was a hunched, squirming thing: no taller than a couple of feet, no wider than a small child. It flew like a mad fly, dancing around Yang's head, then his waist, and then his feet before shooting up to the boy's face while Yang's noise rang out at the same horrendous pitch and volume. With a ghastly ripping sound, the skin of Yang's forehead peeled back, exposing red meat. The shredding spread down to his cheeks, then chin and lips. Skin flew away, sucked backwards into the emptiness. Within seconds, the skin of the boy's neck, chest and belly came loose, shredding like paper even as he shrieked for his daddy to stop it, to help him. Blood rained, staining the white. Yang's arms waved madly, spraying more blood. Skin, muscle and sinew tore loose, leaving bone smeared with red. The destruction raced down to his groin, his thighs and knees, turning his lower half into a slaughterhouse. Long strips of skin broke free from his shins, ripping them loose. Then, his feet and tiny toes did the same. The bloody flesh hung in thin lines and tiny pieces, droplets falling from each section. Yang's head had become a denuded skull and still the boy screamed. Still, the capering shape raced through the white, and its hands were claws, hands tearing through Yang and the black formed a face for a tiny breath of time, a child's face, the mouth open in rage and burning hate.

Dao was upright. Without moving, he stood. There was no time to wonder at the change. He threw himself forward, flying for a second.

He hit the door with a thud and collapsed to the floor. The space and his tortured son were nowhere. Neither was Huan's spirit or the terrible things it had done to his brother.

Dao closed his eyes, tears leaking from the corners. He wept without making a sound, palm over his mouth, his own hot breath baking his palm.

Rod had been right and wrong. Wrong about being in another dimension and right about something being *off* here.

They were in Hell.

Dao opened his eyes and cried soundlessly in the dark.

Chapter Twenty-One

Underneath the three coats he'd taken from the staffroom, Simon shifted position. Bending his legs made the coats rustle, the sound seemingly louder in the middle of the night. He froze, breathing through his nose, listening. None of the others stirred. He straightened a leg and stared into the dark. It felt as if hours had passed since night fell and they'd begun their series of watches at Rod's suggestion. Simon had gone for the idea in a big way, wishing he'd thought of it. Not much of a surprise he hadn't. Ideas were in short supply now. All he had was a big nothing.

Same as ever.

Simon stifled a snort. Whether or not any of the others were faking their sleep as he was, he had no idea, but didn't want to risk waking them. Better to look into the dark and wish for more moonlight to break through the thin blinds in the next office. Enough came to turn the section of wall at the foot of his sofa into a faint grey, revealing the outline of the sofa the girls lay upon. Beyond that, Rod could be anywhere. His chair was invisible in the dark. Simon had listened to the faint murmurs of conversation between the big Welshman and Dao, catching almost none of it and unsure if he actually wanted to. Whatever was going on in Greenham Place, they wouldn't work it out while they were scared shitless and hiding in an office overnight. He'd lain still while they talked, giving no sign he was awake when Rod crept into the seating area and took the chair Dao had vacated. Now, all Simon had were his thoughts and the soft whisper of Rod's breath. Not to forget the possibility of cold eyes watching him as he pretended to sleep, watching from any of the office's corners. The girls' dad, whoever was after Rod, whatever Kelly saw out the window. Dao's son.

Except none of them could be here and, even if they were, *why the fuck could he not see them?*

Because you've got nothing to offer them so nothing to be afraid of.

Was that it? The others had their fears here; that was pretty obvious. Did nothing scare him, so nothing could… what? Haunt him like the others were being haunted?

Simon stared straight up and imagined something crawling over the ceiling, something looking down at him as he looked up at it. Some horrible *thing* up there just beyond the dark, tensing its muscles to launch from the ceiling and land on his face and chest.

Come on, then.

Nothing happened.

Nothing's up there. All you've got here is you, two men and two women. This place is empty.

For him, yes. For the others, no.

Empty. What a word. What a horrible, shitty word. And a shame it covered more or less everything in his life. Job, his flat, his potential, his past. Empty. Maybe he should have told the others about it all earlier or maybe they would have just thought him a total dick with too much time on his hands.

And that was exactly it: too much empty time in his flat that looked exactly the same as it did in the morning when he returned home each night. The same few cushions in the same places on the sofa; the same bit of washing up beside the sink; and the same half tube of loo roll next to the toilet were all there. Not just his flat, of course. The weekdays of work, colleagues, and doing his job with almost no thought even when it involved trekking halfway across the country to some town he'd never heard of to sell a company he didn't care about. Then the dead weekends of TV, going to the cinema alone, getting a pizza, and resisting the urge to go online and check out people from his past. No point. Anything he'd known before moving from a nothing and nowhere village in Northamptonshire to Oxford was long gone. All the photos of little kids' birthday parties and married couples' cats wouldn't bring his past back. And what if it did? What good was the nothing of his past to him? About as much good as his nothing future. Thirty-nine and staring at a great big hole of all the dead years ahead. It made no difference if the company relocated from Oxford to Willington and ended up that much closer to London. He'd bring the same nothing to another city, and the weekends of sitting in the cinema by himself and then channel-hopping would begin anew.

Dead present. Dead future. And hey, while we're at it, a dead past. Yep. Dead days of a childhood long gone. Even when he finally had a home after those long, lonely months of care, even when his Aunt Rachel welcomed him into her house and told the six-year-old Simon he didn't have to be scared or worry about his mum anymore, a small insect of doubt bored its way into his secret heart. While he knew that six-year-old boy was long gone, as was any chance of his drunken mother hurting him. Simon also knew that insect remained. It was the reason he couldn't make friends, the reason he lived to work and kept anything else far away where it couldn't get in.

Would they get all that if I told them, or would they think I was a giant wanker? Dao's got his son and he's scared shitless for him. Rod's got the same fear about whoever that guy is, and the girls have got some issues going on. Kelly's got a secret and Alex knows it, even though she doesn't know what the deal is. So, they've got all that and would they give a toss about your life, about keeping everyone out like you're so fucking mysterious and troubled when you're actually just a boring twat with a job you don't care about and no life outside it? You really think whatever you're scared of matches a man who's scared for his kid? Or for a woman who's seeing her dad walking around a deserted building when she knows he's in a coma? You think you're close to that fear? Bollocks.

The thought held no vehemence or even much energy. It seemed he'd lost the ability to shout at himself, and maybe that was okay. Maybe he could let go of wishing he was a kid again, welcomed into a new home by an aunt, instead of a man trapped outside the world of what mattered to everyone else.

Simon turned onto his side, almost dislodging the coats as he moved. He righted them and gazed at the spot near the doors where Dao kept the second watch of the night. If the man was awake, he made no sound. Dao's turn now; Kelly's next. When she went to the little patch of carpet by their barrier, Simon would have two hours' kip before his own watch began. Not that sleep felt like it was anywhere nearby. Not with a head full of the past and an empty today; not with the possibility they were all dead, burned into nothing by some mad bastard's nuclear attack just as those nutcases from Korea had done in Los Angeles last summer. 6/13. The day that made 9/11 and 7/7 look like practice. The day that led its slow, inexorable way to today, when the Brothers of Jeong-ui apparently wanted to turn

London into a crater but had to settle for a city whose only claim to the world stage was an American air force base not too distant. They had to make do with blowing a few hundred odd thousand people off the face of the Earth and now here he was with four others, and those four others were being haunted by their personal nightmares while he saw nothing, felt nothing, *was* nothing.

Jesus. That's a bedtime story.

The forced humour to his quick thought didn't help. As mental as considering the idea was, he had to see it as a possibility. If they were dead, it explained where everyone else had gone. The bomb had detonated, turning Willington into a blinding flash of a new sun and he was as dead as the girls, Dao, and Rod.

They were dead—and this building was Hell for the others and emptiness for him.

Are you sure it's not Hell for you, too?

In answer, he heard the faint murmur of the lifeless wind again. It blew from the direction of the double doors, brushed over the floor beside the sofa, and rose to make the thinning strands of his hair shake.

Simon closed his eyes. In seconds, the breath became a breeze, steady and flowing from his head to his chest and playing over the coats. Still, he kept his eyes closed. The draft grew into a gust, then a full wind hammering at him. It blasted into his ears, smothered his nose and mouth with its stink, and it wasn't a wind anymore; it was a breath, an exhalation of something long-dead. The stench set up home in his nostrils, blocked from his lungs only by his refusal to inhale. His chest became a fire. He grabbed his thighs, digging his nails into his skin, fighting pain with pain. Still, the wind thundered over his body, a centuries-old gasp blown out of a massive throat. A tunnel stretching from his feet all the way down through the formless black to the mouth of whatever had exhaled its last lungful at him all those long years ago. And all he had to do to see its face was drop through that tunnel and race down, down, down, and take forever to reach the nothing he had in his past, present, and most definitely his future.

There one second, gone the next. The wind left him as if it had never been. Simon opened his eyes and let his breath out as quietly as possible. His heart thudded all over his ribs and in his ears. He focused on the steady pounding and stared towards the ceiling.

There was nothing else to do in the dark.

Chapter Twenty-Two

For the fifth or sixth time, Kelly directed her shrill thought at the doors.

Go away. Just go away and leave us alone.

Scratching in the dark; scratching on the doors.

The first noise had come a few minutes ago: the faint sound as quiet as a cat's paw lightly tapping for entrance. Back to the wall and legs bent so she could hug them, Kelly froze. Enough time passed for her to convince herself the sound either hadn't existed or was only something in the wall or floors settling. But then, another secret hiss, faint but unmistakable from the landing where nothing walked.

Scratch.

Across the floor where the others dozed in their thin sleep, someone stirred but didn't wake.

Someone else— probably Rod—let out a gentle fart.

Scratch again on the doors, loud enough to make Kelly squeak. Surely the others would wake; surely, they'd hear *that*. A moment passed with Kelly left in thick silence and the sensation, the certainty that whatever scratched on the doors was listening to her listening for it. It was playing with her.

Fuck you. Fuck you. You're not here. We are and we're together so fuck you.

Together? That was a joke. She knew just one of these people and wouldn't have had much to do with the rest outside this mental place. The guys were all right in their own ways, but their lives were not part of hers, and chances where they'd say the same about her, so pretending they were *together*—as if that created some kind of magic spell to ward off terror in the night—was crap.

The scratch came again, but now more of a scrape of metal on wood; some thick chunk of pipework eating into a rotting piece of tree and tearing through it so it could stab its way out the other side. And that's what was coming right now; someone wielding a pipe, the end sawn off into a jagged edge so it was able to hammer into the doors, splinter them, and knock their pitiful barrier and all the furniture aside before it tore the tender skin of her face into shreds.

Kelly attempted to kick herself away from the door even as she tried to yell for Alex to wake up. Neither action worked. She swallowed a particular scent, something warm and pleasant: the distinctive aroma of aftershave.

Oh my God. No. No fucking way.

In memory, she saw his face coming closer to hers, mouth opening while her own mouth was filled with the sour taste of all the drinks she'd downed over the last few hours and the fresh cold of a night in late October while the throb of the music in the club through the bricks and the ground into her feet, up her legs, and to her crotch. Her secret throb made her open her mouth and inhale the smell of his vodka shots and the layers of his aftershave.

No. You are not here. No way are you here.

She heard a tiny breath; her name whispered by a man who could not be in the building. A man who could not have been naked and floating outside a window, God knows how many feet above the ground.

Send him away, Kelly thought incoherently. If there was sense to be made from it, she didn't give a shit. *You can send him away. Just think, you stupid bitch. Fucking THINK. THINK OF SOMETHING ELSE. FUCKING THINK OF SOMEONE ELSE—*

Memory took her back to hours earlier, when they'd run from the burned people congregating on the pavement and pressed the ruins of their faces against the glass doors; they ran from them and the awful thing yelling at Rod.

Alex's dad on the stairs, a small man made smaller by his injuries, bandages, and the dangling strands falling from his oxygen mask. Kelly saw him while a squat, inhuman shape pressed its fingers against the doors and relished the girl's terror. She saw Desmond Sinclair gazing back at her with his still, calm face; his eyes were warm and friendly. He was a decent man, memory said. One of the world's good guys, and while they shared no blood, he loved her as if she were his own daughter. He formed part of her extended family and made that family a safe place where her own dad had once been Desmond's close friend. Before he'd become so far gone into his dementia, he had no idea who Desmond was. He loved her as he loved Alex, and he would keep her safe from the thing outside that wanted to come in, to come in and sink its mouth over hers.

The old man's face altered almost imperceptibly. He remained on the stairs a few floors below while the late afternoon light coated his skin and dressings with equal warmth. He remained motionless and he remained human, but something terrible darkened his eyes, and Kelly named it in a heartbeat.

Disappointment.

No, please. I didn't mean it. It was a mistake. I fucked up, okay? Everyone has and I'm sorry for it. I'm so sorry.

Kelly left her memory, but she couldn't shake off the image of Desmond's disappointment. She sat against the wall, as she had done for at least half an hour, and quiet sat with her. Whatever skulked in the corridor beyond the office no longer scratched for entry. It seemed her brief but horrible vision, or whatever the hell had happened, was over. Convincing herself nothing had actually gone on was surprisingly easy, due mostly to the mind defending itself in the simplest way: denial. Known horrors that made sense—crime, violence, accidents— could be incorporated into sense and logic. Even the awful possibility the terrorists had managed to set their bomb off out in the fields and empty roads near the air force base could be taken in, as long as she didn't try to think of the devastation and death that would come from it. The idea or the tiny possibility of a man out on the landing, wanting to break through to their hiding-place, couldn't be true because it threw up the potential for this hell to get much worse.

So, her defence was simplicity. It hadn't happened.

Nope. Not at all.

Kelly tried to relax but couldn't quite manage it. She settled for focusing on her breathing while another soft fart sounded from across the room. She tried to make out their precise shapes. Too little beams of light from the moon broke through the blinds, and there was definitely no illumination coming from any other building on Greenham Road or the streets snaking from it. Kelly refused to blink until her eyes adjusted to the gloom. Dao. That was Dao in the chair while Alex slept on the sofa opposite of the little table they'd placed their phones on. Were they sleeping, or was Alex lying awake, thinking about the sight of her dad and the things he'd shouted? Did she worry about Charlotte and Louisa, the girls somewhere beyond Greenham Place? And what about Dao? How the hell did he sleep when he kept hearing and seeing his son being hurt? Kelly had rarely given any thought to the idea she might one day have kids; it seemed like an alien concept belonging to a future far removed from working in a library and living alone in a shitty bedsit. Even so, she found putting herself in Dao's place to be easier than she might have imagined. The fact that the guy was still able to walk and talk when faced with this shit was pretty impressive. Not to mention what he'd said about his other son dying a few years back.

He said it was today. It's his anniversary.

Disquiet pricked at her. An anniversary. Yeah. She could see that. Two years for Dao, and a year for her. A few days before her nineteenth, and a year to the night she'd had a party for her eighteenth. A year to the night she'd got smashed, danced, drank more, and had a little hit (just a little). No need to overdo it. She felt herself letting go of giving a shit, aware of doing so, aware she could stop it, and totally aware she was letting go willingly because it meant she'd have an excuse for what was coming—what she was about to do.

What she *did.*

And all at once, realisation fell on Kelly. A year for her; two for Dao and neither fact was a coincidence. Neither was an accident.

A second realisation crashed down.

The stink of the aftershave was back, cloying and too close, way too fucking close.

Kelly whipped her head around towards their barrier. At the same time, the darkness moved, a precise shape closing in on her mouth and bringing the reek of its aftershave and too many drinks into her nose as it brought a hot hand to her crotch.

Chapter Twenty-Three

Simon woke when Alex placed a gentle weight on his shoulder and shook him. He jerked forward, cramps biting into his back and neck. He'd slept in a sitting position, wedged against the wall with the only soft comfort coming from the carpet.

"What is it?" he said thickly while turning his head back and forth. Tendons cracked, and he winced.

"Morning." Alex looked around as if to convince herself of the fact. "Just."

Groaning gently, Simon tried to rise. His legs had yet to wake up. Alex took his hand and helped him. He kept hold of her for a moment, aware he should let go, welcoming the warmth of her skin in his. Alex raised an eyebrow. He lowered his hand.

"You didn't wake me," she said, and Simon blushed.

"Slept through my watch, too. Not a great lookout."

The others stirred in the chairs; coats and jackets slid from them as they rose.

"I won't tell them," Alex whispered. "Just say we both kept watch and nothing happened."

Simon nodded. "Thanks."

"Did anything happen?"

"No. Not a thing. Kelly seemed odd when she finished her watch, but I didn't—"

"Odd?" Alex interrupted. "How?"

She glanced behind at her sister as the other woman sat and rubbed her palms against her eyes.

"Quiet. Wouldn't say much. Just told me to keep a look out. Which I managed to cock up."

"Yes, you did." She gazed at him, and he blushed again. At least ten years younger than him, she managed to make him feel like a geeky teenager. "But we're still here, and we get out of here this morning. Agreed?"

"Gets my vote."

She left him to cross to Kelly, speaking in a low voice as the men dropped their coats. Rod stood, stretched, and walked to the kitchen area. He opened a few cupboards and let them close with a soft thud.

"Not a lot for brekkie," he said while filling a glass with water.

"We get out of here and breakfast is on me," Alex said. Rod managed a smile even though every muscle, including the ones in his face, ached.

Shaking off the last of the sleep in his limbs, Simon followed Dao over to the window. On the sofa, Kelly gazed up at her sister.

"You okay?" Alex asked with his voice low.

Kelly nodded once.

"You sure?"

"Shit, get out of my face, will you?"

At Kelly's yell, the men froze in their movements: Rod with a glass almost at his mouth, Dao and Simon not quite side by side as they approached the windows and the murky light of dawn. Seconds of nothing, not even breathing, or so it seemed, passed by. Kelly shook off her improvised blanket and stood. Alex had to step back to give Kelly room.

"Sorry." Kelly knew the apology didn't come close to sounding genuine. Not that she had it in her to give a fuck. Giving a fuck had taken a nosedive out of the window in the middle of the night when the darkness moved—

"I didn't sleep, and I feel like shit. Sorry."

Alex nodded as if she believed the story. "It's okay. Just as long as you're all right."

She left her sister, heading towards the furniture they had moved the night before, and doing all she could to focus on the idea of moving it. Doing that meant she didn't have to think about the hurting tears that wanted to fall, or the way she listened for the chill clang of a church bell that could not be in the building.

"Hey."

Simon and Dao stood at the windows, side by side and both staring outside.

"It's normal," Dao said. "It's all normal."

The men pressed their faces against the glass as Rod and Kelly rushed to join them. Alex approached slowly.

Five floors below, an early Saturday morning in Willington began to play out. While there was little traffic and not a great number of pedestrians, the streets no longer resembled the first sketches of a drawing from an artist with little talent. Shadows moved as clouds came and went over the sun, and those shadows had life, rather than looking like stains on the ground. The wind had picked up since the day before; it took a discarded can of Coke from outside a takeaway to the gutter and rolled it down towards a drain. Outside Edwards, the breeze caught a few squashed burger containers and sent them skittering into a shop doorway. In the alleyway between the still-closed branch of Tesco and a bar converted from an old cinema, two porters for an old hotel five minutes' walk away came into view, emerged on to Greenham Road and crossed for Banks Lane without needing to check for taxis or buses.

"Simon," Dao said. "Keep looking. Don't even blink, okay?"

Simon had to lick his lips a few times before speaking. "Okay."

"On three, everyone but Simon look away." Not giving them chance to ask why, Dao rapidly said: "One, two, three."

He, Kelly, and Rod turned, all focusing on the opposite wall. Not quite close to the windows to see below, Alex stared past the others to the fading grey of the sky and wondered if the kids were awake yet, awake and maybe looking out of their bedroom window and wanting to know why Mummy hadn't come home last night.

"Is it the same?" Dao whispered.

"Yeah." Simon pulled away from the glass as Dao, Rod, and Kelly crowded around him. Below, the scenes of familiarity continued, unaffected by a nuclear attack or by the mad disappearance of everything that made sense.

"It's playing with us," Rod muttered. "That's why everything's fine one minute and gone the next."

"*What's* playing with us?" Kelly said.

"I have no idea, love, but it explains a bit." Rod pointed to the window. "Why we see nothing and then it's all normal."

"I don't care about that." Alex was already moving to the blockage they'd set up. "I'm out."

"We going for the front door again?" Kelly asked, and Alex hesitated.

"There'll be another door somewhere. Maybe through the cash office." She glanced back at them. "At the other side of the ground floor. There must be one near there or at the back of it or somewhere."

"Which means we still have to go down the stairs and to the ground floor," Dao said.

Rod took charge. "Let's just get this lot moved." He joined Alex; both gripped one of the tables and started dismantling their barrier. It took several minutes. Grunting and aching, they carted the desks and chairs into the staff area and left them piled messily. Sweating freely and aware of how red his face had become, Rod leaned on the wall and took a few breaths.

"You okay?" Dao asked him.

Rod nodded. "Not as young as I used to be."

Or thin or little or quick when you run, right?

Rod shivered. The thought was his own—he was sure of that—but it sounded as cold as a January day when the last of the day was fading into a biting sunset.

He pointed to the doors. "Out, down and then outside however we can. A window, a door. I don't care. We'll jump from the first floor if need be."

The others nodded their eager agreement.

"Everyone got a weapon?" Rod asked.

Weapon was pushing the term, Simon thought as the others nodded. Between them, they held a few small kitchen knives, a letter opener stolen from one of the offices, and the snapped handle and blade of a guillotine—the last, a replacement for Dao's scissors. He supposed their makeshift defences were better than nothing, but not by much when put against whatever walked in Greenham Place.

"Quickly and quietly." Rod took hold of one of the doors. Alex did the same, holding the cool handle with a keenness to get moving that frightened her. It was almost out of control. The only reason she wasn't sprinting to the stairs and down was because nothing about this was right. While she knew she'd knock down any spectral visions or phantom horrors if they got in her way, she still didn't want to encounter her dad, blood-soaked and crying out for death or he'd—

No. I won't think about it. Dad's not here. He never has been, and he would never say those things.

In reply: *Kill me, Alex. I'm hurting. Kill me, baby.*

Alex yanked on the door. Rod did the same. They parted without a sound. For what felt like a long time, a thick quiet lived on all sides. Then Rod's single sob broke it.

They stared at the object sitting on the floor of the landing and nobody dared speak.

Chapter Twenty-Four

Alex found herself taking hesitant steps from the offices before she realised she was going to move.

Each step brought the bench closer and gave her more detail of it.

While the sun shone less strongly than the day before, perhaps because it was still early, enough yellow warmth coated the wood for her to see how rotten it was. Brown flakes patterned the white floor. Crumbling splinters jutted from either end and in two dozen or more places on the main section. While the five or so feet of bench gave enough room for a few people to sit without being wedged together, it didn't look as if it would support a child's weight, let alone the weight of several adults. All too easy to see the middle snapping under any pressure, the supports and feet below the main section breaking in two and sending their broken fingers of wood scattering. And the smell. God. While Alex had little experience of woodlands, she knew the particular aroma of old trees soaking after a storm. Pleasant at first, natural and healthy and full of the outdoors which was always welcome when compared to being stuck in a city, even out in its suburbs. Still, it was an aroma that didn't take long to become cloying. It coated the tongue and clung to nostrils, and it was all too easy to picture tiny spores of moss clinging to the fine hairs inside her nose. No, not a smell she liked to take in too deeply or too often. The problem was she couldn't *not* smell it. The scent seemed to live in the walls as well as float upwards from the floor.

"What is it?" Kelly whispered. Surprising them all, Rod raced forward, one large foot rising as if he was about to kick a football. His trainer connected with the underside of the bench, launching it from the ground. It tipped over and clattered down with a mighty crash. One of the supports snapped free, sending more flakes pattering down. Panting hard, Rod turned away and strode to the other side of the landing. He rested on the railing beside the window, drawing breath while the others could only gather together, pressing their bodies to each other and all too scared to speak.

Abruptly, Rod let out a yell full of nothing but rage. *"Fuck you, you bastard. You hear me? Fuck you!"* Howling like a wounded animal, he raced back to the overturned bench and grabbed it.

"Rod." Desperate to make the other man stop, or at least calm down, Simon took a step forward. If there were any words to make it happen, he didn't have them. All he could do was shout the Welshman's name again. *"Rod."*

While fat covered much of Rod's body, muscle was hidden beneath the weight. He lifted the bench as if it weighed nothing and flung it through the air. The underside hit the railing, and a small chunk broke free as the bench tipped and plummeted from sight.

Seconds later, they heard it explode into dozens of pieces, and with an inner vision that grew in strength powered by their mostly unspoken fear. They saw the shards of the destroyed bench fly across the floor and slide through the early morning shadows where nothing they wanted to consider might be ready to pick up each piece and try to put the bench back together.

Rod collapsed, legs sprawled, his shadow pooling over the smooth white of the floor. There were no tears. He looked like he'd switched off, and Alex found that more frightening than any weeping or raging yells.

"Rod? You okay?"

He gave no reaction. She could have been addressing a lump of rock.

"Rod?"

Nothing.

Alex glanced around at the others, saw little help from them and took a few hesitant steps towards Rod. The smell that was closer to a stink of decaying wood remained, even though the bench was five floors below and in pieces.

Hopefully still in pieces.

Alex ignored the thought and moved closer to Rod, treading carefully. Simon nudged Dao's elbow and caught his eye.

What do we do? Simon mouthed, and Dao shook his head. Not from a lack of ideas, Simon realised, but in negating any plan of moving from the entrance to the sixth-floor offices. Between the two men, Kelly tried to keep as motionless as possible, despite the urge in his legs to sprint by her sister and Rod and get down to the ground floor *fast*. Something inside that was no more advanced in thinking than any cornered animal ordered Kelly to remain with the others. Without thought, she obeyed the command and watched Alex approach Rod.

"You still with us, Rod?" Alex muttered, and he finally moved, shifting his head a fraction to stare up at her.

"Where else would I be, Alex?" he whispered She crouched and took one of his hefty hands between both of her own. His skin, while obviously pale, struck her as a shade beyond white. It looked bleached, alabaster, the way she imagined a clean bone would appear. Shaking the image off—it came from the contrast of their skin colours—Alex said: "What happened, Rod? Talk to us."

Rod closed his eyes. When he began to speak in a low, struggling voice, Alex found that to be more than welcome.

It was a blessing.

Chapter Twenty-Five

"I was nine, fifty years back now." A flicker of a smile ghosted across Rod's mouth. It held no happiness at all. "We lived in a village near Cardiff. My dad was a farmer. My mum and dad knew a bloke. Kind of a friend, but not really. He was a man everyone in the village knew, but nobody liked him the way you like a mate. 'A good man to know,' my dad said, but that didn't mean he liked him." Still with his eyes closed, Rod dropped his kitchen knife beside his leg. His free hand swallowed both of Alex's; they held each other, black and white fingers linked.

"Martin Williams. Rich man. He'd done well in property, I think. I always knew he had a lot of cash, but never knew why people didn't like him."

Stepping away from Dao and Kelly, Simon approached. Alex willed him to keep quiet. He sat on Rod's other side, four or five feet away. Kelly remained on a sofa. The leather creaked under her slight weight. Not making a move from the double doors, Dao gazed at Rod, and in his calm eyes, Alex saw the faint light of understanding beginning to gleam. She had to look away because she knew the same was in her own eyes.

Tell me I'm wrong. Please, God. Tell me I'm wrong.

"Maybe he threw his money about too much. Maybe he was just one of those blokes people don't like. I don't know. He lived in a house down the road from our farm. I was out one morning. Cold that day." Rod bowed his head and shook. "Didn't really feel like winter but it wasn't really autumn, either. Just cold and grey and bloody miserable. I'd been walking our dog in the woods at the edge of the farm in the morning and came back over the fields. I remember how grey the sky was and how *big*. It was always big out there, but this was huge. I felt like a dot. A fly. I walked over the field with my dog and my house. . .*I could see it.*"

Rod gave a huge sob. He took in a whooping breath and shook from his ankles to his broad shoulders. Still with his eyes firmly shut. Madly, Alex wondered if it would make any difference to Rod whether they were open or not. He wouldn't see Greenham Place or the growing yellow of the sunlight. He'd see what was in his mind and what had broken his heart for almost his entire life.

There wasn't a thing she or the others could do to help him because Rod was miles away, lost under a massive sky of grey and buffeted by a fierce wind. She saw the sky; she felt the snapping, biting gusts, and could only shiver as they turned her adopted coat into a cover no more substantial than tissue paper. Any greenhouse effect from the wall of windows died. She walked in the last stages of winter. She breathed in its sharp chill and tasted the promise of a frost overnight out here where the fields spread, where the hills grew tall, and where the cities and roads were their own business, not hers, nor the business of the land the men worked on and knew. They loved and hated when the crops grew like sickly children, or when the foxes got into the chickens, or when it rained all night and all day, driving children to do nothing but stay inside and press against their faces against the windows and watch fat drops roll down while the dog snuffled at the door. When the rain finally wound down, you'd put your coat on and open the door to smell the earth and fresh air *and oh my God, I am here. I am here with him.*

The office had vanished, taking Kelly, Dao, and Simon away with it. Alex lived on spacious grassland in the Welsh countryside, sent back through the years of her life and even further beyond to a world that could have been another planet.

The countless blades of grass waved and danced, none of them green or healthy. All were a flat grey; the unbroken sky had fallen and stained the land. This wasn't a farm; it was a dead place away from sunlight and any human warmth.

Beside her, the boy walked his dog. The animal strained on the thin lead and sniffed the sharp taste permeating the air. The boy, clad in a thick coat and some dark trousers, kept his attention on the squat farmhouse perhaps a mile away. He'd given the dog a long walk today. He spent over an hour across to the woods and through the trees where the birds chattered angrily. And if he'd spent longer than usual outdoors because he was pig sick of being stuck inside this half term, well, so what of it? The dog was happy; they'd both got some air in their lungs, and maybe, after lunch, he could get his bike out and head up the road into the main village and spend the afternoon with Tom and Barry.

Living inside his thoughts, he didn't see the man coming to his side until the last second. Even the dog failed to register the approaching figure. The animal gave a quick bark, maybe embarrassed not to have seen the man, then resumed his quick breaths and pulls at his lead.

"Hello, Rod," the man said. The sound stung Alex's ears. There was too much life to it, too much forced jollity. It was like being greeted by a boorish drunk at a wedding.

"Hello, Mr Williams," Rod said. "Walking the dog?"

"Yes, sir."

"Good lad."

The man's big smile fell away. Alex's fear, a squirming worm in her chest, raced for her mouth, and yet nothing emerged.

The man's face could have belonged to a corpse. Without the too cheery smile, he was totally lifeless, even as he scanned the area. The smooth motion of his head and the tracking of his eyes were robotic, inhuman.

"Are you going home for lunch, Rod?" he asked.

"Yes, sir."

The boy Rod might have seen something odd in the man. He remained where he stood, but his body turned towards the direction of his home.

Run, Alex screamed in her head. *Run for your life, Rod.*

The man checked his watch, a chunky device that should have flashed but instead remained as grey as the grass and sky.

"It's only twelve. What time is lunch? One o'clock?"

Rod nodded slowly. His fingers wrapped around the lead, stilling the dog. Again, Alex willed him to sprint for his home and to yell for his dad as he ran.

"It's cold. Come back to mine for a cup of tea, then we'll get you home."

"It's okay. My mum wants me home—"

"Don't worry. Come and have a cup of tea in my shed. You can get warm, then I'll drive you up the road."

Alex's shriek echoed around her head but didn't touch her mouth. It didn't even come close.

The man seemed to ooze over the grass rather than walk. One wide hand found Rod's back and pushed with unmistakeable insistence, turning him away from the farmhouse so that he faced another building off in the distance. It sprawled over the field, a thin road on its other side. A tall fence separated it from the grey grass; Alex's vision landed on a gate in the wood.

That's where they'd go, through the fence and into the house, and this was so wrong.

His hand still on Rod's back, the man pushed the boy firmly, and Rod could do nothing but walk alongside him, pulling his dog and keeping his head down.

Helpless, Alex followed. There was no sensation of walking, and no sensation of feet on the ground. All she had was the sharp wind on her skin and a silent cry inside for Rod to run.

The man chatted, the words coming as if they were in a foreign language. Alex heard him mention Rod's parents and their farm, the unseasonal chill, and whether or not that would have a bad effect on the crops; then on to the boy's school, and while all the subjects made sense, the one-way conversation became close to meaningless. All through the man's discussion with himself, Rod kept his head down and held tight to his dog's lead. The animal was safe, Alex saw. The pet was *home* and while the farmhouse was still in sight, all the good and comfort of it were miles out of reach and getting further away with every step they took towards the fence.

The man changed their course, taking them from the gate and fence to the rear of the property. A bramble hedge lined the garden, with a large shed sitting directly in the centre of the perimeter.

"In there. We can have a sit down and a nice cup of tea."

Rod spoke, and Alex knew it was his last attempt at getting away.

"I really should be getting home, Mr Williams."

"Don't worry." Again, with the too loud voice, the statement that left no room for argument. "I'll get you home soon."

I'm sorry, Rod, but I can't see this. I cannot.

Alex tried to turn; she followed the boy and the man to the shed door. Powerless to move away, she closed in on the man's back as he unlocked the door and clearly pushed Rod inside.

Oh Jesus. No, please. I don't want to see this. Rod. Rod, I'm sorry. I'm so sorry.

Into the shed, into the gloom that was almost pleasant, and into the shelter from the wind still audible through the small holes in the wood panels. It whistled through them, high-pitched and steady; the sort of sound a small child might find scary in a fun way.

"Have a sit down," Williams said, pointing to a ledge. Wordlessly, Rod sat, still holding his dog's lead. The animal tucked himself under the ledge, curling up.

Williams lit a gas light, then a camping stove over which a large kettle sat.

"There. Tea on its way."

Oozing again rather than stepping, he crossed to the door and pushed it firmly closed. Her back to the wall and touching nothing, Alex tried to close her eyes. They refused to obey. She had no choice but to see what was coming; all the horror ahead—all Rod's horror—was hers to share.

Williams chatted, not giving Rod chance to answer before moving on to another subject. While the kettle boiled, and while he tidied away a few small tins of paint on the shelves opposite Rod, he went from the boy's classmates to the summer that felt like a long way off, to his most recent trip to the town to do a bit of business with Mr. Moore, the landlord of The Six Bells. All through the prattle, Rod stayed silent and kept his head down. The door was only two feet away, but he made no move for it. Alex understood perfectly. He was a child; Williams was the adult, and what the adult said was the law. If that law was nothing more unusual than 'sit in the shed and have a cup of tea,' then the law was solid and unbreakable.

"There you go." Williams placed a chipped mug of steaming tea on a small table and rummaged in a cupboard. He pulled a tin free, turned back to Rod, and smiled much too widely.

"Biscuits," he whispered, taking the lid off the tin.

"Help yourself."

The biscuit tin went next to Rod's cooling cup of tea. Williams returned to the cupboard. He reached inside and spoke in a softer voice.

"Rod. Can I ask you something?"

The wind sang in the holes and steam drifted from Rod's tea. Alex had never in her life wanted to be somewhere—*anywhere*—else as she did then.

Kelly, if you're there, if you can still see me and Rod, then hit me. Smack me in the face and get me to wake up or come back or something. Get me out of this. Alex drew a mental breath and screamed for her sister. *KELLY, GET ME OUT OF THIS RIGHT NOW, YOU BITCH! GET ME OUT!*

Nothing at all changed, and Alex knew it would not. She'd see what was coming and she'd see it through to the end.

"Rod?" Williams murmured.

"Yes, sir?" There was fear here, fear and a small boy's trust in an adult to do whatever was right.

"The girls in your school... do you like them?"

Oh my God.

"Like them?" Rod frowned.

"I mean, are they nice? Are they fun?" Williams still had his back to Rod and his forearm remained in the cupboard. He could have been a statue. "Do you feel good when you're with them?"

"I don't know what you mean." The bench below Rod creaked; the small muscles in his legs tensed. Alex willed him to stand and run, to *sprint*. The bench creaked again, and Williams turned.

He held a folded magazine, enough of the front cover visible for Alex to groan without making a sound. She made out one word of the title—*WIVES*—and a woman's leg clad in a black stocking before Williams flattened the magazine and placed it beside Rod's tea.

"It's a secret," Williams muttered. "Don't worry, lad. Your mam doesn't need to know. Don't worry about your dad, either. He wouldn't mind."

Rod's gaze ran from the woman on the magazine to Williams and back again.

"Nothing wrong with a bit of fun, is there?" Williams sat next to Rod, blocking the door and the steady wail of the wind blowing through the holes in the wall.

You bastard. Alex wanted to scream it into his face, to take hold of the tea and throw it at him so his eyes and cheeks would be a scorched mess and Rod could run. Her legs were as useless as her eyes.

"Here. Have a look." Williams opened the magazine and turned page after page. Rod stared at the naked women, more so than the letters he couldn't understand. The adult world laid out and totally exposed before him. Alex watched his wide eyes and the slight tremble in his fingers. She cursed Williams and cursed her useless body. Again, she called to her sister to stop the vision. The only reply was the creak of wood as Williams shifted position. He stopped turning the pages, leaving the magazine open at its centre. A smiling woman, cupping her heavy breasts with her legs wide gazed up at Rod, and Rod stared back.

"It's nice, isn't it, son? Nice to see ladies like this."

Rod swallowed.

"I tell you what. There's something else nice. Something *very* nice, but it's one of those things. It's kind of a secret, you see. Do you want to know what it is?"

Rod managed to speak. "Mr Williams. Sir. I need to go home."

"Soon, Rod. Soon. Don't worry about that." Although the shed was not hot, a distinct layer of sweat covered the man's forehead. It looked like clear oil. "Here. Let me take that."

He placed the magazine, still open, on the table, and then slid an arm around Rod's shoulders.

"Sir, I need to go."

Rod pulled away and Williams pulled him back, hard. He panted; the sweat shone and a rotten stink of fear and animal-need filled the air. Nothing human remained in the shed; there was only a monster.

Grunting, Williams punched Rod's crotch. Rod gave a tiny scream, and Williams' squirming fingers found the waist of Rod's trousers. Under the bench, the dog whimpered and tried to curl into a smaller ball. Trapped in someone else's hell, Alex could do nothing but see and hear every single second. She called desperately for Kelly, for Jesus, for Rod, and none answered.

Through the now exposed holes in the wooden walls, the whoops of the wind merged with the muffled cries and grunts in the shed.

Chapter Twenty-Six

Her hands were her own again. Without making a move, Alex no longer held Rod's hot fingers and there was no contrast of their respective skins because she was fumbling to get away, mouth closed as tightly as she could, desperate not to vomit.

She managed to rise into a shuffling crouch and turned back to Rod. He regarded her, still pale but no longer *bleached*. His tired face and slumped shoulders made him look as if he'd strained rarely used muscles moving more heavy furniture from the doors to the office.

"Are you okay, love?" he croaked.

"What happened?" Simon asked. He stared at Dao and Kelly. "Did you see it? It was like they were… faint."

"You actually saw something. It's a miracle," Alex muttered and tried to pretend she didn't see the look of hurt cross Simon's face. Whatever was going on, it wasn't his fault, and if the man didn't see things as the rest of them did, maybe that was a good thing.

"I saw it," Kelly said. "Just for a second. You kind of turned see-through."

"Yeah," Dao murmured.

Alex stood straight and willed her legs not to give way and her stomach not to reject the little food she'd eaten the night before. It took thirty seconds of focus to still the shaking in her mid-section and arms. All the while, the horrific images in a shed that no longer existed lived behind her eyes. And all her ears heard was the muffled wail of a boy with his face pressed into a dirty floor.

"Rod?" she said, not sure if she could manage more than his name.

He wiped the flat of his hand over his bristly cheeks and rose, grunting as he moved. "You saw it. The worst thing to happen to me. That shed, that bench." He faced the others. "He hurt me. When I was a kid, Martin Williams hurt me on the bench in his shed."

Tears might have been expected. Instead, Rod's features were still and contained. He couldn't say he felt good or anywhere close to it, nor did he feel lighter; there was no letting go of any weight. All he had was the slight sensation of freshness. The closest comparison he could make was the smell of his garden in the middle of a particularly hot summer three years back; the baked earth and wilting flowers refreshed by a fierce downpour came out of nowhere and brought the scents of *green* to the cloying air. This was similar, and he'd take that.

He jabbed a finger over the railing. "That bench was the same one. God knows how but it was."

"This is mental," Simon said, peering over the railing to the little visible of the wrecked bench. "How the hell can this be happening?"

"You think I'm making this up?" Rod asked. For the first time, the rest of the group heard a dangerous note to the man's voice. Anything light and calm was made dark by a controlled anger. Dao readied himself to move between the two men, although he didn't relish the idea of getting in the way of Rod's fists.

"What?" Simon shook his head. "No. Not at all. I'm just saying it's impossible."

Dao stepped forward, his own anger rising seemingly out of nowhere. "You think I'm not hearing and seeing my son being tortured?" he yelled. Keeping the peace was forgotten; the idea might never have existed. "You think I'm imagining it? Or the man shouting at Rod is in his head? Or Alex's dad isn't here? You think we're making this up?" He didn't give Simon chance to answer. "What's wrong with you? These things are real so why can't you see them?"

"I don't know," Simon roared. It was his fists, not Rod's, bearing down on Dao's face. And Dao's racing mind welcomed the blows because it meant it gave him an excuse to let go of his

control and give in to the terrible fury swimming in his chest.

Out of nowhere, Alex was between them. Simon's fists missed the side of her face by a fraction. She flinched but held her ground.

"That's enough." Shaking off the image of Rod's rape for any length of time felt like it might be impossible, but she'd do her best if it meant escape. "Enough," Alex whispered.

Face flushed, Simon backed away. "Sorry," he muttered. "I'm an idiot."

Trembling, Dao let Kelly lead him a few steps away. He leaned on the railing beside Rod and took a moment to breathe and think of nothing. A moment passed before Rod broke the silence.

"I think I know why Simon doesn't see and hear what we do... apart from the people down there." He pointed over the railing.

"Oh, yeah? Fill me in," Simon replied.

"It's because you're not scared. You don't have specific fears, guilt, or an event in your past that defines you now." He paused, letting this sink in. "Right?"

Simon spoke in a slow, deliberate manner. "I've got nothing. Not a thing."

"Then you're lucky." Rod had to stop for a few seconds. Naming it was one thing. Speaking of what Williams did to him in that shed as if it were a fading childhood memory was another. "I've got what that bastard did to me. Dao... mate... "

"I've got Huan."

Rod nodded.

"Alex? Your father."

"No," she said. "I mean, yes, that's a thing, but it's not… "

She broke off, utterly unsure of how she should phrase it. "It's not what's here for me. Not really. I think if there something wrong here, it's using my dad to get at me."

A church bell clanged, the chime low and lonely, leaving a fading echo. Alex hugged herself. "You hear that?" she whispered, convinced in the second before they answered that they had no clue what she meant.

"Yes," Rod replied.

"I did," Dao said, and Kelly gave a quick nod.

"That's what's scaring me. That church bell." Alex met her sister's eyes. "You remember St Margaret's? When we were kids."

"Yeah." Kelly sounded near tears, and a gentle alarm went off in Alex's head. Her memory shouldn't upset Kelly. Taking that thought any further was too much to focus upon; she had to verbalise what haunted her in this shitty office block.

"It was a church we went to with our mum when we were kids." Alex spoke to the men without looking at them. "It was a nice place. Good people. Happy people, but in my head, now, it's changed. It's a dead place." She had to lower her head and fight off the idea of something listening to her a few floors below. Something still and watchful. Something wearing her dad's skin and face.

"I saw it. Yesterday. Like a vision or something. I don't know. It was in the middle of nowhere. Cold. The building was falling apart." She lifted her head and said the word that had drifted around the edges of her thoughts for a day and a night. "Doom. That's what I hear when that bell rings. It's over the top and melodramatic, but that's what I hear. I hear doom for me and my family and my life." Struggling, she gave life to the worst idea in the world. "I hear never seeing my girls again."

Wordlessly, Dao reached for Alex's arm. Although they didn't touch, silent understanding passed between them, a shared fear of harm coming to their children.

"Now you know," Alex said. "That's what is here for me."

"You've got nothing to worry about," Kelly said. "You get out of here and you've got the girls."

"And your husband." Rod offered Alex a smile. She didn't see it. Her attention remained on Kelly, who'd shifted on the spot. While her body remained facing Alex, she'd moved her head to the left, which meant Alex could no longer see her sister's eyes. And that was—

secret, Alex. It's a secret.

Simon walked to the top of the stairs and faced the landing and corridor below. "Whatever's happening here, I say bollocks to it. We get out and nothing stops us. Right?"

Again, Alex pictured her father, clad in his hospital gown and bloody bandages. He was down there, waiting for her, waiting for her to relieve his suffering.

In her head, the church bell rang out, welcoming the mourners from the freezing fields, ushering them inside to gather around the coffin.

Whose coffin, Alex? Who's being buried? It's you, isn't it? Your death. Your doom.

"Can I say one more thing before we go down?" Rod asked.

"What is it?" Alex replied, voice thick and heavy like mud.

"Today. The twenty-fifth of October." He pursed his lips as if considering. "Fifty years for me. Fifty years to the day."

When Dao spoke, there was no surprise for Rod.

"Two years." He had to clear his throat. "Huan. Two years today."

Standing on the first step down, Simon sighed. "All I can tell you about today is it's my birthday. Thirty-nine today. That's it. No big deal."

"Your birthday?" Kelly sounded startled, although Alex's heightened awareness picked on a slightly overdone note to the question. The first fully conscious thought Alex had about her sister in a long time stated without any fanfare:

She's faking it.

"My birthday. It's not a big thing. No horrible thing in my past. Just my birthday." He gestured to the stairs. "Can we go?"

Without waiting for a reply, he set out. As Dao and Rod moved to follow him, and while

Alex refocused herself on getting down to the exit, Kelly peered down to the street below. Her shout of joy stilled all of them.

"The police. The police are coming."

On Greenham Road, a convoy of police cars and vans streamed towards the office building, their sirens singing the most welcome song in the world.

Alex was the first to start running.

Chapter Twenty-Seven

The tenth floor.

At the stairwell and looking straight down, four figures watched the sprinting, yelling people run for each set of stairs, dash across the landings, and take the next flight. They watched Rod's face turn redder, they watched Dao overtake Alex, they watched Simon bounce off a wall and come close to stumbling, and they watched Kelly glance back but not stop to help him. Huge beams of sunlight coated the steps as the group raced on. If they registered the savage warmth in that sunlight, they did not stop, and they did not look outside to the yellow air. The wail of the sirens was enough to make them keep going. Those watching from the tenth floor were deeply amused by this.

Blood flowed from the bandages and dressings covering one of the figures. It soaked the head and face, turning the dirty white into the rich red before long lines streamed down the body, met one another, and formed blossoming pools. They ran over the floor towards the stairwell in a puddle and found the edge. A bead of gore hung for a second, motionless an inch beyond the railings, then fell in a red raindrop. The shape beside the bleeding figure—a naked man—opened its mouth and said Kelly's name without making a sound. And, still running fast, Kelly looked straight up from seven floors below as if someone had bellowed to her. At the same instant, the four shapes—three men and a child—vanished from sight and left the empty space as so much freezing air.

Seconds later, the drop of blood hit the ground floor and sank, and the ground seemingly turned into water. In the foundations of Greenham Place, movement spread from all corners.

A rising movement.

Chapter Twenty-Eight

Dao jumped the last three stairs and crashed to the landing on the second floor. Through the nearest set of windows, sirens howled, the sound welcome and terrible. He'd seen a fraction of the street as they raced down. People out there; actual people walking and talking and *normal* and he ached to be beside them. Simon and Alex were a step behind him. Dao sprinted into the growing pools of sunshine, then skidded to a stop. Simon crashed into his back. The men went down in a tangle of arms and legs, both crying out senseless noise. Dao shoved Simon away and scrambled over the floor.

"Dao," Rod panted like a dog. "What's wrong?"

Groaning, Simon tried to stand; his legs gave way and he reached blindly. Alex's hand found his and pulled him upright. He tried to mutter his thanks but had no voice. He held his side, ribs aching, and looked upright for no reason.

Nothing up there but empty floors. Nobody watching.

The noise of the police sirens and ambulances went on and on. They sounded as if they were coming from miles distant and coming fast. Sweating and shaking, Kelly fought off a wave of confusion that wanted to know why the sirens were still going when Greenham Road wasn't *that* long.

"We need to move," she said, and tried to pull Alex's free hand.

"Yang," Dao whispered. "I can't leave him here. I can't—"

"He's not here." Rod grabbed hold of Dao's shoulders. While Rod was no taller than a level six feet, he seemed to stretch, his form blocking out the morning light. *"Something is trying to hurt us, Dao, but your son is not here, so get bloody moving."*

Dao remained on the spot, swaying, and Kelly had to wonder if he was going to faint. A voice inside, made cold by distance, told her to run if he did. Let go of him and the others and run for safety. Kelly focused all of her energy on ignoring the voice, but it remained. *Run,* it said. *Run away and let them die here. Oh, and by the way. Who said your name a second ago?*

She knew who.

"What the fuck are you doing? We need to run." For Kelly, tears of fright, anger and confusion were close. Getting a grip, even a weak one, on the situation was impossible.

"What is here, Rod?" Dao whispered, barely loud enough for Rod alone to hear. The sirens on the street had become a hysterical shriek.

"I don't know." Rod moved his mouth to within kissing distance of Dao's ear. "It's playing with us. It wants to hurt us but we stick together, and it can't, okay?"

Shaking, Dao nodded. "We can make this right, Rod."

"I know," Rod replied, not sure of what exactly Dao meant and not caring. "Now, move, son."

They ran, Dao in the lead and Rod falling behind the others. Their shadows raced ahead. The sunlight danced and capered on all sides, its heat growing into a scorching summer instead of late autumn. A mix of loud voices came with the police sirens. While words were impossible to make out, every one of the group recognised the sound of order and control. The police had come. The world of logic and order had come.

Dao took the last of the stairs to the ground floor corridor, not stopping to study the mess of the black stain. If that had been down to Alex's father collapsing into so much oil or mud, then so be it. He'd think about it once they were out; he'd have time to wonder if he was nuts. Now was all about getting the hell out and—

Ahead, the doors that led to the main foyer were gently closing. Nobody in sight; nobody going through them and yet, they were still closing.

Yang or Huan? Who was it, Dao? And who do you want it to be?

The terrible question brought a shriek of outrage and grief to Dao's mouth. He upped his sprint to a maximum, bringing both arms up to smash them into the doors and flood the corridor with pure sunlight.

Chapter Twenty-Nine

They'd stepped into a painting.

Simon aimlessly wandered around the reception area, his body temperature already rising in the unbroken sunlight and warmth while his mind paid it no attention. Focusing on a single thought was like trying to grip liquid. He could plunge his hands into their situation all he wanted to; it still squirted from his grip.

"I… " he began before letting the rest of the sentence, whatever it might have been, die in his mouth. He had nothing to say, anyway.

While the sun shone on the pavements and road, it shone on no people or police cars. Building fronts, trees, and the few benches opposite the front of Greenham Place cast no shadows. All his eye could focus upon was the lack of… of…

Energy.

Yes. *Energy.* Outside had no energy. It was like reading a centuries-old book, the paper torn and brown, the stink of decades' worth of dust and trapped air wafting from the cover. Everything from the paving slabs to the weeds growing from cracks—none moving because there was no breeze, let alone a wind—to the windows on the pub and takeaways over the road turned featureless had no life.

He stood at the exit, both sets of doors sealed. Above, the sensor was a blind eye. Simon booted the glass; it shook but held, and the door remained sealed.

"Fuck," he muttered.

Standing at the centre of the floor, Dao locked to all sides, no longer fully registering the others. Rod saw this and decided to let the boy be. He stood beside the sisters, trying to think and hoping nobody was going to lose it.

Playing with us, aren't you? Well, I don't think I'm in the mood for games.

Dao spoke, voice almost soft enough to be unheard. "I am going to find a chair, and I am going to break every fucking window in here if I have to."

He drew breath, waiting. Whatever had yelled its obscenities to Rod the day before gave no reply. Dao wondered if it was listening, before realising that was beyond stupid. Of course, it listened. It'd been listening to them the whole time because it was everywhere.

"Are you here?" he asked. Rod moved a step closer to Dao, unsure if he should speak.

"Fuck you," Dao said, exhausted. "Fuck you. Fuck you. Fuck you."

Nothing replied. The inside of Greenham Place was as silent as the rest of Willington.

Heading towards the cash office, Dao walked without looking back. He only stopped when Kelly shouted after him.

"This is your fault."

"Kelly!" Alex yelled, reaching for her sister. Kelly pulled away and pointed to Dao.

"It is. If he hadn't stopped, if he hadn't waited, we'd be fine, we'd be out, we'd be—"

She choked on her anger and frustration. More, trying to swallow the knowledge that what she was saying made little sense and trying to cling to the idea it did.

Dao turned, and everything else came out before Kelly could stop it, the words fast and hot as she sobbed. "You want your son; you stopped; you're keeping us here. *You,* Dao. You're hearing your son, and that's what trapped us here. We'd be outside if you hadn't stopped. It's your—"

She bent double. The cramp in her stomach flexed claws deep inside, and Kelly had a horrible mental image of her period *flowing* down her legs and soaking into her boots.

What the hell is this shit? she thought miserably.

Standing straight and holding her mid-section, she gazed at Dao with vision blurred from tears.

"Kelly, that isn't fair," Alex murmured. "I think you should—"

"Don't you fucking say it."

Alex recoiled from Kelly's shriek. Almost unfelt and unseen, a shifting in the air floated from close by Alex's side towards the lift doors.

"Don't say it, Alex. Don't fucking tell me to apologise."

"I wasn't going to."

In her shock and panic, all Alex could do was lie because suggesting Kelly apologise was *exactly* what she'd been about to say.

"You are not Mum," Kelly hissed. "Don't fucking forget that."

She staggered away, eyes and stomach hot, sweating freely.

Almost forgotten by the others, Simon rested against the warm glass of the doors. "I hate to get in the way of your family shit, but can we focus on getting the fuck out of here?"

Nobody replied for a moment. Dao turned away. "I'll get a chair."

Simon pushed himself off the doors. "Wait. I'll go."

He wasn't sure why he wanted to get away. Maybe it was due to feeling disconnected from the others. Maybe he wasn't as much a part of them as they were with one another. Maybe he just needed to feel as if he was doing something instead of being a useless lump of shit with no plans and nothing to offer and—

Simon tore the thought in two and tried not to consider the level of vitriol inside it. He crossed the floor towards Dao. "I'll go," he said again. "Stay here."

Without much idea of where he was going, Simon headed for the low wall of windows forming the front of the cash office. Beyond the tinted glass, a wide space sat empty apart from chairs, the odd filing cabinet and a few desks. While none of the chairs looked particularly heavy, they'd have to do. While another office was near the back of the lift, this one open-plan like the others on the floors above, he couldn't bring himself to wander too far away. The others were still strangers to him. Even so, they were all he had for human comfort right now.

He pushed at a heavy door to the left of the darkened windows. As with all the other doors, it relied on an electrical fob access. And as with all the others, nothing powered it now. Whispering on the carpet, it slid open. Simon took a moment to study the area, telling himself it was to get an idea of anything they could use and not to check for movement. If the others were talking, they were doing so in low voices. He entered the office; the door began to close, and he grabbed it with a shaking, nervous grip. While he couldn't even guess what Greenham Place and its phantom sights and sounds was all about, the last thing he wanted was to be locked away from Rod and the rest.

He placed a small bin between the door and frame, keeping it wedged open, and crossed the floor. The blank monitors watched him walk, and the tinted glass overlooking the main foyer was easier to see through on this side. Kelly rested against the reception desk, holding her knife;

Alex stood at the exit, palm on the glass as if she could push the doors open. Against one of the thick pillars, Dao and Rod stood together; Dao's head bowed, his little knife looking forgotten in one limp hand. Simon turned from them, gaze falling on one of the heavy chairs. That would do. He could wheel it out, then throw the fucking thing through a window or the doors. Either way, they were getting out. Making sure he had a firm grip on his knife, he grasped the chair's back and froze. Dao's voice came. Impossibly, madly, it came as if the man was in the office with him, and Simon didn't have to look through the cashier's windows to know Dao was speaking to Rod in barely a whisper.

"It's my fault. Huan. It's my fault. I wasn't paying attention. And not just for a few seconds, but for *minutes*. Minutes, Rod. He's playing in the playground; Yang's sitting on the grass by my feet and he's talking; he's telling me about the grass and the sunshine. I'm on my phone; Huan's climbing on the frame while I'm not paying him any attention, and he's falling, Rod. He's *falling* while I'm talking on my phone, and it's my fault, and that's why I had to stop upstairs."

Dao's little tale collapsed into fresh tears. With his mind's eye, Simon saw Rod placing a strong hold on Dao's shoulder to offer an awkward comfort. He saw the women watching this display, Kelly embarrassed and sorry for her outburst a moment before, and Alex's head and heart full of worry for her own children. Simon saw it all without making a move.

From the air, a cold voice spoke.

Funny, isn't it? There's a man with a reason to grieve. He has a reason to hurt and wish for a different life. What have you got?

With wide, staring eyes, Simon focused on his hands. He wanted to blink. He wanted to scream. Both were equally impossible, so was the voice beside his ear and in front and at his back. Surely nobody could sound so empty; nothing with such a total lack of emotion could speak.

I can speak, Simon. I can see. I see you. I know you. I know you're pointless. I know your life isn't worth half of Dao's and your sorrow is nothing compared to that man's. Or Rod's. Or Alex's fears. Or Kelly's guilt. You might as well not be here for them. You might as well not be.

Now there was something that wanted to be emotion but couldn't quite manage it in the voice. Call it mocking; call it sneering. Whatever its name, it was ugly. Worse than the voice, worse than its judgement, was its truth.

Simon managed a weak sob and tried to tighten his hold on the office chair, if only to have solidity in his grip. He failed to do so because—

Because—

The knife dropped to the carpet.

His hands were fading. His fingers, knuckles, and his wrists were all losing colour and detail. The red leather of the chair replaced them in a soft pink that grew stronger with every second— growing stronger because his skin, bone, muscle and the flowing blood below them all was becoming transparent. He pulled away from the chair, unable to make a sound because the fading had spread from his arms, to his shoulders, and into his chest and lungs. It sunk into organs, turning liver, stomach, and kidneys into nothing more substantial than fog. Lost inside his head, Simon howled as he left the world, or as the world left him, leaving only air in the shape of his body and the contemptuous voice that had no body, just as he had none, spoke from a faraway nowhere.

There is nothing of you, Simon, because there never was. Your worries and sadness aren't worth the space your body took up, so let us take your body away. It's better that you're not here; better for the others; better for you.

As Simon's face slid into the motes of dust and the rays of sunlight shone through the space he'd once occupied, there was no physical pain, only the agony of being wiped away. The scornful tone mocked his desire and need to stay, to be part of the world that didn't care whether or not he'd ever lived.

Stay I want to stay I want to I want to stay let me stay I am here I am I am—

I.

The soft touch of the carpet welcomed Simon as he collapsed. He buried his face against it, welcoming the gentle scratch on his cheeks and chin, crying into it and doing all he could to not hear the freezing wind of the voice as it fell into the same nowhere from where it came. *You are worth nothing, Simon. You offer nothing. Remember that. Remember.*

Simon sobbed. He couldn't do anything but.

Chapter Thirty

Although Kelly stood too far from Dao and Rod to hear Dao's tearful story in great detail, she caught enough. More than enough. Here was a man destroyed by his grief, and what he saw was a failure on a scale beyond anything she could imagine. And while she wasn't to blame, pushing at him in her stupid rant hadn't helped, just like losing her shit at Alex a moment before hadn't helped. So what if Alex was bossy and a patronising cow, sometimes? She meant well; she didn't mean to be *Mum*.

For the first time in months, Kelly pictured her mother before the illness. She saw Carla Brown in her kitchen, cooking dinner for her girls and her granddaughters in the living room while Kelly offered to help, and Carla gave a look that said *stay out of my way in my kitchen, baby,* and all Kelly could do was laugh.

I miss you, Mum. I really do, but I'm glad you can't see this mess.

Letting go of the image, Kelly told herself to go over to the men and speak to Dao, say sorry if it would help. Even if he told her to fuck off or cried more, she had to do something. Sorry to him and then maybe sorry to Alex too.

Kelly remained against the reception desk. Facing Dao's pain and offering some tired apology for having a go at him was beyond her. Same with Alex. All she could do was look at the floor and make sure she didn't meet his eye by accident or Alex's on purpose.

What a fucking mess.

With little thought or plan, Kelly boosted herself forward and took slow steps to the building's front. The image of the horrible burned people, all crowded around outside, played over and over behind her eyes. So many frightening, mental things had happened since, she could almost convince herself those people hadn't been there in the same way the guy Rod's falling chair killed hadn't been there when they all looked. Or the way the police and ambulances hadn't been there, come to save her and the others.

She stared out to the empty pavement and road, expecting the scorched flesh to appear out of nowhere and hearing every ruined mouth wailing that they were burned. The detail of the memory from the day before filled her mind: the palms on the glass, smearing blackened blood, and torn shreds of skin; the cheeks melted into lips, the faces turned into bubbled messes, and every visible inch of skin a deep red, the red of a fierce sunset when the sun went down in a ball and cooked the sky.

Kelly shivered. Nothing appeared outside. If the burned people were out there somewhere, they were keeping their distance. Even so, she scanned the buildings on the other side of the road, eyes unwilling or unable to pause for too long. As Dao and the others had said, the road looked fake. It made her feel off balance, unwell. She reached for support and found only glass. At least that was solid. At least it was real because they were in the middle of a drawing… and what happened if that drawing was erased?

A sound made her turn. Simon wheeled a chair from the corner on the far side of the lift, coming slowly and not meeting anyone's gaze.

"All okay, mate?" Rod called.

Simon nodded once and that was all. He pushed the chair to the centre of the floor, head hanging, the rock-solid hold on the chair's back visible to Kelly even with the distance between them. Nobody spoke for a moment. Dao sniffed a few times and wiped the back of a hand over his eyes while Rod pretended not to notice. Alex took a moment to study her sister, wondering if there'd be another explosion of anger any time soon. Kelly looked smaller somehow; she looked younger, and Alex wanted to go to her and listen to anything she had to say, to not talk but just to listen.

When we get out. When we get home, I'm going to do that, she promised herself.

"What's the plan?" Dao asked, motioning to Simon's chair.

"We throw it," Simon replied. A change had come over him; they all heard it in his voice. If asked privately, none of the others would have said Simon had much strength. While it wasn't strength they heard now, they did hear resolve.

"We throw it," he said again. "And then we get out."

"Sounds good to me," Dao muttered.

Kelly turned from them to face outside again.

In the middle of the road, a double bed sat with the covers thrown back, and the man lying on the mattress totally naked. He managed to move without seeming to change position. Lying flat one second, sitting on the edge of the bed the next. His legs were wide open. His erection jutted. He smiled.

Kelly screamed and she named her fear and her guilt.

"Carl."

Chapter Thirty-One

Alex raced over the floor, her panic drowning out any idea of what to say. Kelly was still backing away from the front, silent after her cry. The pavement and road beyond were as lifeless as always. But Kelly was still backing away.

"Kelly?" Alex yelled. "What is it? Where is he?"

Knowing she wouldn't see him, Alex stared outside, desperate for her husband to be there and desperate for him to be nowhere in sight. Because if he was… oh, God. She couldn't deal with that. Not even a tiny bit.

Dao and Rod ran to her. Only Simon remained still, holding his chair and wondering idly what would happen if he screamed, wondering if he'd be able to stop.

"What's happening?" Rod asked.

Alex yanked her sister around. Kelly came close to stumbling to the floor but managed to stay on her feet. "Where's Carl?"

"I don't know."

"Where the fuck is he, Kelly?"

"Please." Rod tried to push his way between them; Alex pushed back, blocking him.

"One last time, Kel." Alex had quietened and that was all the more dangerous. The men moved away a few inches. This wasn't their business; they understood that. Getting in the middle of it would be the worst idea in the world.

"Where is my husband?"

Kelly found her voice. She had no idea how, but it came like a miracle. "I don't know. I saw him. He was there. Outside. Looking in. He's gone."

Alex stepped closer to Kelly, a bare inch between their faces. "Why did you see him, Kelly?"

To that, Kelly had no reply. None she could give. Alex opened her mouth. Closed it.

Something was coming.

In the air and ground and windows, in the sunlight and silence coating each street, in the dead and flat land of the city the sisters and Dao knew inside out, something was coming.

It began as a soft hum. Perhaps the sound of a bored child who'd discovered the noise they could make simply by pressing their lips together and blowing. It remained at a constant pitch and grew slowly in volume, high and clear without being sharp. The group stared upwards, then to the pavement. Nothing came into view.

"What the hell is it?" Rod said. Before the others could reply, he stabbed a finger toward the reception desk, its polished marble a smooth black in the morning light. "There. Move. We have to get our heads down."

He and Dao ran for the desk. Alex turned but remained with Kelly, her head racing and unable to get a hold on the situation, let alone any questions. Across the floor, Simon remained with his chair, the muscles in his face slack. The noise changed from a hum to a throbbing, rich and thick. It grew from the floor, making their legs shake. On the public side of the desk, Rod gripped its edge and tried to tell the others to get down. He'd lost his voice, or the sound had stolen it. The shaking grew worse; dozens of windows shuddered, making the light dance madly. The throb became a low, constant beat, a dark pulse oozing from the floor, falling out of the walls and raining from the tunnel formed by the stairwell. Staggering, Kelly fell to the wall where the reception area met the front of the building. Alex reached for her, missed, and both women crashed against the wall. At the same time, Alex again saw the ruins of St. Margaret's standing bowed and decayed in winter light. Nothing but dead grass and rotting trees surrounding it while the last of the blood-red sunset died in the sky. She wept inside at the vision, the hurt done to a place she'd loved; a home from home with her mother back in her childhood when the world made sense. She howled at St. Margaret's face, and the church gave nothing back because it was dead, dead, dead. It had sunk below its doom and she would do the same. She would be crushed by loss, by having all that mattered to her taken away, *stolen.*

The sonorous tone paused for a fraction of a second as if drawing breath. Then the toll of a church bell crashed out, down, and up like an explosion. The sound of all the bells there were beating as one. Alex collapsed, hands over her ears, dimly aware of Kelly doing the same. Rod cried out; Dao tried to yell, but he'd lost his voice. Simon made no move at all.

The echo of the tremendous clang dashed across the floor and collided with the windows that should have shattered but remained whole. A few tears fell down Alex's face.

It was here. Call it something as melodramatic as *doom;* it didn't matter. It was here for her.

The next sound was nothing compared to the mighty thud of the church bell, but every one of them heard it.

The gentle ding of the lift doors opening.

Chapter Thirty-Two

Rod saw it first because he was facing that way, and he knew this made no sense because he'd been facing Dao with the front doors at Dao's back only seconds before. But here it was. Here was the yawning darkness inside the mouth of the lift; here was nothing at all peering out at him.

He stood straight, the old anger already coming, and that was good; that was wonderful. He'd take that anger and he'd shove it deep into the darkness. Let it choke on his tired fury. Let it *choke*.

"Are you there?" he asked. To his own ears, his voice sounded nasal and blocked. Maybe the explosion of the church bell had hurt his hearing. What of it? He'd get a hearing aid if need be. He'd wear it and be an old man and not give a toss about this business.

"Are you there?"

A low chuckle, the sound secret, dirty, answered Rod from the darkness and caressed his feet and legs with cold fingers. It seemed that was all the answer he'd get, and the sheer arrogance of this—to think the bastard believed he didn't even have to reply and Rod would take that—went beyond infuriating. It was enraging.

"Are you there?" Rod roared. He raised the blade from the broken guillotine, holding it like a club.

I am here.

The answer was as cold as midnight in winter. Any of the forced jollity in the voice from the day before was long dead. Rod stayed in place, promising himself that whatever happened in the next few moments, he would not back down.

No bloody way.

"I heard that," Simon whispered more to himself than any of the others. None of them were close enough to catch his voice, and it didn't matter. He'd heard the ugly chill of whatever was speaking to Rod, and it sounded almost exactly the same as the thing that had reduced him to literally nothing in the cash office. It appeared his horror was Rod's. In a silent flash of understanding, Simon knew there was only one force in Greenham Place; one force with as many faces as it needed.

Close to Kelly, Alex inched towards Rod, desperate to call his name, desperate to know why he'd appeared to her sister and not to his wife and what awful thing that meant. There was no time to seize upon either speeding thought, and no way to reach Rod without running to him because he was advancing on the lift door.

"It was not my fault," he bellowed. "You hear me? Not my fault."

Something laughed, richly amused and still cold like a wall of ice.

Your fault, Rod. Always your fault. Now come in here and sit down, you little fuck. I'm telling you what to do and I say. COME IN HERE AND SIT NEXT TO ME.

Kelly let out a tiny hiss, and Alex froze in mid-step. The voice spoke again, softer now, and that was no better.

Come in and we can talk about guilt, Rod. We can talk about secrets because everyone has a secret. Everyone is ashamed of something. It giggled, the innocent laugh of a happy child turned into a low, corrupted noise. It was like hearing dirty rainwater falling into a drain clogged with leaves. *Everyone is scared of something. Scared and ashamed. Isn't that right, Kelly?*

Kelly's breath caught in her throat. Vision flashed a deep red and she felt, actually *felt,* her heart rate judder. She bit down on her tongue, and the colours of the morning returned into focus.

Alex stared at her sister, still unable to take hold of her sprinting thoughts. Or perhaps unwilling to, because that meant making sense of the worst things in the world and *that* meant screaming and screaming until she burst.

Ignoring the voice's change of focus, Rod managed another step closer to the lift. Unaware of Simon frantically attempting to signal he should move away, Rod addressed the darkness.

"You are a monster. You are an animal. You are burning in Hell for what you did to me." Tears raced down his cheeks. He was no more aware of them than he was of the others. Everything had become clear. He stood on a road free from traffic, the clear space ahead extending right to the horizon and a pleasant sunshine colouring the sky yellow. Everything was open to him now.

"You are *filth*. And it's about bloody time you saw that. And about bloody time I said so."

At Rod's great shout, the void in the mouth of the lift made no move and gave no sound. Even so, Rod felt it considering. Then movement above, coming fast, and Rod had barely a second to move out of the way before the child's body plummeted to the ground. It struck the floor with a hollow thud. Yelling his shock, Rod dropped his blade and staggered backwards. He expected the shape to rupture into so much flying blood and broken bone, even though nothing of the sort had happened on impact. Not an inch of his body was free from cold sweat; his heart boomed; his mouth was a flood of electric spit and his senses felt as if they'd jumped up a level. Awareness of the men and the sisters returned in spades. They were off to both sides and at his back, not daring to come any closer, only Alex making any sense as she called for him to get away from it. He had to wonder if *it* meant the body, the open lift, or the twitching fingers and shaking legs as the body moved into a sitting position.

The body that was him as a child.

The child Rod jerked to his feet, his body whole even though it should have been smashed into mess by the fall. He swayed like a drunk, face and eyes slack. Rod tried to find a word, *any* word, but had nothing. He saw Dao from the corner of his eye: the man creeping forward, reaching, crying, and the part of Rod's mind still living in the world of real things. Rational thought knew Dao expected to see his boy, the child torn apart and smeared in his precious blood. Not for Dao, though. This was all for Rod.

Come and have a sit down, son, the thing inside the lift said. *I have a magazine to show you.*

The child Rod met Rod's eyes and there was no light there, no hope.

He turned away and walked towards the gaping hole where the darkness was swimming and dancing.

"No," Rod whispered. "No, wait."

His child-self kept moving.

"Wait. Please."

It was no good. Rod could do nothing to stop the boy he'd been from passing beyond the long beams of sunlight into the nothingness of the lift. There was an idea of watching the child enter a long tunnel, the walls smooth and lit by flames and the floor soaked by stagnant puddles. Rod strained to see deeper into the image and caught the suggestion of the tunnel dipping out of sight, falling away into the mouth of the earth where a terrible stink of a monster's breath wafted.

Nice to see you again, Rod. It laughed. *And I don't want your new friends to worry. The others are here for them. Their daddies, their husbands, and their children are all here for them.* Again, the sound of gallons of rainwater swallowed by the mouth of a rotten drain; again, the awful, mocking laugh.

I let them in, you see. I opened the door and let them in. I gave them a safe place from the fire outside, and they brought their burns to me. They gave me their ruined flesh, and I ate it. I ate it all up because they owed me after I kept them safe from their fire because it's fire outside, fire for all of you. Abruptly, the voice went from a conversational tone to a mad raging. *ALL OF YOU WILL BURN IF YOU GO OUTSIDE. GO OUTSIDE. GO AND COME TO ME. COME TO ME SO I CAN EAT YOU. I CAN TOUCH YOU AGAIN. I CAN MAKE YOU BURN, BURN, BURN—*

Then all Rod had was himself, crying and running forward. He howled his grief and hurt, both rising from his barrel chest and burning in his mouth.

"Not my fault, it wasn't my fault, it wasn't my fault, you bastard."

Filling the lift door, Martin Williams came from nothing, a smiling face, opening arms ready to hold, hug, and never let go. And Rod's perspective changed; it dropped to a lower point because *he* was dropping; he was lowering.

He was a boy, again: a running boy now running over the fields of his parents' farm while winds gusted. The winds didn't bring the scent of the morning's rain, but rather the scent of a wild animal closing in an animal's mouth wide open that he was sprinting straight for.

The mouth became a tunnel, and the tunnel became a slope falling through the dead stink of a monster's breath, and Rod fell with it.

Chapter Thirty-Three

It was only when the ache in her chest registered that Alex realised she was holding her breath. She let it go. On all sides, the building settled with an almost audible sigh. The echo of the lift doors snapped together as they closed faded into silence.

"Rod?" she whispered.

If there was a reply, the sound was far too indistinct to be named. She ran past Kelly, yelling for Simon and Dao. All three hit the lift at the same time.

"Get it open. Get him out," Alex shouted.

Grunting, the men dropped their improvised weapons and dug their fingers into the tiny crack between the two doors. They pulled. Nothing happened.

"Pull harder," Dao yelled.

"I am." Simon's face was already a bright shade of red while the thin cords of tendons jutted from Dao's long arms.

"Bastard," Dao spat. *"Fucking open, fucking—"*

He fell back, and Simon jerked his hands clear, as if the metal had abruptly grown scalding hot.

The sound Alex caught a few seconds before came again, clearer now because she was closer to it. Faint screams. Rod's faint screams.

Moving as one, they backed away from the lift. Alex wept silently, Dao shaking his head and Kelly wanting to answer Rod with her own cries. They were trapped inside, and maybe she should have been grateful for that, but letting them go and giving up seemed like her idea of heaven when compared to what she was seeing and what they all saw.

A tunnel underground, black and damp. Mould and moss grew over the walls, rising to the low ceiling and turning the air into a redolent stink. The cloying stench coated each uneven section of the floor and swam on the surface of dozens of puddles. A drip fell with a regular tap somewhere in the poor light while shadows cast by sputtering flames capered over the walls, and Rod's voice was a holler in the distance; his begging for help fell away from this gloomy space because wherever the tunnel dropped, Rod was right on the end, surrounded by the reek of the mould and unable to stop himself from staring straight into the mouth below from where the wind blew and its stench played with his thin hair.

All of that before the mouth below swallowed him, and the last of his cries were a dying echo, bouncing off damp walls to drown in the puddles.

Kelly bent double. While her stomach hitched and all the saliva in her mouth became a thick paste, the savage cramp passed. She blinked repeatedly until her vision levelled out; then she managed to stand straight for a moment, and her back found one of the pillars. Grateful for its support, she slid straight down, legs splayed.

"Rod?" Dao reached for the lift. He didn't dare touch it and eventually lowered his hand.

"He's gone." Alex backed away, glanced down at her sister and heard inside the echo of Carl's name. Had that really only been a few moments before all this? Keeping hold of the idea of normal time was as hard as keeping hold of *any* idea. Everything she wanted to touch was slick like oil.

"It took him," she finished and wandered over to the reception desk to rest her face on its cool surface. That was okay. That was heaven. She twisted her neck, trying to get her cheeks, nose, and chin onto the smooth surface. Let it take her sweat and stink. Let it wipe her clean.

"I saw it." Simon drew closer to Dao, unsure of why he needed the other man to know it, and unable to stop himself. "I saw... it." But had he? *Something* filled the entrance to the lift a moment before Rod ran to it, and that something might have been the shape of a man. He couldn't be sure of a fucking thing right now, least of all whether he was now a part of the others or still so much skin fading into thin air.

No. I saw it. I am here.

He spun Dao around, and Dao's mouth opened and closed without a sound emerging.

"I saw it take Rod."

"Great," Dao muttered. "Now you see what we see. Now you see what's trying to kill us."

He walked to the main entrance and kicked at the glass. As before, it shook but didn't come close to breaking. Back still resting on the pillar, Kelly gave no reaction when Simon wandered over to her and dropped onto his haunches.

"You okay?"

She knew he was speaking and she knew she should answer, but words were outside the world. All she had was the image of Carl out on the road, overlaying the image of Rod shrinking into the body of a running child, and a grinning man with his arms open wide before both of them fell down the lift and the doors closed.

Simon tried to take Kelly's hand. Alex ran to them and knocked him over. "Don't touch her."

Not giving Simon chance to reply or move aside, Alex knelt and took hold of Kelly's shoulders.

"You talk to me, Kel. You tell me why you saw Carl outside."

While there may have been no words left in the world for Kelly, there were still lies. She found one and let it free.

"I don't know."

Barely even a murmur and it was all she could manage.

"Bullshit."

Kelly's eyes rolled, then found her sister's. The women stared at one another, Dao and Simon forgotten. High above, a curious gaze landed on the split group, amused by their arguments as it was amused by their guilt. It waited for the truth to come, not disappointed when it didn't. Now wasn't the right time. Not yet.

"I don't know," Kelly repeated in a flat tone. "Get the fuck out of my face, Alex."

Alex backed away. She spoke to all of them but kept her regard on Kelly.

"I don't care about anything but getting back to my children. Not one single thing."

With that, she turned towards the side of the cash office, heading for the open door of the building's ground floor offices. Simon took a few hesitant steps after her, then looked back at Dao.

"What do we do?" he asked.

Dao left the entrance. Kelly was struggling to her feet. All at once, Dao registered the pain in his fingertips from their attempts to open the lift. His palms were sore, too. A few useless smacks of the doors had done nothing but hurt him. Along with that soreness, muscles throughout his body demanded rest. Not enough food or sleep and a non-stop fear had combined to almost wipe him out.

No. Not yet. Not yet, you hear me?

Peering over the railings of the tenth floor, the shape of a little boy let out a soft laugh that registered in Dao's heart and not his ears.

"We follow her." Dao held a hand to Kelly without looking. She took it and stood. "We find any door on this floor or a window on the next if we have to, and we get out. Ghosts, dead things, monsters. I don't care. We are getting out."

Gathering their dropped knives, the others followed Alex, who was already through the open doors into the back offices. And all wished in their own way that Rod walked with him.

***

The reception, empty again. The reception, waiting.

Chapter Thirty-Four

Beyond the wide space of the back office, with its waiting area and its desks and phones, they found their way into a curving corridor. The walls from floor to ten feet above a smooth, featureless white and no doors lining them. Windows filled the remainder of the wall area, bringing in daylight. Dao let the door shut behind them, morbidly convinced it would lock with a gentle, mocking clicks the second they let go and leave them trapped. With the others focusing on the floor and walls, he gave the door a soft push. It opened. Relaxing as much as possible, he let go of it again.

"You know where we are?" Simon asked Alex.

"No."

Seemingly not bothered by this, Alex strode over the floor and stared straight ahead. Simon offered Dao a raised eyebrow and followed. Dao gestured for Kelly to move. She tried to smile and failed. He followed her, listening to the soft tap of their shoes and boots. The corridor flowed in a long curve and formed a semi-circle that he imagined went around the entire ground floor. All he could do now was hope they came to a fire exit, or another office that in turn led to an exit. Seconds ticked by; Lin spoke up inside Dao's head.

Keep going. There has to be a way out. She was calm and together while his insides jumped. *I know it's bad, but you can find a way out.*

I will, he promised his wife.

Good. Make sure you do. And do whatever it takes to get out.

Dao slowed, not aware he was doing so. Lin's voice sounded harsher than normal. While his wife was not afraid to say what was on her mind or challenge anyone, she was not aggressive with it. Right now, a note of ruthlessness came, and although Dao knew on all levels he was simply talking to himself in Lin's voice, it didn't alter the tone. He trotted to keep up with Kelly while Simon and Alex were already ahead. The tap of their feet grew hollow; the walls remained a pure white and still no doors or windows, still no way out other than back the way they'd walked, still one short now Rod was dead, still—

He sweated, suddenly too hot, despite the cool air. A shout for the others to stop trembled on his lips while his peripheral vision wavered; the walls flowed into a bleached stream and the floor became a silver river eager to sweep him away before it closed over his head and filled his mouth, lungs, belly.

Calm down, Lin told him.

Wonder of wonders, Dao returned to the reality of the solid walls and floor and the rest of the little group a few paces in front. Although it felt like he'd been losing it for minutes, no more than a few seconds could have passed.

That's right. They're all still here and you're *still here, Dao. Keep your eyes on them, on Kelly. Watch her back and keep focused, okay? You can do that, my love. It's easy. Just one foot in front of the other, okay, Dao?*

Okay, Dao replied.

Good. Keep going. You're doing well, Dao. Stick with the others and keep moving. Keep your eyes on them, okay? Keep watching Kelly. Kelly. Kelly.

With each repetition of the girl's name, Lin's voice altered, dropping lower and becoming rougher as if she had a particularly sore throat. He had the strange sensation of Lin grinning in an ugly manner before she spoke again and her voice was a choking, *wet* mutter.

Now watch her, watch her, watch her arse.

Dao managed to hiss. The sound failed to reach any of the others. He tried to yell his horror but could only manage another hiss. No moisture coated his tongue or lips; the corridor had become a boiling oven, and the walls were a blinding white. He would burn. They'd all burn in the oven, and that might be welcome if it meant getting away from the nightmare yelling right in his ear.

Watch that little arse right in front of you; she's right in front of you, that arse, that little bitch, that fucking whore with that sweet arse. You want it, don't you? It's okay, I know what you want. I can't blame you. It's sweet, so small so little like a child's—

Inside, Dao cried for Lin to stop. She would not.

—that arse, it's small like Rod's was when he was a boy, so look at it, Dao. look right now and imagine fucking it. Imagine fucking her. I bet she loves it like that. She looks like she does. I bet she's had it loads, and that's why they don't get on because Kelly's nothing but a little slut a slut who takes it off anyone who offers it. The fucking little bitch. You could fuck her right now and she wouldn't mind—

The raging screeches descended into an image Dao could not lose; his wife hammering a picture into his skull of himself sprinting forward, clambering onto Kelly's back and shoving her to the pure white of the floor while she shrieked, and his fingers found the waist and zip of her jeans and Simon and Alex cheered him on.

(daddy stop it)

Dao managed a small grunt as if he'd been punched. One foot twisted, knocking the other. He tripped and went down, hard.

Pain.

It was a welcome pain because it had one immediate effect. Lin's image vanished in a silent explosion, and that explosion was the hurt flowing through his body.

Groaning, Dao rolled over. Rod's blade clattered as Kelly's toe kicked it. Spots filled Dao's vision, all dancing. He blinked until his surroundings returned to normal, and Kelly's face loomed over his.

"Dao?"

He had a brief flashback to his attack and her cries before he managed to push the image away. Lin was not with him. Only an ugly thing with no name and no face that belonged to his wife spoke here. Let it speak. Let it rant. He would not listen to it now or again.

"I fell," he muttered. Then stupidly: "Sorry."

Alex and Simon arrived at his side, Simon reaching for him with one hand, clutching the blade and his knife with the other.

"What happened?" Simon asked.

"Tripped." He coughed, a flame burning in his chest. Simon helped him up and handed over the blade. "Sorry," Dao said again,

"Don't worry about it." Simon glanced at the women. "We walk in a line, yeah? Not apart?"

For a moment, Alex's face suggested she was going to simply ignore this and walk ahead alone. Then she relented by giving a single nod.

Not surprising Dao, Kelly took his left-hand side while Simon walked on his right, leaving Alex to take the far end of their small line. The sisters were as far apart as they could be, and Dao asked himself when whatever truth festered between them would come out, rather than if.

As long as it doesn't get in the way of us getting out, then I don't care, he thought in his own voice. Lin, or whatever had pretended to be her inside his head, had gone, and that could only be a good thing.

They walked for another minute, the corridor sliding to the left instead of right as might have been expected. At its end, a fire exit filled a large chunk of the wall.

They stopped.

"I think this leads to the car park," Alex murmured. "Sternfield Street is on the other side."

"You sure?" Simon asked.

"No." She rubbed her forehead. "I *think* so. I don't know."

Alex lowered her hand. While no sounds reached them, Simon and Dao wondered if she was hearing her church bell again, which led Simon to hear the autumn wind blowing down the long flight of stairs, caressing the door behind them, and sneaking through cracks.

Leave it. You're almost free.

Something right beside his ear laughed. He refused to turn or acknowledge the wave of icy cold swallowing his body from his toes to the top of his head.

Dao and Alex moved at the same time, striding forward while Kelly and Simon trotted to keep up. The four reached the fire exit and stopped as one. Alex tapped the cool metal of the grey bar crossing its centre.

"If this is locked, I don't know what I'm going to do," she whispered.

"We'll knock the fucking thing down if we have to,"
Kelly said.

Alex's hold on the bar grew firmer.

"Wait a second," Dao said. He placed a hand beside Alex's and looked at Simon and Kelly. "All of us."

Four hands found a space on the dirty grey of the bar. Simon's question—*what do we do if those burned people are out there?* —lived only in the panic and confusion of his head, and maybe that was for the best. Verbalising it would do nothing for them.

"On three," Alex said. Then in a mad rush: "One, two, three."

They shoved on the bar.

Chapter Thirty-Five

For the third time in many minutes, Simon pushed on the useless door. Again, it was like pushing at the floor and expecting it to give way.

"You need to stop doing that," Kelly said, her body against the wall. She sat, and was made smaller than usual by bringing her legs up to meet her resting chin.

Simon kicked the door. "Why?"

"Because there's no point." Alex took a few breaths. "It's not going to budge, Simon."

He struck the bar hard enough to hurt his fingers. "Fuck."

Sitting beside Dao seemed to be the only option. Dao had slumped down a few seconds after it became clear their joint shoving on the fire exit bar was pointless. He hadn't spoken in long minutes.

The men and women faced one another, nobody speaking. Simon placed his knife beside his knees and studied the floor instead of looking at the door blocking their escape. Better to do that than think about there being no way out of this place. Better to do that than think of their walk through this corridor, and it's quite pregnant with threat leading to a great big anti-climax.

Another gentle laugh brushed his ear, the sound as bleak as the voice back in the cash office that turned his body into a fading bag of skin and bones.

Go away. Leave us alone.

It chuckled; a secret joke shared between him and it.

No. It's not just for me. It's here for all of us.

If the thing laughed at him again, he didn't hear it. "We have to go back," Dao said to nobody in particular.

"Why?" Kelly replied. "What's the point?"

"So, we just sit here and do nothing?" he said, and Kelly had nothing to say to that.

Story of my life, Simon thought. At once, a burst of anger hit him. No. That was not fair. While he had no friends and no life outside his job, he *was* good at what he did. He could plan and organise, sort and *do*. The managers back at work didn't like him; he knew that and hadn't really cared in years. He was good at expanding the company because he knew what to say in work-life. It was only in real life that he failed miserably. He'd been sent to Willington to sell the company. All he had to do was apply his work skills to this.

"Up," he said and stood. Nobody else moved. "Come on. Get up. We're moving."

"Where?" Alex asked.

"Wherever we can." He smiled and, wonder of wonders, it actually felt real. "We moved, and we don't stop until we find a way out that actually works, one that isn't this." He rapped on the fire exit. "Think about it. Whatever's happening here… supernatural or what, this is still a solid building. Glass, brick. It's physical, yeah? We can affect it. Rod did when he broke that window and, even if something was messing with his head to make him think he killed someone, he still smashed the glass. We do the same if we have to. Okay, we can't do it to these windows." He jumped, reaching for the high glass. The tips of his fingers managed to stretch a foot or more below the windows. "We do it on the first floor instead of the fifth. We can break and smash whatever we want because this is real." Grinning and feeling as close to good as he could manage, Simon rapped his knuckles on the floor.

"You're full of shit," Kelly said, and some of Simon's determination faltered. "There's no way out of here and nothing to get out to. It's nothing outside." She lowered her voice to a dull whisper. "Nothing out there."

With a soft grunt, Alex rose. "We're not helping ourselves by not moving." She eyed the men, but not her sister. For Alex, Kelly was no longer completely there because…because…

Because she couldn't think about that. She didn't dare. The fear of what it meant to do so was much too great. Almost as much as the terror of not knowing if her kids were safe somewhere out in the world beyond this hateful building.

"Simon's right. We move, and we don't stop."

Wordlessly, Dao reached towards Kelly. She eyed it as if not quite sure what it was before grasping his skinny fingers and rising.

"Back down here." Simon pointed to the curve of the corridor. "Side by side, yeah? We keep together." The next few words were a struggle. Reaching out to Dao, Alex and Kelly were human things, things that mattered. Not his job, fake smiles, handshakes for deals, and agreements that he didn't give two shits about. This was as human as it got. Life and death right here.

"I know I'm not seeing everything you're seeing. I know whatever fucked up thing is here, it's not for me like it is for you, and I don't know why. All I think is we're here together; we stay together, and we get out together. All right?"

Red flamed in his cheeks. He stared at the wall between the sisters' heads, not daring to meet their eyes or Dao's at his side.

"All right?" he whispered.

"All I want is to get back to my girls." Alex pushed herself off the wall and began walking back the way they'd come to the sealed exit. Dao watched her go for a moment, then, knowing Simon needed something, he whispered to him.

"She's just scared."

"You're scared," Simon muttered, not caring if Alex heard him.

"Yeah. I am. Come on."

Simon between Dao and Kelly, they followed Alex. They'd barely managed ten steps before she glanced back.

"What is it?" Dao asked, peering past her.

"I hear something."

Nameless dread spread over Simon's back, turning him cold. A quick look at Kelly and Dao said they felt the same. She was beginning to back away, turning her body towards the fire exit.

"Wait," Simon whispered. "I—"

The smell hit his nose before the cool wind found his skin. While the reek of the phantom air had never been pleasant, whether in his imagination or blowing out of nowhere, this was a stink of rotten flesh. This was a huge pile of bodies, their skin sliding off bones, falling into a puddle of liquefying flesh, and all of it clinging to the teeth and gullet of a monster.

Blocking her nose and mouth, Alex retreated, joining the others.

"What is that?" she cried, voice made nasal by her hand. Behind the others, Kelly ran for the fire exit. She knew on all rational levels that it wouldn't open, but still forced herself to try. She hammered at the solid metal, not feeling the pain in her hands from each blow. Her hair flapped madly around her head. The wind gusted with a savage roar, and the corridor formed a tunnel for it. Bent double, Dao tried to walk. He failed and skidded backwards, one arm catching Alex in the chest. She reached for the wall, fingertips finding it briefly before she had to pull her arms in simply to keep her balance. The gale stormed down the corridor; the reek choking them, and their cries lost to each other.

Kelly smacked into the fire exit. The metal bar crunched against her lower back, making her cry out. She inhaled a deep lungful of the terrible smell and choked on it. Tears squirted, and in her blurred vision, she thought she saw the shapes of two men advancing with the steady wail of the wind. One man, well-built and totally naked, was taller than the other; the second man was dressed in a hospital gown.

Kelly screamed.

Alex collided with her sister, forcing Kelly against the bar again and sending bright bolts of agony radiating throughout her body. Reaching without thought, Dao and Simon found one another, and both men slipped over the floor towards the women, the wind propelling them gleefully and the stench coating their skin and hair.

The four spread over the fire exit, all crying out, fingers splayed and nobody able to get a hold on another. Their backs pressed against the bar as their hands had minutes before, and the bar slid inwards, and the wind was a storm on their wide-open mouths.

Chapter Thirty-Six

Up on ten, the pure yellow of the sun shone on the floor and expensive sofas lining the walls of the corridor. The door to the office of a Mr. Alan Letts remained closed. The crack in the wood from the crash while Dao could do nothing but watch it remain as a twisted line running from top to bottom. If anything existed in the office, it was a silent, contemplating force.

Beyond Mr. Alan Letts's door, the corridor took in the entrances to the meeting rooms and the executive management's offices. All remained firmly closed because nothing lived beyond them. The creature making its way through the tenth floor paid them no attention. Its business was further along: past the junction and at the end of the corridor where the lone door to the roof stood.

It paused at the junction, watching, waiting.

Any thermometer would have registered an abrupt change in the temperature, a rapid lowering to winter- like conditions while the sun's light flowed in and reached almost every inch of the floor. Any person up there would have retreated quickly from the biting cold, but no flesh lived on the tenth floor. Nothing walked.

The creature moved an inch forward.

At once, the door leading to the roof flew open, crashing into the wall with a hollow bang. A shape emerged. While it had no human-like body, it did have a face. One of many. It opened its mouth and smiled.

A glacial blast barrelled down the corridor. The creature who'd come from the terror and confusion of the fire exit. The reek blown towards the men and women took the Arctic air.

Then, in a mad howl of rage, she gave it back.

Chapter Thirty-Seven

Striking the rock-hard floor and sliding over it sent Kelly back to the day before. She was flying, shoved by a massive pulse at her back, and now she'd landed; she'd stand, see that all the lights were off, and she'd think something was very wrong before a door opened. A big Welshman would introduce himself as Rod Moore, and then everything would turn into a nightmare.

But that had already happened.

She pushed herself along a few inches before finding the strength to stand. Upright, Kelly had a dim, aching wish she hadn't bothered making. At least still on the ground, she could believe the obvious hadn't happened.

They were back in the main reception of Greenham Place, everything so much the same as earlier, so they might not have walked away. She stood between two pillars, facing the entrance. Alex, Simon, and Dao were in front, all in various stages of rising, looking around. Kelly's own disbelief was reflected in their faces and her need to scream, too.

Cradling her throbbing elbow, Kelly looked behind, half-expecting to see the fire exit jutting open. Instead, the lift was at their back. The doors were firmly closed.

It had swallowed them from the fire exit and spat them out like they were bits of fat. She staggered from it, eager to put as much distance between herself and the innocuous metal of the doors.

"No," she whispered. It couldn't be true. Could *not*. If it was, they might as well sit on the floor, wait for their second night in Greenham Place, wait for whatever lived here to grow tired of its snide games and crush them into dirt. If wherever they went brought them back here, then there was no point in believing they could escape and definitely no point in actually trying to get out.

The woman, her exhausted mind whispered. *Who was the woman?*

Kelly stopped, memory coming in fast. She'd seen a woman, only for a second, before the fire exit opened. A skinny woman, obviously ill, formed out of the storm firing down on them. Who the hell was she?

Pressing on his ribs, Simon stared past Kelly to the lift. Except he wasn't seeing the lift.

"Who was she?" Kelly's question came out of the same nowhere that must have formed the skinny woman. A nowhere of stinking air and dead hope.

Simon flinched. "Who?"

"The woman." Kelly advanced on him, body still aching from the crash to the floor. "I saw her."

"So, did I," Dao said. "A woman. She looked ill."

"Shut up." Simon turned to the front. It looked exactly the same. Nothing moved out there. Nothing lived. They faced a sketch of a town.

Wanting to look anywhere else, Kelly met her sister's gaze. Alex gave a quick nod but said nothing. Silence, dark and throbbing, spun out. It seemed Simon would keep quiet while they waited, and the reception was as it'd been in the horrible moments after Rod's disappearance.

"My mother," Simon said abruptly. "It was my mother."

"Hey, congratulations." Kelly had never heard Alex's voice sound so ugly, so savage. "You see the same shit we do. Lucky you. Now we're definitely all in this together."

With that, Alex sat at the reception desk, head in his hands. She might have been crying. Kelly didn't know. She didn't know a thing.

Knives.

Shit. Their little weapons were nowhere in sight. Whatever shoved them from the fire exit and out of the lift had kept hold of their knives.

All they had to defend themselves now were their fists.

Dao drew closer to Simon. "Why are you seeing your mother, Simon?"

"Shut up," Simon replied without much strength.

"No. Talk to us. Why are—"

"I said shut up." Simon threw a blind punch at Dao and struck him in the shoulder, more by luck than aim. Dao staggered and took the blow without fighting back or moving aside.

Weeping, Simon crossed to the doors and windows at the building's front. "Let us out," he whispered. The words were barely audible to himself, let alone the others. Kelly caught the sound but not the sentence. She stepped closer to him, eyes on the road outside.

"See anyone, Kel?" Alex called. "See anyone I know?"

"No." Kelly fought off waves of anger and guilt. "It's not my fault, Alex. What's happening, it's not my fault."

Alex let out a laugh that sounded more like a bark.

"I'm not blaming you for *this,* Kel."

If there was more to be said, Alex held it inside, and Kelly didn't have the courage to take their argument further. She stood as close to Simon as she dared, keeping five steps between them. He splayed his fingers over the warm glass, still crying. Watching them, Dao banished the disappointment that their attempt to get through the fire exit had been pointless, and he pictured

248

the woman's face in the corridor while the wind hammered at them and the fire exit began to give way. The image had been in front for no more than a few seconds. His focus had been trying to keep upright and not choke on the stink of the gusting air. Even so, he'd got a decent look at her. Again, he saw the strained skin and the jutting cheekbones, neither were from lucky good looks but rather from illness. The woman was diseased. The sickness had turned her pale skin the colour of dirty paint, made her long hair thin and straggly, and eaten into the body below her clothes. Cancer? Something worse?

"My mother. It was her and it wasn't. Like she was… different, but the same." The sigh Simon let out made his chest tremble. "Like she was just to the edge of the person she was. That make sense?"

"No," Alex muttered. Dao gave Simon a quick nod, encouraging him.

"She died when I was five. She drank herself to death. Literally. Her liver was nothing by the end. My aunt adopted me on my sixth birthday. Thirty-three years ago, today. In case you were wondering."

He pulled away from the windows and faced Dao, then glanced at Alex who remained on the desk. "That's who was in the corridor. Fucked if I know why. That's who we saw."

"She was that wind." Alex fell silent, the rest of her sentence uncomfortably clear. *And the stink.*

"No." Simon shook his head. "I don't think so, anyway. She was there after it. That wind, that fucking stench… that's something else."

Alex emerged from the other side of the desk, and when she spoke, she was Alex again. No mocking; no savage anger. She was the woman Kelly knew and loved in her own troubled way.

"Why would your mother be here, Simon? My dad, or whatever's pretending to be him, wants to hurt me. Same with Dao. But your mum didn't hurt you. Not now."

He wept again, decades of tender wounds making their languid way to the surface and stabbing him every step of the way.

"I don't know." He sniffed, the sound loud in the quiet. "She had a problem. A big one that she couldn't beat. I found out when I was twenty she'd been abused. Her dad. She drank. She drank herself to death." The hurt he'd kept at arm's length for more than thirty years was more than close; it was his skin and bones. He'd become that agony and it was glad to have taken over his heart and mind. "She… made me… she made me do things."

There. It was out, exposed to the others, exposed to whatever shitty thing walked the corridors of Greenham Place. He'd named the worst thing in the world.

"Jesus Christ," Alex whispered. Any anger and frustration she'd forced herself to feel as a distraction from her terror collapsed into so much ash.

"I haven't seen her here like you've seen your dad." Simon looked at Dao, eyes wet. "Or your boy, Dao."

Simon took a shaking breath. Dao walked to him, arms open. Simon stared at the other man: a small, sad part of him wondering when someone had last done this for him. Years, maybe.

Letting go of the thought, Simon embraced Dao in a rough hug.

"We'll get out of this," Dao whispered.

"Yeah."

They let go of one another, both feeling awkward. Simon sniggered.

"Going to offer to buy me a drink?" he asked.

Dao smiled. "Maybe later."

He walked to the doors, standing in the same spot Simon had a moment before. "Two options. Just like before," he said, looking at the others. Kelly rested her forehead on the glass. "Either we try again to find something that smashes this." Dao tapped the doors without looking from Simon and Alex. "Or we go up one floor, smash a window and jump. Maybe break an ankle or a leg." He shrugged. "At this point, I don't care about a broken bone."

Alex nodded, eager to believe and agree. There *had* to be a way out; all they needed to do was find it. So, the fire exit plan hadn't worked. So, what? What Simon said back in the corridor about Greenham Place being a physical place with its windows and doors made sense. They just needed to find the right door.

Pretending she believed her own encouragement all the way down, Alex studied the foyer for something they might have missed. It didn't take long for her forced hope to wilt and die.

Nothing here. No way out here.

Tears came. Furious, she blinked until they ceased and wondered what her daughters were doing in the world outside Greenham Place.

Still staring outside, Kelly scanned the fronts of the shops opposite the office block and pictured the wall of people from the day before with their faces and bodies scorched into so much destroyed skin, all the open wounds, all turning into something inhuman. The memory flooded her inner eye; she saw them pressed on the other side of the doors and windows, their mouths distending like glue and the voice turned into a Voice.

We are burning.

Kelly shivered. The reek of all that burned flesh stung her nose, the smell as much a memory as the sight of the people on the pavement.

Forget about it. They're gone.

Hoping that when she opened her mouth, she'd say something that Alex wouldn't jump on, Kelly turned from the window.

The stink hit her first. Then the sight.

Between her and Dao, beside the useless entrance and Alex and Simon, a wall of burned bodies stood. The choking stink clamped down on Kelly's mouth and nose. The bodies at the rear of the main group, three men with their eyes turned into lines by the melted skin of their foreheads, turned towards her and Dao.

Cold logic cut fear off. Kelly's sensory perception exploded; sight and smell merged into one force. In a second, she took in the damage done to each body; she inhaled the sweet aroma of flesh cooked in an oven, and the ice of the logic in her head said there was no need for fear because the people could not possibly be real. They were simply images in the same way Alex's dad had been an image on the stairs. Horrible, frightening, but not solid.

Not tangible.

Then a hand, stripped down to blackened bone, found her face. Hot fingers gripped the skin of her cheek; jagged nails tore that skin and began to pull her into the oven.

Chapter Thirty-Eight

Dao shoved forwards, yelling, aware of nothing but the command inside that said *run away*.

Three hands struck his head, pushing him backwards. He stumbled and twisted around. The creatures a matter of feet away became a blurred reflection—bodies too damaged to possibly stand, let alone walk. The hands pushed again, shoving his face to the glass while he bellowed his horror.

The outside had vanished. In its place, a great wall of flame threw itself from the ground to the top of the sky, the fire making no sound and generating no heat. It was like looking at a TV screen that filled every inch of his vision. The force pushing on his head and back increased in pressure: squashing Dao's nose to the hard surface of the glass. He flashed back to the moments up on the tenth floor when the same thing had happened before the glass parted like water.

That wasn't happening here.

The pressure remained steady. The dead people wanted to break his face on the door and smear his blood all over it while the silent fire cooked the world beyond Greenham Place. Breathing was next to impossible. Dao's vision began to bleed a deep shade of red. Red like all the skin at his back. Red like the flames barely two feet away.

Help me, Dao shouted at his wife. She said nothing. He was on his own and that shouldn't have been any surprise. He'd been on his own since he sprinted to this building while the entire city tried to run from the bomb.

The pain was a growing beast. Soon, it would eat all of his sight and all that remained would be the thick blood-red of his eyes forced from their sockets by the pressure on his head before his skull cracked open like a broken egg.

I am sorry, Yang. I am so sorry. Be safe. Be happy.

"*Dao.*" Kelly's cry broke through to Dao. He reached blindly and found her fingers. She tugged.

Dao pulled away from the glass, the force loosening for a second. He sucked in a mighty breath and threw a punch without looking. He struck the remains of a man's face. Skin sloughed off, coating Dao's hand, then splattered to the floor. He shrieked. The twisted scar of the man's mouth opened, tore the wound open and stretched further.

He was trying to smile.

We burn, the man said. *You burn.*

Outrage detonated inside Dao. Its force shoved him forward and made him punch without looking. Shrieking, Kelly did the same. Her small fists sunk into scarred flesh. She pulled it from the bodies and punched again. Her horror and panic, even the cloying stink of her own sweat, were buried beneath the desperate need to get the burned people away from her. A tall woman loomed above, the dangling tissue of her neck making her head hang as if it were on a spring. The darkened stubs of what had been her teeth snapped together in a blur and Kelly heard a metallic clang at the same time.

It's the lift, she thought without hearing it. *It's* laughing at us.

The woman closed in. Kelly voiced her fury and swung a fist. The woman's teeth missed Kelly's fingers by less than an inch before fist met cheek and pulled. Caught in Kelly's nails, scar tissue shredded, horror-struck, Kelly punched again. A knuckle caught the woman's eye. For a second, Kelly came close to simply letting go of her sanity.

Her knuckle poked through the woman's eye. Hot fluid coated it, then something else. The terrible heat of a never-ending fire.

Kelly yanked her hand free and shoved the woman back as hard as she could. Four of them went down. At the same time, agony claimed her hip.

A child, no older than five, clung to Kelly's side fastened there like a leech. The boy pulled his mouth from her skin. Blood stained his lips. *Her* blood, she saw with an eye turned dispassionate by the weight of her horror. Trying to smile, the boy bit her again, face burrowing like a rat with a piece of meat.

"Motherfucker."

Grabbing the child, Kelly yanked him free from her bleeding hip and flung him. His head collided with a pillar. Even with the storm of shrieks and yells almost deafening her, Kelly caught the wet thud of skull on marble, saw the boy's skull shunted forward by the impact. She slapped a hand against the wound in her hip, utterly convinced she was infected with the building's disease.

An elderly man, his clothes turned into little more than rags by the fire, got hold of Dao's shoulders and pushed him back towards the entrance. Dao kept hold of the man's forearms; skin slid off. Dao spun on the spot and launched the man. He struck the doors, bounced and looked up at Dao.

Even though his features were destroyed, Dao saw enough to know the man was Chinese and to know the man had come for him on purpose. Or had been sent by whatever controlled the building. Sent to mock. Sent to remind Dao of his roots and the long dead but still clear misery of his early years in England when all he knew at school was the looks from the other kids, the causal racism and the desperate desire to be home in a world of friends and family he recognized, rather than the cold, grey tedium of England. Misery was dead since he left his childhood behind, dead since meeting Lin, starting a new life beyond growing up in China, and travelling thousands of miles and years away from all he understood. Now, misery reflected in the old man's twisting mouth and what remained of his eyes.

Shouting and shrieking were forgotten. Dao grabbed the back of the man's head and smashed it against the glass in the centre of the door. Again. Again. Again.

Bone split. More skin fell free. Gore coated Dao's forearm up to his elbow. He bounced the man's head off the glass again. The Skull, stained red and black, broke through rents in the man's forehead and snapped into fragments when Dao put all of his strength into another blow.

Glass cracked. An awful mixture of joy and fear flowed through Dao.

"Kelly." He hit the door again.

The crack spread in a spider web-thin line. Dao threw the man who no longer had a face to the floor and booted at the crack. A chunk of glass fell out to the pavement. At once, a burst of boiling heat streamed in through the hole. Dao jerked backwards. The space around the entrance was becoming its own mini-sun. The dead people pulled away from Dao and Kelly; Dao's vision teared, and his saliva dried, leaving his tongue and the insides of his cheeks like parched rags.

Staggering, Kelly reached for Dao. His flailing hand caught her on the cheek. Pain and dizziness came at the same instant. Through a mouth made numb by his blow, she shouted: "Run."

Half a dozen of the burned people moved on her and Dao, all speaking without opening what remained of their mouths while the air grew insufferably hot.

We burn. You burn. Burn with us.

Kelly shoved Dao. They ran to their left, skidding over pieces of reddened and blackened skin, and Dao struck one of the pillars. He groaned, not hearing it over Alex's voice from the other side of the massing bodies.

"Kelly. Where are you?"

"Run, Alex. Both of you, run," Dao yelled, taking Kelly's arm as she made a move towards the centre of the floor. While at least twenty feet from the invisible fire at the doors, both could still barely breathe in the heat.

"Let go of me." Kelly tried to pull free from Dao. Her hip and leg felt like fire. Her whole body was one giant throb. Dao held her firm and jabbed a finger at the door to the cash office.

"We have to go. They'll tear you apart."

Ignoring Dao, Kelly stretched for the milling burned people, convinced that if she saw Alex through any gap in the bodies, she could keep her safe and undo all the wrong things. Four men, none with anything recognisable as a face, advanced on her, arms up and their fingers together.

Burn with us.

"Alex!" Kelly screamed.

At the main doors, more glass broke. On the outside, a man smashed his fists into the small hole, widening it, reaching through and catching his fingers on a jagged shard. Enough of the charred people parted for Kelly to see not a single drop of blood fell from the long gash in the man's torn skin, then to see his face, leering at her as he lifted a naked leg to kick in more of the hole while streaks of flame burned the air outside.

Carl.

Her brother-in-law smiled.

Kelly ran for the cash office, Dao remains a step behind. She struck the door a second before him, aware she was sobbing, aware Alex was calling her name over and over from the far side of the ground floor and not giving a shit about either.

Carl was here. Carl had come for her.

Dao struck the handle. "Open the fucking door."

Nothing happened. No power in the building and all the fob accesses dead, which meant every single door should be open to them. But this one was not.

"Fuck." Kelly booted the handle with the toe of her boot. It shook, but that was all.

She looked back and immediately wished she hadn't.

Carl pulled himself through the hole. While it was barely big enough for a child (*Dao's boy,* her mind whispered), the naked shape of Carl was still coming. Shards dug deeply into the thick muscles of his arms and hips. In terrifying detail, Kelly saw rents open in his skin. The flesh parted to reveal nothing. Black stared out of the wounds in Carl's body, and the uneven cuts flapped in hanging chunks.

He was still coming.

Dao shoved on the handle again. It had no effect. He looked around, eyes huge. There was no way through the bodies. To get to Alex and Simon, they'd either have to run back to the scorching air and the naked man coming through the door or try to fight their way through the barrier of the burned. He readied himself to tell Kelly that they had to fight when she dashed straight at the nearest figure. An old lady, wizened, dried to a husk by the fire.

Kelly ran with the woman, head on her hand. She propelled her straight at the small pane of glass in the centre of the cash office door. Dao threw himself to the floor. The woman's face struck the glass, breaking both. Kelly shoved the woman aside. What remained of her face slid down to her narrow chest. The outer layers of it stuck to the broken glass. Banishing all thought but the need to escape, Kelly punched through the wrecked pane and reached.

"He's coming, Kelly," Dao whispered.

She didn't hear him and didn't need to. Carl was here for her.

Kelly's dancing fingers found a handle. She shoved hard and yanked her arm free as the door opened. More shards cut her wrist and a faraway pain sang.

She was first through, Dao right behind. He shoved a few office chairs to the door.

They ran.

Chapter Thirty-Nine

When the screaming began, Simon was facing away from the others, his attention on the lift doors and his mind on the image of them blown through the fire exit to be blown out of the lift, as if the two were connected.

Blown away by a hurricane with your mum watching, he thought, and the world turned into a volley of cries, all sharp and bright like broken glass.

Simon whirled as Alex dashed from the reception desk. For a second or two, Simon couldn't process what he saw. A crowd had come from nowhere to fill the main area of the ground floor. They flowed between the pillars, men and women and children all dressed in torn and shredded clothes. Not shredded, he realised. Burned. Burned like their skin.

Simon backed up, trying to speak, failing. He reached the smooth wall beside the lift, conscious mind unable to process the sight of fifty or sixty people, all clearly dead, almost in touching distance.

Unconcerned about Simon, Alex dashed from the reception desk. She could run. She knew that. Despite being out of shape, she knew she could move. She stayed where she was, though. Door to the stairs off to her right; a clear path between her and it, and a wall of scorched bodies between her and Kelly.

"Kelly," Alex whispered.

It was as if her quiet voice was a trigger for chaos.

A great chorus of voices, babbling together, exploding from all sides; men and women screeched that they were burning; children crying for their parents to stop the hurting, to put out the fire. Alex's lone cry was drowned out by dozens of others. The nearest people came for her, their melted hands trying to reach and unable to grip because they had no fingers. Nauseated, Alex lashed out and knocked a man to the side. Her fist collided with a woman's hot face; the woman's teeth snapped together. A tooth caught on the tip of Alex's finger. A bright flare of agony raced up Alex's hand into her arm along with a mental shriek of horror *(oh god I'm infected she's infected me with fire),* and blood pattered down to the floor as Alex swung her arm back. The air burned her lungs as she drew breath. It was like inhaling the raw heat from an open oven. The skin of her face tightened and the fine hairs on her forearms curled over, turning crispy. Coughing, Alex skidded backwards, desperate to be away from the invisible fire.

The burned people kept coming.

"Get away from me!" Alex bellowed, searching for help. Simon stood against the wall beside the lift, mouth hanging open. No help there. No sign of Kelly or Dao, only Kelly's screams from somewhere on the other side of the horrible crowd.

"Get the fuck away from me."

Clang.

The church bell boomed above, mocking her, ready to bring all the endings there could be, eager to take her life—her family and love—away and give her a world of aching loss in a dead field while the sunset burned the sky with cold fire.

No, I will not. I will not. My girls. I am going back to my girls.

Terror powered by unthinking rage sent Alex running forward, raising her solid fists, despite the horrible pain radiating from her injured finger. She collided with the nearest of the burned flesh, sent two of them to the floor and landed a blow on a man's nose already spread across his face like butter. It squidged below her fist; she felt it *slide* over his destroyed features, and gagged. She sank her fingers into an arm with no idea if it belonged to a man or woman, and she yanked it down from the elbow as hard as she could. While it didn't break, it hung at a horrible angle. The wounds in the skin split further as burns tore open. Blood, shockingly bright crimson, spurted from each gaping hole. It sprayed Alex's chest and hands, then rained down on the white floor. Gagging, Alex jumped backwards. A staggering figure loomed from her right—a teenage boy with no face except a swirling mass of blisters and burns—inches away. She managed to let out a single nonsense noise before his fingers clamped over her mouth and she could smell him, *smell him cooking.* What might have been his mouth, but was now just a slit in the ruins, split wider.

He was smiling at her.

Another hand found one of Alex's arms and grasped. It pulled hard. Sickening agony bolted through her and she shrieked against the stink.

The boy lifted his free hand and brought it down to Alex's breast. Her horror juddered, rising to a level she understood was as close to insanity as she could go without falling into the dark and never finding her way out. Mocking her, the lift doors opened, then banged together before opening again. They snapped like gnashing teeth, slamming and jerking open a second later while the great tunnel of darkness stretched from its mouth to the far end of everything. And the only sound was the steady drip of dirty water.

Mummy, come home.

Whether the voice was real or simply existed in her head, Alex had no idea. All that mattered was Charlotte speaking to her afraid and confused.

Instead of pushing—she understood that would achieve nothing—Alex pulled back as hard as possible, feet propelling her and the boy over the floor. She struck the wall, bouncing an inch off it upon impact. The hold over her mouth loosened. Alex lifted her one good hand and smacked the boy's arm away. It swung as if it made of goo. He gazed at it, then turned back to her.

Unable to verbalise her sheer horror and disgust, Alex threw her fist into the boy's face. Skin split. She did it again, not giving a thought to the pain from each blow, stopping only when the boy's face dented and bone split. He fell, just so much dead flesh brought to life by this horrible place.

Far away, she heard Kelly calling her name. From even further away, she heard herself crying for Kelly to run for her life.

The others were coming closer. The lift doors continued to smack together, a mouth eager to chew and bite and tear.

"Alex."

It was Kelly somewhere on the far side of the floor, lost with Dao beyond the mass, and there was literally no way through. The only way out was behind.

Crying, body enveloped by pain, Alex staggered across to Simon, who hadn't moved from the wall.

"Move," she panted, unable to find the breath or strength for anything more.

He made a noise that was little more than an animal's whine before death took its life.

"Come on."

From its foundations to its highest window, Greenham Place shuddered. The tremor sent the milling bodies to the floor and pushed Simon off the wall. Alex had a chance to see Dao and Kelly running through a door beside the cash office, and a chance to see the smashed hole in the entrance, which let in the blasting heat. Already, the strongest and most able of the cooked people were beginning to find their feet. Already, they were turning back to her and Simon.

Injured arm against her stomach, bleeding from a dozen scratches, Alex ran for the door leading to the stairs. Twisting at the last second meant her shoulder took the impact instead of her wounded arm. The doors flew open, crashed into the walls, and began to swing shut. Without looking back to see if Simon followed or remained on the wall, Alex sprinted for the stairs. The second before she reached the first, someone said her name. Alex came close to hitting the wall. She managed to stop at the last moment and turned.

Kelly stood at the now closed doors, head down, and her hair draped over her face.

"Kel?" Alex whispered.

Without making a move, Kelly spoke. Her words came, and Alex answered them with a shriek. Her mind trembled on the edge of letting go of all sense; she clung to rational thought with her fingertips. This could not be Kelly. Her sister had run the other way. This was not Kelly. Not, *not, not, not.*

Kelly's toneless words ran out. Still with her head down, she shuffled towards Alex, a silent shape made inhuman by its steady pace. Alex backed away, aware, on the most basic level, of Simon approaching the other side of the doors, dismissing him as she spun on her heel a second before Kelly lifted her head to reveal a face that was a gaping hole. No eyes to see her sister; no mouth to speak the terrible things she said.

Alex hit the stairs and ran. She passed the stain left by the vision of her father, and the man came out of nothing. Air one second, a fully formed figure the next.

It's true, Alex. Everything she said is true.

Shrieking, Alex reached the first-floor landing and looked back.

Her dad stood on the stairs, dressed only in bandages, bleeding from head to toe.

It's true, Alex. All of it. Now will you kill me, you bitch?

Alex went over the edge.

Chapter Forty

Was it the sixth floor or the seventh? They definitely hadn't come as far as the eighth.

Simon was pretty sure he'd be on his knees by then. But what else was there to do but keep moving, half dragging and half carrying Alex's limp body. He'd found her, collapsed and almost silent on the first-floor landing after fleeing from the sheer insanity of whatever the fuck was going on below, and no amount of yelling into her face made her move. So, he'd taken her by her heavy arms, grateful he kept in shape, and pulled her to the next flight of the stairs. Then up. Then repeat.

Now here they were, about as far as he could get them away from the dozens of people below, with their hideous burns and clothes turned into little more than baked rags. With the last of his energy, Simon dropped Alex onto one of the sofas, then fell beside her. Trembling, either from fear or exhaustion, from his knees up to his stomach and out to his arms, Simon let it flow, too weak to fight the shakes.

"You okay?"

Alex gave Simon no reply. Nothing he understood, in any case. She made a noise that might have been words if he dared move his head closer. He did not. Let her mumble her terror. He couldn't do a thing to stop it.

Simon rested for a few moments, the sour smell of sweat stinging his nose. His throat ached for water. While his stomach needed food, it was much less of a demand than to slake his thirst. Find a tap, stick his mouth under it and drink until he burst. Then maybe he could think.

Rising, Simon stumbled forward and held the wall to keep steady. For a moment, he considered peering out of the window and working out what floor they were on.

There was probably little point. Whether fifth, sixth, or seventh, so what? There'd still be no help from outside. There'd still be no outside, full stop.

Instead of looking through the windows, Simon leaned on the railing that offered a clear view all the way down to the ground floor, opening to the space in front of the lift. Nothing moved down there. If the burned people remained, they were out of sight.

Coming up the stairs?

He listened. All he heard was his own breathing and Alex's soft mutters of nonsense.

No steps on the stairs. No tread of feet fused into shoes and boots by searing fire. Whatever they were, they'd gone. For now.

A gentle sound brushed his ears—something like a shout from the other side of a field, maybe. He listened for more, straining, desperate. What might have been a murmur came and went in a few moments, leaving silence in its place.

"Kelly," Alex said clearly.

Simon turned.

Alex remained on the sofa in the same position he'd dropped her. She gazed at the floor, head loose. Blood dribbled from scratches on her face, and from a finger with its shredded skin.

"Kelly," she said again.

Swallowing the dry taste coating tongue and teeth while wishing for a bottle of ice-cold water, Simon approached Alex. He stopped five paces from her and edged a fraction closer to the next flight of stairs.

"What about Kelly, Alex?"

Her hands danced in her lap.

"Kelly!" Alex screamed. Simon jumped backwards and crashed into the stairwell railing. Alex stared at him, but she wasn't seeing him. Not in the least.

Heart hammering, Simon raised both hands, unconsciously surrendering.

"It's okay, Alex. It's all okay."

He had to hold a mad laugh inside. Okay? Nothing was okay. Not in this fucked up place.

Alex fell silent. Her hands continued to squirm. She could have been washing them. Maybe in her head, she was.

What the hell am I supposed to do? Leave her here? Keep going up? Go back down? And where are Dao and Kelly? Christ.

Without further debate, Simon knew going back down was out of the question. Not without knowing where the burned people were. Leaving Alex... no. He couldn't. That meant continuing while carrying her. Or dragging her.

Alex made a soft noise. She'd lifted her head and stared at him. Actually, *at* him, he saw.

"Alex?" he whispered. "You there?"

She made the noise a second time. It took Simon another few seconds to realise she was speaking.

It's true. She said it's true.

"What's true, Alex? What's happened?"

She opened her mouth and exhaled. Simon caught the fading scent of the stinking wind that had blown them through the fire exit. It drifted from Alex's tongue and lips, wafted towards him, dissipated into nothing a moment later. He swayed but stayed upright.

"I knew it was true," she muttered. "Always knew it. I didn't want to."

What the fuck is she talking about?

He crept closer to her. She giggled, sounding like a little girl.

"Now I've got nothing left. Isn't that funny?" Alex let out another childish laugh. The sound of this grown woman with faint lines around her eyes, and her somehow comforting bulk turning into a kid, made Simon cringe. If insanity had a sound, Alex's regressed laugh was it.

"You've got your family," he said. "Out there. Your daughters." He searched his memory. Had she mentioned their names? By some miracle, both came. "Charlotte. Louisa. Your girls are out there. We find a way out and you've got them, Alex. Carl, too."

She flinched as if he'd moved to hit her.

"I think I might be insane," she whispered. "How about that?"

"You're not. Neither of us are."

"Then how do you explain my sister appearing down there with no fucking face?"

The words wanted to come. She was desperate to own them and have some feeling of control, however small, over what the apparition of Kelly had said in that horribly dead voice. She wanted to hold those words and stomp them into the floor until they were nothing but the same dark stain they'd run past on the way up to the fifth floor.

"I don't know," Simon muttered.

"There's nothing to know." Alex gazed outside at the dead streets and road devoid of traffic. Again, the sight resembled a photo that wasn't quite right. Maybe it was a shot that was going through edits on a computer; all the detail that made it lifelike had been removed for some reason. Maybe someone was working on the light and shadow; maybe they were fixing it even as she looked through the glass.

Or maybe they were taking more and more from it while she and Simon stood in the dead corridor. Given enough time, it might all just disappear, and they'd be left with a big nothing pressing against the wall of windows.

"I've got nothing," Alex whispered, and an explosion of anger boomed inside Simon.

"Nothing? *You've* got nothing?" he yelled. "You've got the whole fucking world, Alex. You've got family. You've got a reason to keep going. You've got a reason to get out of your fucking bed in the morning. You want to talk about nothing, I'll tell you." As much as he wanted to stop his raging, it was impossible. Something had broken free inside and it meant to have its say. "Nothing is a job you know doesn't matter, but you still do because if you stop it, you don't have a thing in your life. Not one thing. Nothing is no family and no roots because the aunt who raised you after your mother drank herself to death died last year. Nothing is being thirty-nine and knowing you haven't made an impact on anyone and won't. Literally ever, Alex. And you know it's ridiculous, but you don't know how to connect with people, so you don't bother. You're anonymous, Alex, and it's easier that way. It means you don't have to try. It means you've got nothing, so don't fucking tell me you don't have something to get out of here for. Don't fucking tell me that."

He ran out of words and breath. Panting, Simon held on to the stairwell while spots swam in front of his eyes and shaking rolled through his body. After long moments of quiet, he left the stairwell to join Alex. She still stared ahead.

"Alex?" he whispered.

Blood ran from the scratches and grazes on her face. The gash in her finger was a congealed mess. Blood from the small wound stained her trousers. Whether her wrist was broken or simply strained, Simon didn't know. She held it while the sweat and the red dripped from her face.

"Alex? You with me?" Tears ran down Simon's dirty face. He registered the sensation and thought fresh lines of blood were cutting their way down his cheeks. Brushing or wiping them away seemed like too much effort.

"Don't go, Alex. I don't want to be here alone," he whispered. "I don't want… "

Want what, Simon? Don't want nothing? Don't want to know you do your job and go home to your flat and the needling urge to check what people from your past are up to? That urge you ignore by drinking and wanking and watching TV without seeing what you're looking at because if you gave in to it, then you'd find out the people from school or college or anything before today have forgotten you ever existed and even the acquaintances from long ago are nothing to you, and you're nothing to them. Nothing, Simon. That's you. Not a fucking thing.

From below and rising like smoke from a scorching fire, a voice spoke.

"There's one other thing."

Kelly?

"After that business with Dean, something happened."

It was Kelly's voice, clear and whole. There was nothing dead about it, as there'd been from the vision or whatever had been in the corridor seven floors below. This was her sister, human and *real*.

Kelly spoke again, and Alex's world turned over and over, racing faster towards a black cliff.

Chapter Forty-One

They crashed through the cash office. Kelly's injured hip caught the side of the computer monitor and sent it crashing to the floor. For a second, agony replaced all of her senses. Animal survival shoved it away, and her sight returned. At their side, the tinted windows looking out to the ground floor showed a lone figure advancing. She saw him in a snatched look and didn't have time to wonder where all the burn victims had gone. The man was naked. The man was Carl. The man was coming for her.

Dao struck a rear door, yanked it open and yelled for Kelly to follow. They left the mess of the overturned furniture in the cash office and reached a short corridor, lined with more doors. Side by side, they sprinted for the other end. Although it should have been impossible to hear, they both caught the smash of a door opening, the unmistakable din of chairs being knocked over.

He was in the cash office.

"There." Kelly pointed to an open set of glass doors. They raced through. One look around told her they were in the offices to the rear of the lift. Across the open floor was the entrance to the long hallway with the smooth, white walls that ended at the sealed fire exit. They'd come back to the same useless area they'd tried less than fifteen minutes before.

"Fuck." Kelly cried.

"No choice." Dao ran for the doors at the other side of the room. Sure, she was about to pass out, Kelly followed. There was no point in going back to the fire exit, but Dao was right.

No choice.

They bashed through into the corridor at the same time, neither looking back and both aware of Carl's steady approach. While Dao had no idea who the man was, he didn't need to know. He ran from a nameless threat. He ran because Kelly's terror was his terror.

Bouncing off the walls, he upped his speed to its maximum, reached behind for Kelly, and found her sweat-soaked hand. Streaking over the polished floor, they came to the fire exit moments later. It looked exactly as it had before the phantom wind blew them through it, and it was just as solid. Looking around was pointless. No exit and no sign of their weapons.

Kelly held the bar. *Please. Open. Let us out.* Nothing answered her. Not even a mocking laugh. Behind, steady steps drew closer. A voice followed.

I'm coming for you. I'm coming to fuck you. I'm coming to take you outside and make you burn.

"Jesus," Dao whispered. He cringed like a frightened child. "Who is that?"

Kelly named her horror. "Carl. My brother-in-law."

Somewhere still out of sight, Carl giggled. It was the sound of all madness.

I'm almost there. Coming for you. Coming all over you.

Kelly's stomach turned over.

I'm going to burn with you. All that fire outside. All that fire on your skin and in your body. You will scream like the others when you cook.

"Leave us alone," Kelly shrieked, and Carl's laughter floated down the corridor. A moment later, he came into view. He paused, giving them time to see every inch of his naked body: his thick muscles, his wide chest, and his jutting penis.

Kelly's innards seemed to recoil. It was as if they retreated to the furthest point of her body.

"What the fuck?" Dao whispered.

Your boy is with me, Chinaman. He is here. He has a friend.

Carl's mouth opened in a wide grin, exposing fangs.

His brother is here with him, Chinaman.

Dao wailed like a wounded dog and moved towards Carl. In those few seconds, Kelly discovered a level of horror she'd never known existed. It took her thinking into a higher plane and jettisoned everything but the basic fact of their lives coming to an end. And in that understanding, all options bar one fell away.

"Stay here," she whispered and advanced on Carl. Dao tried to ask Kelly what she meant. The horror of Carl's words robbed his voice as Kelly walked away.

The featureless white of the walls became red, all bleeding with her blood, and Kelly understood that it was a premonition of what might occur in the seconds that followed. When Carl's hands came down on her shoulders, and his teeth found her face, her blood would spray onto the walls before he dragged her twitching body into the flames eating Willington—where she would burn, and where she would be given every single one of the millions of degrees of heat out there.

"Carl." It was little more than a croak and it would have to do. She couldn't speak any louder.

Kelly. I'm going to fuck you. I'm going to burn you.

She inhaled, and her gaze darted from the foot or so

of space between Carl's right hand side and the wall.

Have to catch me first.

She ran.

Shooting through the little space, Kelly sprinted for the first time since childhood, when running had been a daily fact. Not running for any grander reason than the desire for speed and to feel wind lifting her braided hair.

Hands that were more like jagged claws came down for her head and neck. They missed by millimetres. She raced back the way she and Dao had come, a single wish—*leave Dao alone*—come and gone in a heartbeat, because Carl was coming for her again. He was no longer taking his time, relishing a steady advance, but coming like a bullet. Carl stormed after her, crashing from wall to wall, making noises somewhere between speech in her head and animal grunts.

Fucking Kelly. Stop you bitch! You fucking whore! I am going to burn you! Fucking stop right now, bitch! Bitch! Fuck! Bitch!

Gasping for every hot breath, Kelly ran into the rear offices and shot towards the open door leading to the main reception. A thought flared like a dying star, too quick to register fully.

If this doesn't work, you are dead.

She skidded to a stop, saturated with sweat, t-shirt stuck to her back and breasts. The burning in her side wanted to come back, wanted to make her stare at it, and wanted to wonder about infection and germs.

He was still coming—all the world's horrors turned

into the shape of a naked man.

The lift doors eased open, and it wasn't *like* a mouth. It *was* a mouth.

Kelly ran with light steps to the pillar nearest the reception desk.

Kelly. Where are you.

The words were not a question, because there was nothing human here. It was like hearing the middle of the night come to life. All the cold and disquiet of walking home at three in the morning was striding across the floor of the rear offices.

I'm coming for you. I'll find you. Carl, or whatever was pretending to be him, laughed in a shrill, mad giggle, utterly unlike her brother-in-law's usual big laugh. Kelly had to bite her tongue to keep in the frightened squeak threatening to emerge.

Doing all she could to banish her fear, Kelly directed her thoughts at the sealed lift.

You want me, don't you? You know what you have to do. You have to open up, you fucker.

The blank surface of the lift doors gazed back. The last she looked, they'd been wide open. Closing without a sound was a trick, a shitty, ugly trick to make her believe her little plan was a failure.

You fucking want me. I know you do.

Kelly breathed too loudly against her palm, unable to stop her panting.

I tell you. That thing isn't getting me, so you can have me instead. Deal?

Nothing from the lift. Its silence mocked her, and tears of terror and frustration blurred the edges of her vision.

Are you ready for me, Kelly? I hope so. I hope you want me to fuck you, and burn you, and fuck you, and burn you and—

"Shut the fuck up!" The screech was out before she had any chance of stopping it. The yell bounced from floor to wall, then up towards the high ceiling, crashing back to her, as mocking as the still face of the lift.

Carl gave another giggle. It sounded like a child amused by a dying animal. A moment later, his footsteps reached the reception area. Without pausing, he drew closer.

"Where are you hiding, Kelly? Come out and see me. Come and see what I've got for you."

Desperately, Kelly tried to picture him in relation to her position against the pillar. If she was lucky, he'd moved in a straight line from the opening into the back offices. That should put him level with the pillar opposite hers, twenty feet away.

Praying she made no sound, Kelly eased away from the pillar and twisted so she faced the lift full on. She crouched. Her knee cracked. She froze as her exhausted thigh and calf muscles protested. Nothing from Carl. She splayed her hands on the warm floor as if about to launch into a sprint, then moved her head forward a fraction so the side of the pillar drew level with her peripheral vision.

Nothing.

He was behind her. She knew it.

Kelly whipped her head around, hair hissing as it flew.

Nothing.

About ready to puke all over herself, Kelly eased forward another half inch. She could just see the line of the far pillar and a section of the floor. No sign of the thing pretending to be her brother-in-law.

Silence closed in, pressing a cold weight over her ears. He was listening for her, both of them not making a move. The only difference was, Carl was playing with her while she literally gambled on her life.

Dao.

She'd left him behind in the white corridor. What happened if he came after her, thinking he could help? She'd told him to stay there, and while that had only been a few moments ago, it would be an eternity to him. If he ran from the back offices, if he appeared now, the Carl-thing would kill him. Maybe his boy would. Maybe they were all seeing their own private fears and guilt, so those fears could kill them as they'd killed Rod.

These thoughts sped through Kelly's mind in a matter of seconds, even though she no longer had a sense of time or place. Everything came down to listening for the monster pretending to be Carl, listening while her bowels became a hot weight. Her stomach was a rising boulder, rolling up into her throat and ready to bring all the screams in the world to her mouth because… because… because…

Because I see you, the Carl-thing whispered from right behind her.

Kelly flew, feet leaving the floor for a second. She crashed as she had the day before, the hard ground welcoming her body and giving her pain in return. She cried out and spun over without giving the hurt more than a second's thought. Carl stood close to the entrance, facing her. Smiling with no trace of humanity on his face. Even though his whisper had come from her back, he stood at the other side of the floor, not caring about the space between them. He had no reason to because she had nowhere to go.

Want to go outside.

Kelly groaned, unable to stop it. Those few words were an echo, a memory. They were a shitty taste in her mouth to go with the remnants of the cocktails she'd downed that night a year ago. One year exactly. And here was her anniversary as Rod's had come, and Dao's with his dead son. And Alex's, even though Alex didn't know it.

She groaned again, teeth and tongue wet with too much spit that wasn't hers alone.

The Carl-thing giggled, seemingly pleased by a dirty joke.

It began to move towards her, taking his time because she was trapped.

You hear me, you fucker? You took Rod. You can take me the same way.

Carl, coming.

Her body hurting and her heart a small ball of regret and her thought—*sorry, Alex*—a brief flare before primitive survival stamped down on everything else.

I know what you want. I know the score, you motherfucker so you do this, you do it right now, you son of a bitch, you do it right now—

Carl's mouth grew wider than the world as he smiled; his teeth became gleaming fangs; his naked body flesh rippling because things lived, things that only exist underneath the earth where no light ever reached and no warmth baked mud and ancient rock—things of dirt, cold, and rot all ready to burst out of his skin the second his hold clamped down on her neck and began to pull her head free.

Carl, howled and barked like a mad dog. Carl, a running nightmare.

"Fucking do it, you motherfucker. You want this. You want this, I fucking know you do. I fucking know you do, I—"

Ding.

Kelly dived to her right, landing awkwardly on a wrist and yelling out in pain as the shape that had worn her brother-in-law's face streamed over the space she'd filled a second before.

Still running, it hit the mouth of the lift. The doors slammed shut.

Kelly's screech of triumph answered the crash of the closing lift doors.

Chapter Forty-Two

Kelly almost managed to make it to Dao before she collapsed.

He took the little impact of her weight, let her rest her head on his neck, and backed up until he reached the windows that looked into the rear offices. The streaming sunlight failed to reach this far from the front windows and that was welcome. He wasn't sure if he'd ever been as hot or exhausted. Not a centimetre of his body was free from sweat; not a muscle was free from strain.

You're still here. That has to be worth something. Dao swallowed a laugh and eased Kelly away. "Are you okay?" he asked.

She made a noise that might have been a reply; he wasn't sure. Shaking, Kelly pushed the hair away from her forehead and slid down to the floor. He eased himself beside her. She took one of his hands, welcoming to simple touch of his skin. Their shared stink of sweat and fear didn't matter. Maybe they'd gone beyond both. For the first time since their sprint from the foyer, chased by Carl, the pain from the struggle with the *things* that had filled the area made her want to cry out. Blood caked her arms. At least it was drying.

"How did you beat him?" Dao whispered.

Seconds ticked by, the moment long enough for Dao to wonder if she would reply at all. That was okay, though. The quiet was welcome.

"I remembered. Yesterday. On the stairs. Alex's dad and that guy. That guy who hurt Rod."

Kelly had to take a few breaths. It hurt to think of Rod. He'd been a decent man. While she couldn't pretend he'd have been anything to her in normal life, he'd mattered here. For the first time, Kelly realised what she'd noticed within minutes of meeting him but hadn't been fully aware of thanks to all the shit going on.

Rod had reminded her of her dad before his dementia took him away. A man who knew what was right and fair. But now the world didn't give a shit about that, just as it didn't give a shit about her dad or Alex's, so hurt, so wounded.

Not aware she was crying, Kelly said: "On the stairs, those two things, they weren't together. Remember? *They are mine. He is yours.* That's what Alex's dad said to the guy who hurt Rod. Everything here... it's part of the same thing, but what we're scared of, what we're guilty about, it's all working by itself. I told the lift it could have me. I lied, and the lift knew that." She wiped her nose with a trembling hand. "It knew it. This place knows everything. It doesn't care how it hurts us in the end, but the things looking for us, they want to hurt us themselves. Carl for me;

your son for you. I gave Carl to whatever the fuck's in the lift. Rod's thing. My thing. Whatever. The lift… ate him."

Dao let Kelly fall quiet again while he chewed on a potential question. Asking it seemed pointless because he already knew the answer just as he knew why the naked man was haunting Kelly. Even so, asking it was the last thing left to say right now.

"Who was he, Kelly? Who was that man?"

She didn't pause or hesitate, perhaps aware there'd be no naming her guilt if she did. "There was a guy." The words should be prisoners in her head; they belonged there. But they were out, and she couldn't stop more from coming. "Year before last. Dean. He was twenty-two; I was seventeen. Nice guy. Kind of." She gazed at the white floor. "You know what's funny? I can't remember where we met. I think it was at a party, but it might have been in a club. You'd think I'd remember after what happened, but it's not there. It's just background. Anyway, we started seeing each other and I liked him. A lot. I mean, he was everything I wanted. He had his shit together. He had a job, and that's more than a lot of my friends asked for in a guy. He worked in his uncle's company. Something to do with plumbing for businesses. I don't know. But anyway, he wasn't some bullshitter. He was the sort of guy you could take home to meet your mum. Mine would have liked him, but… she died when I was fourteen. My dad, not Alex's, he didn't meet him, either. Didn't seem much point. My dad doesn't know who he is most days. Alex's dad met him and said he was a snake. That's what he called him." The anger, dulled by exhaustion and time, flared for a moment. "Said I couldn't trust him. Said he knew boys like that when he was young. Nice, polite, friendly, but always looking for the money, for a way out of things. And if that meant he'd drop someone or do some deals, he'd do it."

She spoke more to herself than Dao and couldn't stop. Dao was there; the feel of his skin on hers was welcome, but her words weren't for him. He might have muttered something, a bit of encouragement to keep going; she didn't hear anything precise.

"Turned out my step-dad was right. It was about six months later I found out Dean was dealing. Coke, mostly. Basically, he sold to whoever was buying. The stupid thing was there was no big scene about it. Like in a film I'd have heard someone talking about it or the police would have got hold of me and asked me to drop Dean in it, but none of that happened. I just walked into a deal. He was at home one Saturday and got his times wrong. He thought I was going around at two, but I went to him at one. I walked into him with a knife on some kid's throat; some boy who wanted to pay less for a few grams. There's me outside his flat, looking through his kitchen window, and I see it all. He saw me, kicked the kid out and tried to explain it all. I just ran."

Kelly shifted position, the muscles in her legs falling asleep. The discomfort belonged to someone else; movement was instinctive.

"He came to mine later. He was all nice, you know? We went out to a park near my flat. We're sitting on the roundabout like we're ten and he's telling me the whole thing. What he deals, what money he makes, what he has to say to people who don't want to pay. He tells me it's like a business and he has to be professional." Kelly snorted.

"Professional. Like he's a lawyer or some shit. He tells me he wants us to be together and he'll keep that side of things under control and away from us. And you know what?"

Dao's reply belonged to some faraway place. Maybe wherever the office block and its horrors went. Kelly had nothing but the pleasant warmth of that August afternoon and the creak of the old roundabout under her bottom and legs. Her jeans scraped on the flaking wood and Dean's shadow stained the paving and tired grass, both dry in the summer's heat.

"You know what?" She had to whisper it. Guilt, shame and anger at herself took away any strength. "I wanted to believe him, so I *did* believe him. I wanted him. I wanted to still be his girlfriend… and something in me wanted to be a dealer's girlfriend. How fucking stupid is *that?* How stupid was I? I mean, shit, I wasn't a kid. I knew better than to act like that. Or think like that. It's something I would've seen a mate from school doing. You know?"

If Dao did know, it didn't matter. The festering self- anger of the last two years was out in a fierce stream. It ran over sharp rocks, growing faster the further it went. Unless she got in its way, it would become a flood. And maybe she didn't want to stop it. Maybe letting it drown her self-disgust for being such a stupid kid was the way to go. Couldn't be worse than picking at what it had led her to on the night of her eighteenth birthday.

In memory or reality—it didn't seem to matter which was real—Kelly pressed her calves against the old roundabout. They'd come here a lot when they were kids, her and Alex. Usually on a Sunday afternoon after coming home from church with their mum. In the bite of a dead January or the dazzling sun of the summer holidays, they'd come here and go on the swings or spin the roundabout as fast as they could. Days like that had lessened as time went on. They'd probably not been here since Alex turned fifteen. The thought of that time before, abruptly feeling as if it had all been decades back and not just a few years, stabbed Kelly harder than she might have expected. Things made sense when she'd been ten and her sister in her teens. Life was known, secure. Now, everything was up in the air and all Kelly had to hold on to were Dean's assurances and the nice light of his smile. It reached his eyes and she'd always liked that. He smiled as she glanced at him, and the peace of the park was broken by a strange cramp in her leg. Burning spread from her hip, reached down to her groin, then lower. Kelly jutted her leg from the roundabout, trying to concentrate on Dean's explanation for what he'd been doing, holding on to the comfort and sense of them even as imagination whispered of the future with him: money, stability and an interesting life, instead of the dull asininity of everyday that almost all of her friends had taken after school and college.

She held her leg, rubbed it, and sank her claws deep into the skin of her hip. Kelly jerked forward. In the movement, air on all sides blew away, taking every mote and line of colour out of the day, bleaching the lovely yellow into a dull grey. Breeze and warmth died in a second; Kelly pitched through a murky light, trying to call Dean's name, swinging her hands forward to take the impact when she hit the hard ground.

Memory snapped in half and reality crashed down.

She was against the wall with Dao's hand in hers, the wall at her back while thin lines of sweat dribbled down her neck and forehead.

"Jesus," she whispered.

"You okay?" Dao asked.

"Yeah. I think so." She swallowed the staleness in her mouth. "Felt like I wasn't here for a second."

"A second? You haven't said anything for a few minutes. You just sort of trailed off and sat there."

"A few minutes?" Kelly stared at Dao, searching his face for a lie or a joke. She saw neither. "Why didn't you do something? Say something?"

"I didn't know if you didn't want to tell me more of your story."

Disorientation made clear though difficulty. Several months had passed since she'd last been drunk; whatever had happened to bury her in memory felt like the brief time between sober and inebriation. Kelly let go of Dao to stretch and take a moment to look around. Everything appeared the same, which meant everything was as fucked up as it'd been since the day before.

She surprised herself with a laugh. The sound and feel were both welcome. Dao smiled, unsure what she found funny, but ready to smile all the same. It beat his tears or his fears.

Not sure if she could explain anything, Kelly shook her head and took his hand again. Another funny thing: Dao, like Rod, wasn't someone she'd have had much to do with outside here, but right now, she couldn't be more grateful to have him with her. Human contact. That's what it all came down to in this place. Maybe the same applied to Simon as well wherever he and Alex had run to upstairs.

"You want to hear the rest?" she asked.

"If you want to tell me."

"It's shit."

"So's everything else around here."

"Yeah." Kelly checked the foyer again. Still empty. While it was possible for the lift to spit Carl back out like unchewed food, she didn't think that would happen. The things here, the horrors, they were all apart from each other. Each one wanted to hurt its target and it didn't give a shit about the others. Greenham Place might have made the walking nightmares, but she didn't think it controlled them.

Unsure if she should be more scared or relieved by that thought, Kelly went on. "We stayed as a couple. Me and Dean. And it wasn't like you might think it would be. Like in a film, we'd be surrounded by gangsters and bad boys with guns. None of that. I mean, I knew that he dealt with some guys I didn't want to know, but he kept it away from me. And with me, he was fine. *Nice.* He was the sort of guy you see yourself with for a long time. You see it going somewhere. Lasting. You know what I mean? Anyway, we were good together. Everything was good for us. That is until Alex."

Out of nowhere, a bizarre sensation hit Kelly. She knew what she wanted to say next: to tell Dao about Alex making her feel like a kid and all that had gone down. Sitting beside him, telling the story, she felt something close to ridiculous. She was focusing on dead issues, on a life mile away from the death and hurt in the building. Whatever was going on here, it was a killing business. The dead life outside it was no more important now than the exams she'd taken a few years ago, or the days at the park with Alex. It was all over.

She sighed. The story needed finishing either way.

"She found out what Dean was up to. Even now, I don't know how, but she did. And she went for him. She wasn't scared of him like you might think, even though he could have hurt her. She came to his flat one night when I was there and went nuts. She lost it totally. Told him if he ever came anywhere near me again, she'd kill him. She wouldn't get the police involved, she would actually kill him. If he hurt me or her, he'd better kill us because she wouldn't stop until he was dead. She was like someone else. She *was* someone else for a few minutes. I've seen her pissed off before, but nothing like that. Anyway, she grabbed me. *Grabbed* me like I was a little kid and dragged me out of there. She got me back to hers and told me to grow up."

The heat of embarrassment baked Kelly's face and head. Stopping now wasn't possible, though.

"She said that a lot. *Grow up*. She said being a dealer's girlfriend was for silly bitches, not for me. She said I was better than that, and I needed to start acting like it or my life would be over. I'd be a waste and I'd *deserve* to be a waste unless I did something about it. I was acting like a kid according to Alex and that... that was the worst thing. She couldn't let me work it out for myself or walk away from Dean in my own time. She had to bully me into doing it and wouldn't let me be an adult when I wanted to. She treated me like she always treats me. Like she became my mum after ours died. Like I'm a five-year-old going to school on my first day."

Anger lived somewhere else. Kelly finished speaking, her tone growing flatter by the word. All that time furious with her sister and she had nothing to show for it.

"There's more, isn't there?" Dao said. "Yeah."

She told him. It was like peeling a huge scab away from her skin. Millimetre by millimetre, it came free, exposing an unhealed wound and letting the stale air trace its fingers inside. There was nothing she could do about that because the words were in the speeding stream from a moment before, boiling and frothing from her mouth. There was no stopping her or the ugly story, no stopping the flood. It was here to drown her because she deserved that; she'd get what was coming to her. Carl had said so.

Trembling and crying and lacking the energy to fight off either, Kelly stared at the wall; she spoke to the featureless surface; she confessed what she'd done and what was now haunting her. When it was finished, she fell into the silence of aching regret.

A few moments passed without a sound. Kelly waited for Dao's judgement or comment. Nothing came from him. A haze struck the edges of her vision: a speeding blur dropping from the ceiling and coming down even as she turned to it. In the foyer, the body fell through the stairwell, struck the floor, and exploded.

Chapter Forty-Three

Simon listened. As much as he wanted to take hold of Alex and run for any door that would lead to a private room where they could shut away the sound of Kelly's voice, he had to listen. He'd become a statue, joined by a rock-like arm to the railing around the stairwell, and he'd stay there until enough centuries passed by for his body to collapse from stone to dust.

"I was beyond angry at her," Kelly said. "It wasn't like anything I'd known before. It was like something I could touch. I wanted her dead. Jesus. I hated myself for thinking it, but it was still true. I wanted my sister dead. I was just sick of her. She'd treated me like a kid for my entire life. Alex wanted to be my mum, I think, and I hated her for it. After all that business with Dean, I just… I don't know. It exploded out of me. I wanted her hurt. So, I hurt her."

Kelly fell silent. Alex's head hung limp and useless. Simon saw with perfect clarity: Alex had given up. Any fight left in the woman after the hours of confusion and torment had quietly died.

"Alex," he whispered.

She gave no response at all. He could have been addressing a corpse.

"My birthday. My eighteenth," Kelly said from below. "We had a party in a pub my uncle goes to. It was a good time. A lot of people. I danced and drank and enjoyed myself but all night, I knew what I was doing and what I wanted." The girl sounded near tears. Any dead note to her voice as there'd been from the ghostly vision that walked into the wall was long gone. Now, she was totally human, and that meant a complete lack of pretence.

No, stop it, Kelly. Stop talking.

"I got drunk and I fucked my brother-in-law out the back of the pub," Kelly said, and that was all. It was as if her voice had been switched off. Alex sagged on the railing; her shoulders shook as sobs broke loose. Simon reached for her and she whipped her head up, eyes mad and staring.

"Don't touch me," she spat, bringing her fingers up to his face, long nails aiming for his eyes. Simon jerked back, dodging Alex's fingers by inches. He eased away, not taking his gaze off her.

"Okay, Alex. It's okay."

Her mouth twitched at one corner. It took Simon a moment to realise Alex was trying to smile. She looked as if she'd forgotten how.

"Okay?" she echoed.

"I know this is bad. It is, but you can deal with it, right? You've got your kids to get back to, right—"

Alex grasped the railing. "They're dead." She stated it as a cold fact. "We're all dead and I won't be with my girls, again."

"Alex—"

"Listen."

Unwillingly, Simon did so. And there it was—the peal of a church bell calling the faithful and the bereaved to a funeral on a bitter afternoon. Alex's doom had come to them and there was no melodrama. Just cold.

He closed his eyes against the heat of his tears. When the voice, Kelly's voice, rose from far below, he tried to open them and could not. He was blinded by his fears and loneliness, damned to listen to the terrible story Kelly was telling while her voice cracked and echoed as it spun up the stairwell to land in front of them like a huge weight powerful enough to shake the building, to seal his eyes and cut away the last sliver of Alex's hope that none of this was true.

She was no longer by his side. He sensed her movement while Kelly's story came to its ugly end, and all Simon could do was open his eyes. Open them, *fucking open your eyes. Open them right now. Open and see, Simon.*

Simon's eyes jerked open, spilling the last of his tears to mix with the blood smeared on his cheeks.

Alex stood at the stairwell, looking over the edge.

"Alex," Simon managed to whisper.

What might have been miles above, a church bell gave a single ring. The last one.

"Alex, wait." He managed to get to his feet and, even as he was rising, Simon knew he'd be too slow. He was a gust of wind, air blown from the sofa, and that gust could shove him in a hurricane or a summer breeze. It didn't matter. Still too slow. Always too slow.

Behind him, a tiny breeze wafted by, created by movement from the slightest shape. He registered both but didn't turn.

Alex swung her legs over the railing.

All he had was the trickle of seconds, his body not moving anywhere near fast enough. Alex pulled herself through the warm air, rising with it and casting no shadow on the white floor as her legs came up to the railing. She turned to see him one last time.

"It's over," Alex said.

She flew forward, then down, a streaming line of light passing each floor without a sound. The mouth of the stairwell swallowed her all the way to the hard ground of the foyer where she changed in an instant, going from a distinct shape to a detonation of red that flew upwards before raining down in huge drops over a blossoming sea of blood.

Behind Simon, the gentle movement came closer. And as it moved, it said one word over and over.

Up.

Chapter Forty-Four

Kelly's wail raced around the ground floor, taken by the floor and walls and the lift, and sent back in mockery. The noise echoed between the pillars, powered by a dozen voices, all shrieking Kelly's agony and layering their reply with a terrible sneering. Kelly registered the derisive sound and banished it from her thoughts in the same instant. The body mattered. The *mess*.

She skidded over the floor, boots tracking through the widening pool of blood, Dao yelling her name as the echo of screams faded. Seven floors above, Simon's face was a tiny white circle, his empty hands still visible over the railing.

"No," Kelly whispered. "No. No."

It seemed to be all she could say. The useless negation spilled out, not doing a thing to change the scene and refusing to go away.

"No. No. *No.*" The last was a roar that turned Kelly's throat into fire for a moment, and meant nothing. Alex's body was almost unrecognisable as formerly human. Kelly dropped to her knees, ignoring the sharp impact on her legs, and reached for what might have once been Alex's face.

"No."

Dao yanked Kelly away from her sister. Kelly shrieked and tried to free herself. Dao held her with arms seemingly made of steel.

The rich stink of all the gore assaulted her nose. Kelly's vision spun, turned into a faint grey, and there was nothing wrong with that because it meant she didn't have to see.

Her mind repeated the heavy thud Alex's body had made upon impact with the ground, and then the wet explosion of all the blood in the world splattering the floor and pillars. It was the sound of rotten fruit bursting; a dead animal run over on a busy road, and its innards coming out; a bag full of kitchen waste fell apart and its stinking contents spilled all over the floor. It was the worst sound in the world and it lived forever in Kelly's head.

"Kelly."

Dao's shout broke through the grey, and Kelly wished it had not. She tried to say Alex's name and could only manage a hoarse croak that brought back the fire in her throat. The ghastly smell of Alex's shattered body clamped hold of her nostrils, coating her tongue and teeth like a stain. The scent of blood, shit, liquids, and organs never meant to be anywhere but *inside* filled the air; they filled the building, and she was breathing in bits of her dead sister.

Kelly tipped, overbalancing Dao. He fell back, losing his hold on her. Kelly's head struck the pillar. Pain bloomed like a flower inside her skull, joining the chorus of hurts singing in her scratched and torn skin and her bitten hip. She reached blindly, found the pillar and held on to it as hard as she could.

Alex, oh my God, Alex. I'm so sorry. So sorry. Sorry, Alex. So sorry.

She'd keep thinking the words for as long as it took. She'd block out everything else in her head and give space only to the apology if it meant Alex wasn't dead and none of this hell was happening.

Someone held her elbows, pulled hard, and spun her around. Dao's face was an inch from hers. "Kelly? Can you hear me?"

She managed to open her mouth. That was all.

"Kelly?"

Dao's hold was like a weight on her arms, pulling her down to the mess of her dead sister, and she had no strength to fight him.

"Kelly."

She slumped against his narrow chest and let out a hacking cry. Her torso felt as if it had split open and all the hurt she'd ever known sprayed out. That was okay. Breathing out meant breathing in, and if she breathed it back in, she'd drown and be dead and all this would be over.

Kelly tried to inhale and failed. She gave another huge sob and her world became hot, dark agony. Thought ceased and her cries belonged in another place far outside the nothing on all sides.

Barely able to think, Dao kept his hold on Kelly and his eyes off Alex's broken shape. He'd seen enough already. The grey of Alex's ribcage jutting through shredded skin met the grey of coiled meat. The back of her skull had become her face for an instant before the exploding bone sent what remained of her features sliding over her neck towards her breasts. Only one arm remained fully attached to her torso. The other had snapped almost free at the elbow and now lay like a curled-up worm,

Dao saw all this as he ran after Kelly, not fully aware of what he was taking in as his gawking eyes rolled from one detail of horror to the next. In the sudden quiet, punctuated by the hiss of Kelly's rapid breath, he saw it all again without looking at Alex. It was there in his head, forever.

Lin spoke, and it was a horror upon horrors because his wife had never sounded as coldly furious.

You heard the little bitch. You heard what she did and now here's her sister in pieces. Look at her. Look at what Kelly's done to her sister, and all because she didn't like being treated like a kid. You know what you should do? You know it, Dao? You should shove her face into Alex's body like a puppy that's pissed on the floor. You should rub her nose in all that blood. You should keep her face inside Alex's stomach. See it? See it all opened up? Shove Kelly's face right in there so she chokes on it, so she fucking chokes on what she did.

Dao closed his eyes and thought of Yang. He thought of his boy as he'd seen him the night before: a small shape beneath his bedcovers, curled slightly with one hand on the pillow, a toy bear sitting at the foot of the bed. Yang had placed it there to keep him safe, Dao knew, and that was the best thing in the world. Not the fear of a monster, but the belief in what could fight that monster—fight it and beat it.

The image worked its magic. The horror masquerading as his wife faded away.

Chapter Forty-Five

It might have been moments or hours later. Light exploded and broke through the black. Kelly blinked over and over until enough of the tears cleared for her to see. The light was sunshine, she realised, and the tang of blood remained horribly strong. Stronger, maybe, because it had time to ooze over the floor and drip down the pillars. Alex's blood, everywhere but inside Alex's veins and arteries where it belonged. "You there?" Dao asked.

Kelly managed a single nod. Speaking was still out of the question.

"We need to move, okay? Just one foot in front of the other, and we'll get away from here."

Okay. That sounds like a plan. Words, trapped inside. Words, refusing to come to her mouth.

She moved on auto-pilot, turning from Dao. She stood in the blood and her boots squeaked on the floor.

The grey threatened to return. As fiercely as she could, Kelly wished it away and turned again so she faced the door that led to the stairs. Ten steps. Twelve at the most. She'd then be at the door Rod had crept through the morning before, a nervous Rod asking if anyone was there, and hadn't she known instinctively that he was decent? She'd known that, yes. It came from him like a scent and she'd welcomed it like she used to welcome a hug from her dad. But now her dad was gone, Rod was gone, and Alex was gone, and all she could do was walk away from Alex's remains. And maybe she could imagine a distant time when this would be a memory instead of the worst reality possible.

One step, and then the rest would follow.

Kelly lifted a foot, placed it down a few inches in front and froze. The doors had opened. Simon stood between them. His eyes were two dark pits in his too pale face. He swayed and had to rest on the wall to keep himself steady.

"Alex." The word sounded as if he'd forgotten how to speak properly. It was mush in his mouth.

"Dead," Kelly whispered. She barely heard herself, but Simon caught the reply. He sucked in air. During his mad dash down the stairs, he'd frantically told himself Alex's suicide was just one more shitty vision in this place. The building was playing another game. He'd crashed down each flight of stairs, the lie in his heart harder to believe the closer he came to the ground floor.

Kelly pushed away from Dao, held a blood-smeared hand to her forehead, and wondered if she was about to pass out. Dao slid off his jacket and dropped it over what he thought was Alex's upper half. While the gesture felt pointless given the severity of her injuries, it was better than nothing.

Resting against a pillar and fighting away waves of faintness, Kelly spoke to the floor.

"It's my fault."

"Yes." The reply emerged before Simon had any chance of stopping it. Face flaming, he felt Dao's angry gaze and tried to ignore it. Kelly gave no visible reaction.

"I mean, we heard you. Up there. We heard what you said about Carl."

"How?" Dao yelled. "All the way up there?" He quietened, realising his question was pointless. Acoustics were their own issue in Greenham Place. If sound wanted to travel and take a painful story with it, then it would. At the same time, if it didn't want to be heard, then it would not. Kelly's confrontation with Carl hadn't made it to the floors above, but clearly, something had wanted Alex to hear her sister's confession.

"She didn't deserve this," Kelly said. "Alex was… she was a pain in the arse, sometimes, but she was all right. She meant the best for everyone. She wanted that." Rage ignited inside and that was just fine. *"She didn't deserve this, you motherfucker."*

Kelly shouted her abuse and anger at the air. Helpless tears made her vision dance and the desperate urge to hammer her fists against the pillar was close to overwhelming. Unable to think of doing more to stop her, Simon called her name. Kelly's mouth sprayed saliva; the thunder of her heart boomed in her ears. She raged at the invisible presence watching them all, fully aware of that appraisal and infuriated by the sense of its amusement. They were toys to it, and Alex was a broken toy. She'd been discarded because her fear had gone as far as it could. She'd lost all hope, and the only one to blame for that was Kelly.

The fury dribbled away. She felt it go as if a tap had been turned off. Gasping for each breath, Kelly subsided and caught a tiny sound—something whispering or hissing. It didn't come a second time.

"You okay?" Simon asked gently.

Kelly lifted her head, tilted it to peer upwards. "Fuck you," she told the air.

A soft laugh answered her. Despite the anger, the laugh turned her cold. It was like an abusive parent amused by their child's attempts to fight back.

"Fuck you," she said again, although she couldn't manage the same strength.

Dao kept at his distance from her, she noticed. Maybe he didn't want to associate with a sister-killer.

Alex, I am so fucking sorry. So sorry.

"What now?" Dao asked.

"Up," Simon replied. "What?"

"Up. We go up." He struggled with explaining or elaborating. "I saw something. I don't know what."

Oh yes you do, you liar. You didn't want to. Never want to but that doesn't change a single thing. You saw her. You heard her.

"Up there." With a trembling finger, Simon pointed to the gap of the stairwell and pictured Alex's rapid descent punctuated by the horrific noise of her body turning into mostly liquid. "Something wants us to go up. As far as we can. I think that might be the way out."

It made no sense. The way out was the street, and the street was probably thirty steps away. So, what if the street was an oven, ready to strip the skin from their bones the second they managed to make a hole in the windows? It was outside.

Dao gave an exhausted shrug. "Okay. I'm out of ideas. Let's go. Up it is."

He extended an arm towards Kelly's back, thinking he could perhaps guide her forward or offer support he didn't much want to give *(her sister's dead and it's her fault, her fault, her fault)* and froze as Kelly did the same. Abruptly frightened, Simon took a step back.

Another slight whisper. Another little hiss.

In his head, Simon said: *We need to move now.* In his mouth, he didn't make a sound. Something was with them and it ate his speech as it ate any hope they might find a way out somewhere above—despite what he'd seen.

From the corner of her eye, Kelly watched for moving shadows on the wall or floor. Neither came. She listened for Carl's threats or his approach. Again, neither.

You imagined it.

No. She had not.

A sliding hiss. The sort of noise someone might make if they dragged their foot over a carpet, or maybe a piece of clothing pulled gently over a floor.

Cold prickled the back of Kelly's neck.

There was only one item of clothing on the floor nearby.

Dao's jacket inched a fraction to its right again. Alex's voice slithered out from underneath the jacket.

Help me, Kelly. It hurts.

Chapter Forty-Six

Later, when only the two of them remained in the building, Simon would ask himself if he'd truly meant to move and shout for Dao and Kelly, or if something shoved him forward. Running back was the thing. Yep. Definitely the plan. Leg it for the door and stairs, and just keep going until he found a way out or collapsed. Whichever came first was fine if it meant being away from the sight of Dao's jacket sliding free from Alex's remains, pulled or pushed by nothing at all.

He lunged forward. *"Move. Fucking run."*

His answer came in the form of Alex's quavering voice. *Help me, Kel. Oh god, everything hurts. My body, Kel. It's broken.*

Alex's jacket was whipped free and flung at the wall beside the lift. It struck, splattering blood and loose pieces of flesh on the surface before dropping to the floor. What remained of Alex's upper half had risen a few inches, supported by the circle of blood and innards surrounding her. The jutting growth of Alex's spine was no longer connected properly to Alex's skull, because the skull was little more than a shattered egg shell, and Alex's eyes and mouth were now on a sliding sheet of her face.

It hurts, Alex moaned, and the word stretched, made of the same gooey fluid that should never see the light of day. *Hurrrrrrrrttttttsssss. Hurrrrrrrrrttttttsssss.*

Dao's hand slammed down on Kelly's shoulder, spinning her around. "That's not your sister."

Daddy's coming, Alex hissed. *He's hurt like me, Kelly. He'll make you hurt, too.*

Kelly's mind banished every single emotion but the burning need to flee. She ran, Dao a second behind.

Simon yelled at them to move and the floor dropped away as if it had become a waterfall.

Kelly hit the edge of a spreading opening with her arms spinning. Her upper half leaned forward, affording her a horrendous view of a tunnel dropping from the floor to the other end of—

Everything it's the other end of every fucking thing. Oh, god. Oh, Jesus Christ.

The growing hole reached the toes of her boots. She threw herself backwards, bringing Dao down. Screaming, they both rolled and struck a pillar. Upright in seconds, Kelly jumped further back from the rip in the floor and a gentle finger ran its way down her neck. She whirled around, fists raised. There was nobody in sight. On the floor where her body fell, half of Alex remained risen from the blood and shattered bones of her hips and legs. A flapping piece of what had once been Alex's arm wavered madly. She was trying to point at Kelly. Miles away, a new sound crashed out of the air; something metallic, the grinding of gears, and Kelly named it straightaway.

The lift began descending.

"We have to jump," Dao roared.

On the other side of the hole, Simon seemed much smaller. He stared at the waterfall below their feet. And Kelly's senses, taken to new levels of awareness by her terror, registered the look on the man's face. It was simple recognition.

Jagged growths shot from the edges of the hole, spreading inwards, twisting and curving together.

They were teeth, and the hole was a mouth.

Kelly, take me with you, won't you? You owe me that. You killed me, so you owe me. Come and take my hand.

She looked. She didn't want to, but she was powerless
to stop herself.

Alex's fingers hung from a dangling hand. Several compound fractures shoved bone through skin and muscle, and fresh blood sprayed as Alex shook the ruined limb.

Give me a hand, Kel, Alex whispered, and screeched mad laughter.

The mouth reached the first pillar. The marble oozed into the black, both seemingly no more substantial than oil. More teeth, gnarled and broken, snapped free.

"Jump it. We have to jump it."

Jump it? How the fuck could they? It would be like jumping a river. They'd fall, and they'd fall into a mouth; when the teeth closed together above them, they'd be chewed into pieces. Maybe even then Greenham Place wouldn't leave them alone.

Kelly took Dao's hand. "We jump," she whispered.

He didn't hear the words and had no need to. What she said lived on her face and in her tears.

Ding.

The lift doors flew open, and Carl, naked with skin torn by claws and bite marks, sprinted from them. A massive rent tore one of his eyes in half and turned a cheek into a flapping piece of skin. Sprays of blood coated him from head to foot; half of his scrotum dangled almost to his knees, the testicle a smear of meat rubbed into his thigh. Through the rents in his chest and stomach, his ribs and organs peered out; a layer of flesh held in place over the centre of his chest by sticky blood came loose. Carl's heart was an exposed fist of red, the chewed edges visible.

He saw them with his one whole eye as Kelly took in every inch of his ravaged body. Each scene was given to her by the mocking sunlight, a gift she didn't want. And then she was pulling on Dao while what remained of Alex cackled its laughter to the walls and teeth. Carl was a lumbering corpse, and Simon could have been on the other side of the world.

Their feet left the ground; they flew hand in hand, hanging for an instant over the centre of the mouth.

Then, hand in hand, they dropped.

Chapter Forty-Seven

Solid ground.

All the miracles in the world, solid ground.

Dao tried to rise and overbalanced. His hold on Kelly had broken, and his empty hands spun desperately. Black raced in from the edges of his vision. He tipped backwards, trying to cry out, and felt his centre of gravity snap.

An instant before he fell to the teeth, fingers soaked with sweat grabbed his bicep and yanked. He fell against Kelly, almost knocking her to the floor, as Simon took hold of both of them, pulling them away from the hole.

Dao shrieked until he ran out of breath, then turned while his lungs ached, and his head pounded.

Nothing. Not a fucking thing.

"What?" he whispered.

There was no sight of Alex's husband or the terrible damage done to his body; no Alex coming from the ruins of her remains, and no mouth in the floor. All that remained was his jacket covering the terrible hurt done to Alex.

"We need to go," Simon whispered.

"Go?" Kelly coughed. "Fucking go?"

Maybe she wanted to yell it, to let her anger loose as Dao did, but she obviously didn't have the energy for raising he voice. Understanding—come and gone in the time it took him to blink—told Dao that Kelly was almost used up. Greenham Place had found a weakness in her tough surface and it was kicking down that door with everything it had. She held her hip, covering the blood now drying. Streaks of it coated her cheeks. Splatters stained her fleece. Dao wondered if he looked as done in as she did.

"Yes." Simon smiled. "Fucking go."

A soft chuckle came from the direction of the lift. Despite his body plunging into winter cold, Dao refused to turn. Let the place laugh at them. Let it find their fears funny. He wouldn't give it the satisfaction of facing it, just in time to see another phantom image— something to replace the hole in the floor or the resurrected mess of Alex.

Not real. Any of it. *Not fucking real.*

"Let's go," he whispered.

"Alex," Kelly murmured.

She's dead, Dao raged inside his head. *She's dead and that's on you, Kelly, so don't say a word.*

He closed his eyes briefly. He wasn't angry inside; it wasn't his voice cursing the girl. Nor was it Lin.

You're inside me, aren't you? You're laughing inside
me.

It giggled. Dao didn't need to open his eyes to know the others had not heard the little laugh, nor had they picked up on the chuckle coming from the lift. Both noises were in the dark underside of his heart. Somehow, the horror of the building had slipped inside him. An undercurrent of anger, and what he had to admit was hate, now flowed stronger and faster than a moment before. Maybe it didn't matter exactly when Greenham Place had found a way into him. Maybe it had come without a sound in the seconds after everyone vanished when the bomb detonated, trapping them in one instant. Maybe it had been with him since, biding its time.

I know what to do about you, he told the stranger who'd set up home somewhere in his soul. *If you don't want me to hurt you, then leave right now.*

He sensed it listening, almost curious. While Dao felt the thing looking into his mind, he knew it couldn't probe as deeply as it wanted to. Perhaps it didn't understand the human psyche as well as it thought. Perhaps the resolve to fight and stay alive was an alien concept to it. Perhaps—

"Dao?" Simon called. "Still with us?"

Dao jerked. Kelly and Simon were a few feet away, both heading for the door to the stairs. Kelly shuffled; Simon walked with a new purpose.

What did he see up there? What did that idiot see?

"Shut up," Dao whispered and then jogged after the others.

Chapter Forty-Eight

While she wanted to run ahead of the men, Kelly simply didn't have the strength to push past them and lead the way. Instead, she staggered from step to step, head down, forcing her to stare at her aching feet. Managing to keep it upright and her eyes focused on Simon's narrow back was hard work.

Alex.

Alex was gone. Her sister who, no matter what she said, had acted more like a mother than a sister, was dead. There was only one person to blame for that. Yeah. Just the one. She knew it. Simon knew it. Dao *definitely* knew it. Although she was aware of her grief fucking her up, Kelly had still picked up on his anger and disgust. It was like a low hum only she could hear. Being angry at him in turn was an attractive idea, but one she couldn't get behind.

Because Alex was dead.

The thought spun in her mind as they ascended, reaching the third floor, then the fourth, and then shuffling up to the fifth. She stumbled on the next flight of stairs, and Simon managed to catch her flailing hands a moment before she almost went down. Dao watched her, unblinking, face set.

"You okay?" Simon asked.

She nodded, mouth and throat too dry to let her speak.

"We need to keep going." Simon peered ahead. For the first time, he registered a niggling sensation, an odd feeling that had lived below his skin since he'd arrived for his meeting the day before. Every floor, every landing and every set of offices were laid out in the same way, and it was fucking horrendous. While he knew they'd come up five floors, something in the décor, a slight change, to confirm it would have been nice. Different coloured walls, different pot plants; differing levels of sunlight through all the fucking windows. But, no. Whoever designed Greenham Place was, in Simon's humble opinion, a total wanker.

He snorted tired laughter and felt Dao's gaze.

"Nothing," he said to the unasked question. "Come on."

He set out again, stopping when Dao spoke. "Wait a second."

Simon looked back. Dao stood between him and Kelly. She blinked hot sweat from her eyes and tried not to hear the whisper of Alex's name echoing through her heart.

"Why are we going up?" Dao asked.

Simon studied his shoes, the toes scuffed. Kelly gathered her strength and slipped past Dao. Not wanting to put too much space between herself and the men, she rested on the arm of one of the leather sofas, too weak to move from the strong sunlight turning her already warm skin to hot.

"Why, Simon?" Dao said.

"I saw someone. I don't know who," Simon added quickly, as if Dao had demanded a name. "Up there when you were on the ground floor. They said to go up. As far as we could."

"What?" Dao pulled himself up a few steps, gripping the rail. "I was up there yesterday." The memory of the awful time trapped in the office while an invisible nightmare tormented him, and his son made Dao shake.

And maybe that's when it got inside you. Maybe then. Maybe earlier. Who cares, right?

"There's nothing up there. And there's definitely no way out. I mean, how can we get out seven, eight, nine floors up?"

"We need to go to the roof."

At first, Kelly wasn't sure she'd heard Simon. *The roof,* she repeated to herself. *That's what he said. Jesus Christ.*

Don't take the Lord's name in vain, her mother's voice shrieked, and Kelly let out a moan. Neither of the men heard it.

"The roof? Why?"

Simon began to cry. It reduced him from a man in his late-thirties to a child. Tears turned the dirt and sweat coating his face into clean tracks. He bent double, agony gripping his chest and stomach. Nothing physical hurt him, and that was the worst thing in the world. An open wound would have been better; cuts and gouges healed. The fire burning its eager way through his belly and bones was worse because it was old. It festered like a sore left untreated, and he understood too many long years had gone by when he should have done what he could to deal with it, instead of letting that hurt take over his life, *become* his life, and stop him from opening the door to anyone or anything.

Too many years. Too much of a lifetime turned into a pit because that was easier than filling the pit with love and light that might one day go away and go out.

And look what that's got you, a woman's voice muttered and it was not without kindness and sorrow.

"Simon." Dao said.

"You saw your mum, again, didn't you?" Kelly asked him. She had nothing else to offer him. All the good things had gone, now.

Simon struggled to speak for a moment.

"I don't know why she's not here to hurt me like what hurts you is here. It's not her. Not totally." Again, he fought for the words. Mercifully, they came. "It's like she's who I want her to be, not who she really was." He stared at them. "She's our way out."

Simon spun, moving to sprint as he turned, and Dao grabbed his shoulders before spinning him back. Dao's face was shielded to Kelly by Simon's head and neck, but she still heard the man speak. She knew his lips weren't moving, because none of the other demons of Greenham Place needed to use their mouths to voice their horrors.

Fuck your mother, Simon.

With a strength he could not possibly possess, Dao threw Simon straight at Kelly.

Chapter Forty-Nine

Simon smashed into Kelly, knocking all the air from her lungs.

The back of his skull connected with her nose, breaking it instantly. The crunch of bone was lost to Kelly's wheezing as she tried to inhale oxygen and suck it down into the fire of her chest. Hot blood exploded over Simon's head, soaking into his hair. At the same time, Kelly choked on more blood. She was utterly unable to breathe, swallowing the hurt from the bite in her hip. The flood of boiling liquid struck the back of her throat, splattered out of her mouth to cover her lips, cheeks and chin.

Simon pitched forward, reaching on pure instinct. His flat palms took the jarring impact of landing on the floor; he cried out, unable to think coherently. Still operating on instinct, he rolled backwards, throbbing head meeting the arm of the sofa Kelly had sat upon seconds before. Something approaching, something turned into an indistinct shape by his tears and blurred vision; something with arms reaching, reaching, reaching to tear him into pieces.

Collapsed on the sofa, thrashing and still choking, Kelly's body jacknifed like a dying fish. She tipped over and hit the floor, face down. For an unknowable time, she existed in a white supernova of agony, then crashed back to awareness.

I can't fucking breathe. Oh Christ, I can't fucking breathe. Help me, Alex. Can't breathe. I don't want to die, Alex. I'm so sorry, but I can't fucking breathe—

She spun on the floor, pushed by an invisible force. Spatters of blood turned the white walls red and trickled like tears. Kelly crashed into a pot plant, managed to lift her upper half and coughed up a huge volley of blood.

Airwaves cleared; she sucked in a lungful of oxygen, and that was when she saw the thing on the stairs lumbering towards Simon.

It was Dao, and it was *not* Dao.

She was looking at a shape devoid of any light as if a shadow had become three-dimensional and swallowed a man's form. Its arms, much longer than Dao's, swung like clubs, and talons grew from their ends.

The talons swooped down towards Simon's face.

Without thinking, Kelly flicked out a foot, and it collided solidly with the centre of the Dao-thing. The impact did something to him, turned him back into the man she'd known for barely twenty-four hours. No shadow-shape or walking darkness, only a skinny guy, head thrown back in agony from the foot striking him in the crotch.

Howling, Dao staggered backwards. His feet hit the top step and he fell. Bone snapped; he shrieked and another bone broke. He hit the level floor of the landing below, blood streaming from his head. His eyes danced, spun over, closed.

Wanting nothing more than to sleep, Kelly shuffled closer to Simon, let the streams of blood fall from her ruined nose, and reached for him.

"Kelly?" he whispered.

She couldn't speak or nod. Both actions were unthinkable. Pain. All the pain in the world and all hers.

"Jesus, your nose." Simon lifted a hand as if to touch her. She pulled back a fraction, and even that little movement was enough to make her want to scream.

Scream all you want later. For now, you need to get out.

She found his hand and then her voice. While it wasn't much more than a husky whisper, it was still hers. "You okay to move?"

"Dao."

Talking was like dropping into a bath of fire.

Stop moaning. You're still alive, aren't you?

The mad thought brought a tired laugh. The sound was so unexpected, she did it again. Simon stared at her, and Kelly wondered if she was still sane.

Probably not, a mournful voice answered her.

"Dao," Simon murmured. Even if the man had been right beside them, Simon's quiet voice wouldn't have reached him. Staggering, Simon edged close to where landing met stairs and peered down. Dao hadn't changed position since crashing down there. He lay flat, a wrist obviously broken, his head almost touching the bottom stair. If he opened his eyes, Simon and Kelly would appear upside-down to him.

But he wasn't going to open his eyes. Not again. There was no movement in the man's chest. Maybe the snap had been his neck. And maybe that was as kind as this shithole could be for Dao. No more terror over what was happening to his boy. No more agony over the death of another son.

Simon moaned. Losing Rod, Alex, and Dao was just too much. Better to sit on the sofa, close his eyes, and let this place do whatever the hell it wanted to him and Kelly.

Come on, someone whispered close by. A woman's voice full of desperation and urgency while something in the air hunted for her. Something furious.

Simon backed away to a swaying Kelly. He tried not to focus too much on the blood coating her shattered nose, painting her face a dark red.

"We need to go," he said. "Dao," she croaked. "Gone. Come on."

They lurched to the next flight of stairs and stared ahead. To both, the landing of the eighth floor seemed at least a hundred feet away. Air, stairs and wall rippled, all sliding away on an upward slope that took the next floor to some distant spot in the perfect blue sky. The clear sheen high over their heads mocked them. Safety up here, it said. Peace and comfort the higher they climbed. Only their stupid legs and aching bodies wouldn't carry them another step, let alone a thousand miles into the blue where the thing haunting Greenham Place—*eating* Greenham Place and wearing the face of all their fears and old guilt—had no chance of getting to them. Oh, no. None of that up above, thank you very much. Above was for being happy; above was for looking down on the secret ugliness that owned Greenham Place and the dark miles below its feet. Above was a sweet blue. Above was out of the way of the streaming river of fire barrelling down the slope of stairs at a thousand miles an hour and sinking its rage into their faces, turning flesh into ash and bone into scorched stone.

"Jesus," Simon cried, and came close to falling to his knees. Head bowed, he panted and tasted the harsh tang of his sweat. It was all he could do to pretend he hadn't pissed himself a little.

Kelly made a noise. Simon didn't catch it fully, and Kelly herself wasn't sure what she was trying to say. Sight made as much sense as her wavering thoughts. She blinked over and over until some sense returned.

Nothing unusual about the stairs. No sea of blue at the other end of the world. No flying red and orange coming to cook her face. She spat blood and wordlessly pulled on Simon's hand. They ascended slowly, neither with the energy to talk. On the last step, Kelly looked back, convinced Dao would be right behind them, ready to tip her over the stairwell. No sign of him, and that hurt in an odd way. While she'd picked up on his anger and frustration, that her childish behaviour had cost Alex her life, and known he'd disliked her for it, he'd still been okay in his own way. She spat again and then looked over the railing.

The open space gave her a view all the way down to the ground floor. At least, it should have done.

Instead of the railings of the floors below and the foyer at the bottom, a shape blocked it all out.

It was a lizard, but one larger than any she had seen before. It stood on its rear legs, hunched and squashed in the relatively tight space of the stairwell, the top of its spine level with the railings of the fourth floor. Its skin, a dirty brown, was spotted with massive patches of diseased flakes. Where the sunlight fell on it, the yellow turned the surface into a sickly white that trembled and squirmed. Not the skin, Kelly realised, the horror finally beginning to close in. The tendrils were like giant worms waving in no breeze; the sightless, squirming things with their tips opening to reveal a thousand mouths, and two spreading pieces of flesh jutting from the lizard-thing. Their skin was thin enough to let beams of sun spear them and rain from their other sides. The appendages were like gossamer: the growths flapping once and sending up a great stink of dead wind. She was looking at a thing that did not belong in any human world. It lived outside all worlds, sleeping and dreaming of somewhere other than its cold nothing. It was an old god buried in the earth; it dozed for aeons and knew nothing of all that time passing because the long centuries and years were simple days to it. Days of sleep and dreams of food in the world of human things.

Whatever grew from its sides flapped again.

It's got wings. Oh Jesus Christ, it can fly.

It heard her.

Its head tipped back to reveal what might have been a face. Paper-thin skin, brown like old muck, stretched from head to neck, broken by no eyes or nose, then splitting in half as a mouth opened.

No teeth. No tongue. Only a hole in its face that contained all the darkness in the world.

With no idea how she managed it, Kelly jerked away and spun to see Simon reaching for her. The understanding was a flash of white light—she'd been staring over the stairwell for no more than two seconds and still long enough to take in all the chaos under their feet—and her flying hand met his.

"Don't look down," she told him. "Run."

A wail answered her. It was Dao.

He stood at the bottom of the stairs, blood coating every inch of his head, broken wrist cradled to his stomach.

"Help me," he moaned.

Not looking back, Simon and Kelly ran, skidding on their own blood and both trying to see clearly through the streams of sweat and dripping red blurring their vision. Kelly crashed into the thick arm of a sofa, barely registered the impact, and lost her hold on Simon's hand. She raced for the stairs, took two at a time and thought: *Getting out, Alex. I'll make it up to you when I get out.*

Movement spun in her peripheral vision. Even as she ran, Kelly turned her head to see. On the wall, a shadow jutted off the surface, reaching for her, splitting open to form a human face and mouth. In the mouth, an agonised voice called her name.

Kelly. Kelly. Help me, please. Oh, God. Make the pain stop. Make it stop. Dear Jesus, kill me. Kill me now. It's eating me alive. It's inside me. I can feel it eating me. Make it stop. Jesus fucking Christ, kill me.

Above, below and on all sides, her mother's mad shrieks blew everything into pieces. Kelly's shame and guilt and grief became dust, leaving her with nothing but horror, horror at what had been done to her mother.

She faced the older woman, Carla Brown's form twisted and *eaten*. Before her death four years previously, she'd stood at barely five foot tall. Now, she'd lost at least eight inches and her already small waist was a line, a pencil slash on paper. She tried to stand straight and something inside ripped. Carla yowled, and blood splattered down her chin and dropped onto her hospital gown. Hisses rose from the floor. With dim horror, Kelly realised her mother was urinating, wetting herself in her agony.

Kelly. Kill me. Please kill your mother like you killed your sister.

Kelly howled.

From somewhere far away, Simon was a running animal, crying Kelly's name while the walls laughed at him and the floor shook like a wild sea and all he could do was watch.

A flailing, spinning darkness struck Kelly. The world went around and around. Sunlight shook with her screams and the windows were blinding squares stretching from miles below the earth to the roof of space. All of the sun's light was a never-ending explosion in the sky, come to cook her into ash.

Shrieking, she went over the railing into the hungry mouth of the stairwell.

Chapter Fifty

Non-stop wailing battered Dao's ears as the agony in his crotch, broken wrist, and elbow howled at him. The yells of his ruined arm and bruised testicles were nothing compared to the horrendous ripped sensation of being invaded by something so alien and so fucking cold. It had torn him in half; it had split him wide open and held on to both pieces. Its ugly bulk kept his mind from simply drifting in two different directions. Now it was gone, and all he had was the knowledge it could come back whenever it wanted because it had somehow found a doorway into him.

Huan, let it in, Lin told him sadly, and the only thing worse than the idea of his dead son wishing him such hurt was hearing only truth in his wife's voice.

Crying, he tried to move over the floor to get away from Lin, the racket of Simon, and Kelly's yells at the other side of the landing. Despite carrying him from the floor smeared with his blood to the stairs and up, his legs and feet wouldn't work properly. He slid as if moving over oil. A horrible wail crashed down on all sides. He'd seen the hunched figure of an old woman; he'd seen her piss herself and the stink of the urine made him want to choke. Escaping it all was the only option.

Dao made it to the wall opposite the stairwell, scrabbled at the smooth surface, and made it to an almost crouch. He looked back. Simon bellowed Kelly's name, and Dao realised he was shouting nothing that made any sense. He managed to move a few inches by kicking at the floor then rolled over to lie flat. Cold floor against his face, cold despite the sunlight, cold despite the burning fire in his throat and mouth from all the awful noise.

Dao staggered to his feet. The terrible racket behind faded to a low drone, all of it pulled down that same dark corridor that took Rod. Moisture ran down walls while stagnant puddles coated the floor and *things* capered in the gloom: things with teeth and claws. Their sole purpose was to please the ancient ruler who'd made Greenham Place its home.

While the shouting remained as background noise, he could focus and think. He could take hold of the rail separating floor from the massive windows and stare out to the blue sky unmarked by a single cloud. Even though the dazzling daylight made him want to squint or cover his eyes, he did neither. Much nicer to see and take in as much of the city as he could. Standing here with the blue spread in front and the entire landing lit and shining, he could let go of the noise behind: the growling barks that weren't quite human. Let that all go. Let it stay at his back while his eyes took in every inch of the thick blue; he relished it in a way he hadn't since he was a child and summer days were long, long, long. He had little to do in this strange, new country full of pale people and kids who thought he was the odd one because of his language and because everything he knew was thousands of miles away, trapped in a country closed to him. His life was sealed now, and all he had was days of sunlight and nights of staring at the window by himself, wondering which way China and home was from the noisy streets of England.

Blue sky. Blue stretching from one end of the world to the other, all of it laid out for him and Yang. His son stood on the other side of the glass, no more than a few feet ahead, his little shoes supported by air and that same air making his fine hair dance. No sign of injury or hurt, only his boy as beautiful as always.

Daddy.

The word had no sound and it didn't need to. Dao saw it on Yang's lips, and his heart cried out for it.

A voice spoke inside, and it was all him, not Lin.

NO. THIS IS NOT REAL. YANG IS NOT HERE. HE CAN'T BE HERE, AND YOU KNOW THAT.

He *did* know that. He knew it as he knew his own name, as he knew he loved the boy, and as he loved his wife. Whatever the building was and whatever was happening outside to prevent anyone from hearing their shouts, Yang *was not here.*

Dao reached for the boy.

Daddy.

Hot liquid burned Dao's cheeks. He was crying. Maybe he made a sound while he did. It didn't matter. Sound had left him. Touch and sight remained; the touch of the morning sun on his skin, and the sight of his boy only inches from his fingertips.

NOT HERE. HE'S NOT HERE SO CLOSE YOUR EYES. DON'T LOOK. CLOSE YOUR EYES.

In reply, another voice spoke to him, this one kind and soft. Dao knew there was no pretence of his mind trying to be Lin and no outside, alien force probing its way into his thoughts. This was something good, the opposite of the sly, ugly force living in the brickwork, glass, and foundations of Greenham Place.

Yes, he's not here, but this is as close as you're going to get to him. All you've got is right here. It's as close as you'll get to Yang again. You know it. Lin would do the same, and you know that, too.

He did. Oh, God, he did.

Swinging a leg over the railing took no effort at all, even though he hadn't done anything like that in many years. The section of landing on the other side was barely large enough for his feet. The gap of a few inches between it and the window was a tiny mouth opening all the way down to the ground floor.

Daddy.

Yang. Oh, God, Yang. Wait for me.

Blurred movement swam close to Yang: a reflection. Something was behind Dao. Something was running for him, someone reaching. And beyond the someone, a voice doing all it could to break through to him. His name. Was that it? His name shouted from the other end of the world? If he turned back, it might be able to break through the bubble keeping him safe; it might pierce that bubble and bring all the terror and confusion with it. He did not want that.

Alex had the right idea. Better to go your own way than to wait for this place to decide it for you. She knew it. She accepted it and you can, too.

Yes. He could.

Yang's not there. You know that. He never was, but this is as close as you'll get to him now.

He knew that, too.

So, go your own way, Dao.

Inside Dao's head, some breaking chunk of thought, hammered and beaten for hours, snapped free. There was no pain. He welcomed the break. He welcomed the freedom it brought.

Go, Dao. Go outside.

Was that Lin? Someone else? Himself?

—DAO STOP. DAO STOP. DON'T DO IT. DAO,

WAIT—

The last thread of Dao's sanity whispered the name *Simon*, then died. He didn't mind. There was no need to look back when all he needed was right in front of him.

Dao took a single step forward. On all sides, his vision rippled, as it had when a claw-like hand forced his face through the window in the office of a Mr. Alan Letts the day before. Again, passing through the glass was like moving through a peculiar mix of water and oil. It slithered off his body in a pulling sensation. He wondered if walking through a huge mound of jelly would feel the same. Wind blew hard on all sides; the sunlight streamed down from the blue, forcing Dao to squint. With his decreased sight, he still saw what was in front of him.

Nothing.

No Yang.

Just blue.

It grew from his fingertips. It spread like paint and coated the dead streets, the silent roads, and the small alleyways between buildings where nobody walked and where no wind blew through the rubbish. Nothing existed in this version of Willington. This dead town. This empty planet scoured clean.

The sky ate the world and turned the space it filled into silence.

Then the blue rushed away, racing up and up as if fired from a gun toward the top of the world. Wind gusted hard in Dao's ears, drowning out everything, so he closed his eyes against what waited for his body far below. He took Yang with him past each window reflecting the sun, each inch of Greenham Place as it tried to mock his life and his pointless yearning for Huan's forgiveness; Dao took his boy as he fell soundlessly towards the wall of fire that turned the street and pavement into a river of flame.

In the end, he took his boy and held him tight as the blue pressing against his eyelids became a deep red and the fire swallowed his skin and bones.

Chapter Fifty-One

Kelly hit thin air, then smacked into a hard object. Pain boomed up her wrists. Instinctively, she closed her fists and her vision cleared.

Somehow, she'd managed to grab the railings. She hung from them, the chasm of the stairwell yawning all the way through the nine floors below.

Kelly, look at me.

She looked up, sweat almost blinding her. Close to being lost in Kelly's wavering vision, Carla Brown loomed over the rail, staring straight down, mouth wide open and pints of hot blood falling like a red waterfall.

It struck Kelly in the face, filthy and full of a dead stink. The final segment of her battered sanity yelled that she could not open her mouth. Do that, and she'd be infected. She'd be eaten alive from the inside.

Still, the blood rained, sinking into her clothes, streaming down the front of her top, sticking to her breasts, hot and full of the promise of sickness all for her. The horrendous agony in her shoulder was almost forgotten in her horror, but the rapidly growing ache in her forearm and wrist couldn't be ignored. She was going to fall and explode on the ground as Alex had. But only if the monster below didn't come back and swallow her first.

No, please. I'm sorry, Alex. I'm so sorry. I didn't want this. I didn't want you hurt. Never wanted that. Please, you have to believe me.

The rain of blood became a trickle, and then stopped. Eyes almost glued together, Kelly tried to see. The fog that comprised Carla Brown was turning away. Kelly raised a shaking arm and gripped the posts of the stair rail in time to see.

A second shadow raced from the wall, barrelling down on Carla like a storm cloud.

Carla let out a noise that didn't come from a human mouth—a machinelike groan, a buzzing growl—and grew a giant's arms to welcome the second shape.

They collided and shot into the air above Kelly. There was a second, no more, of them hanging together before they fell. Hot wind blew past Kelly as the shapes missed her by an inch. They fell further, entwined, and the second one turned over, a face forming for a fraction of a second.

Alex.

Below Alex, Carla gripped her daughter, pulling her down faster. They both fell beside the landings of floor six, five, four, three, two, one.

They struck the ground and blew apart into nothing. A massive tremor raced straight up the centre of the building, and Kelly's legs swung helplessly. The pain in her arms became a roar, lessened only by the knowledge she had no chance of climbing up, so as soon as she let go, the hurt would stop.

Glass exploded from the lift shaft, each section blowing outwards to rain huge chunks of pane to the ground floor. Unable to hear anything but the detonations, Kelly tried to cry for help. Her voice was lost even to her as cannon fire crashed out of the lift shaft. Then, with a screech of twisting metal and bending supports, the lift itself fell from the shaft. Its top hit one of the posts, snapped, and the remainder tumbled straight down. It shattered in a storm of flying glass and crushed doors. Wiring flew loose; sparks danced through the wreckage. Kelly's right hand came free from the railing with shocking ease. She spun around, too weak to cry out at the awful pulling sensation that jarred through her shoulder. Two of her fingers lost their hold.

Alex.

There was no time to think anything else. Another finger came free. She hung, entire body weight held by a lone finger smeared with blood and sweat.

Kelly dropped.

A blast of agony exploded through everything at once. Something twisted her around, and Kelly saw the flat floor of the landing on the other side of the railing, then her feet. A crouching figure, shouting, telling her to hold on. With dumb wonder, she reached up and Simon's solid hand slammed into hers.

Chapter Fifty-Two

Crying out, Simon pulled Kelly up from the other side of the railings. He rose too sharply, bending his back rather than his legs, and a muscle around his coccyx turned into what felt like a burning rock.

Simon let out a dumb noise of hurt, eyes squeezed tightly shut, teeth and tongue parched. Kelly kicked at the tiny space of floor on her side of the railings and managed to slip her small feet between the narrow bars. Coughing on the blood from her broken nose and spitting flecks into Simon's chest and neck, she took as much of her own weight as possible and grabbed his neck. He opened his eyes, every muscle in his back throbbing, and pulled Kelly over the edge.

"You okay?" he yelled, hearing still muffled after the storm of yells and breaking glass and metal below.

Kelly nodded, unable to speak. Holding her as tightly as one might a lover, Simon backed away, slipped in a long smear of still running blood, and Kelly saw over his shoulder.

"DAO STOP. DAO STOP. DON'T DO IT. DAO WAIT."

The cry broke free, sending knives through her throat and nose. Simon spun; Kelly pushed herself from him and they ran across the landing. They both yelled Dao's name as the man stepped from the floor, climbed through the window, and stood on empty air.

A second later, Dao was no longer in sight. All they had in his place was the fresh morning light, brightening the sleeping buildings and roads of Willington's heart.

His hands limp and useless, Simon lowered them. He rested against the railing and stared out at the sky and tops of buildings. The sloping roofs of shops and the expanse of the cathedral all appeared normal, but *normal* was long gone. Same as Dao. All they had now were their strained muscles, the dark throb of cuts, and bruises.

"Christ," Simon whispered.

Aches pulsed in the centre of his head in a way they hadn't since his last hangover. He pressed a palm to his forehead as if testing for a temperature and wiped away sweat. Its salty stink was everywhere.

Walking stiffly and cradling the hand he'd grabbed to stop her from dropping, Kelly joined him.

"Dao," she whispered. Even the single word sounded blocked. Kelly's ruined nose turned it into a nasal drone. "Gone."

His little reply didn't cover it. The man had walked through the glass like it was made of some stretchy material; he'd passed through to the thin air outside the windows and *he'd hung there*. Only for a second that felt like it could have been a few hours, but still hanging there and reaching for nothing before he fell to the hungry pavement.

Kelly lowered her head, not crying, and that was a terrible thing. Tears had died for both of them, and all they had in their place was the silence as the building held its breath.

Simon reached for Kelly and her fingers encircled his. "Can you feel it?" she whispered. Blood dripped from her face. It pattered on the floor with a small, secret sound.

"What?" He knew. Saying it was still impossible.

"We're being watched. This fucking place." For the moment, Kelly's fear had died with her tears.

Simon kept his mouth closed and his gaze on the glass overlooking the city centre. She was right. They were being watched, considered, *judged.*

"It's been watching us since we got here." Kelly kept a tight hold on his hand, and that was the only comfort in the world. Their faint reflections shone, the paleness in his face and the drying smears of blood all over Kelly's face and clothes wanting to destroy that comfort. "The building knows everything about us, Simon."

"Yeah," he whispered.

Briefly, the fire in the centre of her face, the sickening jarring sensation filling her arm from shoulder to wrist, eased into silence.

"Can we burn it?"

Kelly's question came in a light musing manner, as if they were discussing what to have for lunch. Simon listened for what he expected to come: a mocking laugh slipping out of the walls, Rod, Alex, or Dao calling their names, or whatever really lived in the stone and glass of Greenham Place to finally reveal itself and ask just how they thought they could kill it.

"No. I don't think so."

"Why not? Everything out there is burned. This place can cook, too."

Still in the slight, gentle voice. Still no fear.

"I wish," Simon replied.

He glanced downwards through the little gap between window and railing. It seemed impossible to think Dao had balanced on such a small space before walking through glass. A few inches across and a space of nothing at all dropping nine floors straight down. As Simon studied it, the unbroken view folded in on itself, flipping around so he stared upwards instead of down, even though his head remained hanging.

Vertigo swam through his skull and his innards churned. It wasn't real; he knew that. It was simply the building playing with him and a voice far outside anything human broke through the vertigo.

I'm playing with you, Simon. I hate you, Simon. I'll kill you. Kill all of you. I'll crush you. I'll burn you. You can't burn me. You will never kill me. Never burn. Outside burns. Never burn me. Never get out, Simon. Never. Up and down and in and out. No way out. No outside. You stay with me forever and ever. You burn. You burn, you FUCKING BURN. YOU WILL BURN, AND BURN, AND BURN.

A woman's face, pale and drawn, filled Simon's vision. Silence crashed down, and it was a welcome peace. An exterior rage battered at the wall but had no way of breaking through. After long seconds, it pulled away and sank into the formless black of cold night.

Leave me the fuck alone, Simon thought. He blinked a few times; normal vision returned. He and Kelly remained at the window, still linked by their fingers. It seemed no time had passed while his head and insides were ravaged by the screaming voice.

He tilted his head, straining to hear the slightest sound. Their surroundings were soundless; they could have been inside a vacuum. They weren't, though. Not by a long way.

You're here, aren't you? You're watching us.

A tiny breath came from somewhere near the window. It might have been a snigger, or it could have been his imagination.

I heard that. I did.

"Fuck you," Simon whispered. "Come out and show us what you are. You can't, can you, you fucking coward?"

Wind blew out of nowhere, taking Simon back to the moments yesterday after everyone vanished, turning the building into a silence made deafening by its sudden difference from all the panic and fear. It made his hair flap, then did the same to Kelly, coating both of them with its stale stink, running over their bodies soaked with sweat and making them want to seal their mouths and noses against its stench. Refusing to do so, Simon inhaled the reek of dead meat and yelled against it.

"Fucking coward. Let's have a look at you. Right here, you fucker. Right here."

Vision spun, rolling over to send the floor over their heads.

Right here, you fuck, Simon thought, and Rod laughed at him; Rod turned into a savage animal.

You really want that, son? You want to see what did those things to me as a boy? You want all the monsters in the world here to rip the skin off your bones? You want to be lost in all the black with no way back? Lost there with just your mum for company? Your mum ready to do all that stuff again? Well, come and have a look whenever you fancy it, mate. Whenever the fuck you fancy it.

The breath of the wind faded into stillness. Kelly said his name with no strength. Feeling abruptly powerful and welcoming any new sensation that was not misery or fear, Simon spat a thick wad of saliva against the glass. It struck with a foul splat before trickling its slow way down the window.

"Fuck you, coward," Simon said.

If anything truly was listening or watching, it gave no reply.

"We should go outside," Kelly murmured.

He turned to her and she spoke to the window.

"We should leave. The air outside. The heat. We should just step outside."

She means you should die.

Simon listened for argument, but none came. The thought was his and his alone.

"No, Kelly. We're not doing that."

"Why not? Maybe we deserve it. Maybe all of us did and that's why we're here. We could have gone anywhere when everyone started running." She pointed to the smooth blue of the sky, and Simon saw with sickened wonder that the vomited blood from the shape that might have been an old woman in a world that made sense had managed to coat Kelly's arm all the way up to her shoulder. She looked as if she'd showered in gore.

"The bomb out there and everyone legging it. We ran but we came here. We didn't have to, but we did. We could have gone anywhere. Maybe it wanted us here. Maybe it's been watching us outside."

"What is it?" Simon whispered.

She shook her head. "I saw something." The volume of her voice dropped a level. The slightest sound would drown her out. "Below. Before." Kelly's entire body gave a brief shudder. "Before my mum." She touched her face. "Before all this. Something down there. A creature. A monster. It's here in the building. It's everything here."

She subsided for a few seconds, continuing before Simon had chance to think of a reply.

"Maybe it's been watching us and brought us here to play with, because we *deserve* to be here, and we deserve to just go back downstairs, break a window, and go outside."

Simon stared at her, at the twitch of her eye, at the tremble in her mouth, at the lack of tears.

It's inside her. You stopped it somehow, and it's gone for her.

"Kelly, listen to me." Ignoring the protest from the strained muscles in his back, he turned her around and pressed his face as close to hers as he could without making contact. Despite the lack of skin-on-skin, it was good. It was a human thing more important than the reek of blood or sour sweat.

"There's something here, right? We know that, but it's all pretend stuff. It's not physically here. Nothing can touch us or hurt us unless we let it. We can't be beaten by whatever's here. Your guilt and your fear, it's working on that, so don't let it. We've fucked things up. I know that, but we don't deserve this. None of us did. Okay? Whatever's here is playing with us. It wants to hurt us, but it can only do that if we let it. You hear me?"

Kelly's eyes remained wide open during his tirade. He closed his mouth and remained close to her face, searching it for any sign she understood and, more importantly, accepted it. Kelly blinked, a weak light shining deep down in her pupils. Then she kissed him. The touch was only for a moment; her lips remained sealed and they were as dry as a winter wind on his. Even so, Simon welcomed the slight pressure with more gratitude than he'd have thought possible.

"Okay," Kelly breathed. "Okay." She pulled away. "So, how the fuck do we get out?"

It was time to say what had been in his head since the terrible seconds after Alex's suicide was here and now. Simon leaned close to Kelly's ear; she tilted her head.

"It's my mum. She's the way out."

Kelly pulled back. "What?"

"I don't know what's going on. I don't know how she's here, but she is. Or whatever was good in her, *that's* here and all the rest of her, the part that hurt me, that's gone." He had to close his eyes for a moment. "I don't know what she is now, or even if it's really her."

Gaze clear and open, he stared at Kelly. "It's like she's more than she was."

"*What* is she?" Kelly whispered.

He shook his head. "I don't know. She's not a ghost." Simon managed a smile. "I don't think ghosts work on me here." Tears of regret or hurt or whatever the fuck he could call it were close, too close. If they came, he might just collapse and never get up. "She said to go up. All the way."

Kelly appeared to consider. It was a cover. She listened for the mad voices of dead people—guilt given the power of speech—to mock Simon's belief and hope before the lizard-thing with the mouth filling its entire face to swallow them whole.

Silence answered, but it was a waiting silence. A silence listening to her as she listened to it. Worse than that was the sensation of something huge on all sides. It dwarfed her and Simon; they were no more than dust to it, in the same way an ant would be to them. Scurrying around its feet, two tiny dots it could crush or let live depending on its mood. Whatever listened, it went beyond the framework and windows of Greenham Place. It wore the building like clothes and it sank its body into the earth for miles underneath into the pitch-black silence. It looked up to the world of people, their stupid beliefs, and their fights over nothing. It ate their fears when those dreads dripped through the mud and rivers. Sometimes it rose into the light of the human world when it grew hungry, and sometimes the perfect meals were ready for it with a bit of guidance towards its plate.

Or mouth.

I don't want to think about this shit, so I won't. Simple as that. It's nothing to me. This whole fucking thing is nothing to me, so I'm not going to think about it. It's not in my head. It's not around me, and it's not a fucking thing. Not one fucking thing.

Believing all this was easier than Kelly might have expected. It was almost as if invisible, probing fingers pulled away from her head.

"Okay." She nodded and wished she hadn't. Her shattered nose felt like a grenade had gone off in her face. "Up."

Leading Simon, Kelly stepped away from the window and towards the next flight of stairs.

Below, the building exploded.

Chapter Fifty-Three

The tremor speeding from below hit them before Kelly had chance to grab hold of any support.

She dropped, Simon coming with her. They hit the floor as the building roared, the sound drowning out their screams. Swirling dust slipped over the railings at the stairwell. It ascended in a grey cloud, filthy and choking. Kelly coughed as her throat burned. She spat to clear the taste from her mouth and nose, grit crunching between her teeth. She managed to stand, and Simon came with her. The dust cleared and the rumble of the collapsing stairs beneath rolled on. Staggering, Simon ran through the fog. Kelly followed, squinting as her eyes teared. They crashed into the railings around the stairwell together and the mucky air parted at the same time, blown apart by no wind.

At least the first two floors and sets of stairs had collapsed, sending brickwork, glass, and shattered masonry raining to the destroyed foyer. Huge mounds of rubble lay in piles, obscuring the floor and rising alongside the pillars. Of the lift, there was no sign, and it was the same with the ground floor windows and exit to the street. Even if below had been a way out, it was totally sealed to them now. More waves of dust made their way up the ruined stairs. The echo of the explosion followed, the noise oddly hollow. It could have reached them from underwater, muffled by pressure and the gloom. The cloud flowed out from the stairs into the gap directly underneath her and Simon, then grew thin to show the tallest mound of debris.

Carl stood on top of it, staring straight up, the muscles in his face utterly slack. Whatever had attacked him after his run into the lift had done more damage. One cheek hung in a huge flap, the insides looking like undercooked beef. Down his neck and into his chest, claw marks revealed sinews and the grey of bone. Her shocked eye traced the length of his body, saw the pumping fist of his heart cradled between his snapped sternum, and the forearm dangling from an elbow, held to the rest of the limb by tearing flesh and a bundle of veins and arteries.

"Jesus," Kelly whispered, and Carl's voice boomed from all around, even though his lifeless face and mouth remained still.

I'm coming for you, Kelly. You fucked me, so I'm going to fuck you.

Carl winked out of existence and, while nothing took its place, *something* lived down on the wreck of the ground floor. She caught a tiny glimpse of an outline of the lizard-thing: misshapen and hideous in its deformities. There was the suggestion of a twisted spine dozens of feet long, a head as large as a bus, and too many eyes peering up at her.

The mouth opened for her, now revealing hundreds of jagged teeth and its tongue flicking out to taste the air, taste her terror, and taste her guilt, *relishing* the feelings and drawing sustenance from them.

The dust cloud sealed the thing from view. The echo of the explosion began to fade, and Kelly realised she was holding her breath in exactly the same way Greenham Place was.

Holding it, waiting.

Blindly, she reached for Simon and once again found his hand. In the poor light, the white of his fingers against the black of hers became a dirty grey. Even the horrible smears of blood all over her clothes turned into a murky no-colour. The splashes on her face and drying in her hair could have been paint. They *could be*. All she had to do was pretend. Doing the same with the wounds causing those splashes was hard to the point of impossible. She'd try, though. It was the last thing left to do.

This is not real. None of this is here. I am outside on a nice day, the sun is shining, and there's green all around me. There are no buildings, streets, or roads. I am alone, and it's a nice day.

Kelly craned her neck. Above. The stairs. The roof. The sunshine.

The crash of church bells, icy-cold and terrible, rained down from above. Kelly shrieked, hands against her ears, which did nothing to block the sound. Simon staggered as if punched, and still the bells clanged with mercy. All the bells welcomed family and friends to a wedding where the guests would be unable to stop smiling, their faces turned into rictuses of mocking joy while more arrived. They all crammed through the doors to bring their dead, to shove the bodies to the priest's feet, each corpse a mouldering wreck of tattered flesh and grey bones. The wedding and the funeral, were both announced to the whole world by the thud of the ringing bells.

As if replying to the bells, something new came to the air.

There were three distinct voices, all crying together,
all in agony. Rod, Dao, and Alex twisted into a single shriek, deafening Kelly and Simon. He fell against her then stumbled to the railing, head whipping back and forth in desperate negation. The three lost to Kelly and Simon, all taken by the building, shrieked their pain.

There were occasional words in the howling. Blame, fury, and judgement all wrapped in the shouts for Kelly and Simon to suffer as the others had for them to cut their own throats, to stab their fingers into their eyes, to pull them free, and to let the fire cook the sockets before it baked their brains. To do all that and scream as the people they'd let die did the same.

Kelly bounced off Simon, her knees buckling. She spat, letting tendrils of saliva dangle from her mouth and mix with the blood still dripping from her damaged nose. Simon clutched the railing, keeping himself upright only through leaning on the cool metal. He no longer had the strength to cover his ears; the pound of the church bells would deafen him before long, and he could only take all the hate Greenham Place could throw at him and laugh at the faint belief that escape was possible—escape offered by a woman who'd given him up as a boy and was doubtless dead, along with every other person in this city he didn't know and wasn't home.

Dead and burned into nothing more than hot ash.

The roof, Simon. Come to the roof.

Silence crashed down, cutting everything in half, the lack of sound so sudden that Simon thought his hearing really had been destroyed by the noise. Then he caught the tremors of his breath and the murmur of Kelly's sobs.

"Kel?" he whispered. "You there?"

She reached for him, still crying, and took his hand without a word.

"The roof. We need to get to the roof right now."

Wiping snot from her upper lip like a child, Kelly nodded. The roof. Yes. Even if it wasn't *out,* it was something.

Side by side, they made it a single step from the railings before a new noise roared down and up and to all sides.

The agonised wail of a little boy. Simon and Kelly stared at one another, understanding on a level far below rational thought that the sound wasn't Dao's boy Yang or the memory of his dead son Huan: the image of him brought to Greenham Place purely to taunt the man.

This was the real Huan. They were hearing the cries of a boy condemned to fall from a climbing frame, over and over, fall and hit his little head on the soft and springy grass that was no help in keeping his neck whole and unbroken. They were hearing the loop of a child's violent exit from the world, and Greenham Place had managed to bring it to them or them to it. Either way, they'd been given Dao's hell.

No, Huan. Oh, God. Help my boy. Help him.

Kelly closed her eyes for a moment, sure she was going to start screaming and never stop. The sheer insanity in Dao's cry had to be contagious. No way could she hear that without losing her shit forever and ever.

The roof, Simon. The command managed to drown out the boy's tears for only a moment. *Get to the roof and stop this. Stop this for all of them.*

The woman's voice smashed its way down the stairs, something beyond human. It was like hearing trees talking. There was power in the command, maybe even more power than whatever horror powered the creature with the giant's mouth and the stink of its ancient breath.

Kelly ran. Matching her step-for-step, Simon ran with her. Together, they sprinted for the tenth floor.

In answer to their dash, a roar shook the building from the roof down to the rubble coating the ground floor.

Then the landing and offices of the third floor fell to join the remains of the first two floors. The shriek of snapping metal and the thunder of breaking glass were beyond anything in the world. Thousands of tons of masonry rained down, bringing the mashed leftovers of office chairs, desks, and computers down through the clouds of thick dust. The little remaining of the lift shaft exploded, vomiting chunks of glass as big as boulders and as small as the blades of kitchen knives through the smoke. Huge cracks raced along the windows, turning the non-stop sunlight into a dance of white beams while the racing smoke climbed quickly, obscuring the mountains of broken floor and ceiling, even as water from pipes sprayed down and sparks of shattered light fixtures were flashes in the fog.

Then the fourth floor collapsed.

Chapter Fifty-Four

Kelly fell a few inches from the last set of double doors, and so Simon hit them by himself and stumbled through. He turned as they swung closed, and dread fell on his shoulders with a freezing caress. They couldn't be parted. Not now.

He threw himself at the doors and fell to the hard ground beside Kelly. Only then did the impact on the doors and the floor register. It almost didn't matter. Everything was pain. More bruises and more cuts to spill more blood.

"Come on," he panted, not quite able to hear himself over what sounded like a bomb going off on the lower floors. "Up."

He reached for her. Their hands damp with mingled sweat and blood stuck together, and Simon pulled. Kelly made it to her feet, and Simon's strength abruptly gave out. He slid down; she slapped an arm against the wall, balancing herself. He saw her eyes become two growing white balls as she stared behind him, and he choked on the swirling dust and smoke a second before he saw it.

The cloud broke over the top of the final flight of stairs and closed in on them eagerly.

It's here, Simon thought from the spaces outside his head. *Whatever the fuck's inside this building, it's in that smoke. Its mouth is right here.*

As Kelly dug her fingers into his shoulder and yelled for him to get the fuck up, he saw a section of the dust cloud part. Two lips spread wide, curving at their edges in a mocking smile, gave him a view into the mouth and tunnel that had swallowed all the people yesterday, and had taken Rod, Dao, and Alex today.

Fuck you, he thought.

Then they were up, staggering through the doors again, their lungs hot like coals and exhaustion threatening to spill them to the floor.

Ahead, the long corridor of the tenth was lined on both sides by office doors just as Dao had said.

They both realised it at the same time.

Dao was up here. He found the way out and he didn't even know it.

They held one another and lurched forward, neither looking back as the first fingers of the cloud slid underneath the doors and came after them.

"Where the fuck is it?" Kelly yelled. She struck one of the office doors with a bloody hand. It swung open over a plush carpet to reveal a huge desk, sofas, and cabinets. Daylight on the other side of the window mocked her. No help here.

"Where's the fucking roof?"

Simon slipped in his own blood, shoe squeaking.

They dropped to their knees, both crying out.

Simon looked back. The advancing cloud was no more than twenty feet behind and coming fast. Anything beyond it might as well have not existed.

"Move." Another detonation from below threatened to drown out Kelly's voice.

What floor's that? Fifth? Sixth? Seventh?

It probably didn't matter. Greenham Place could spill their bodies through its yawning mouth as soon as it wanted to. The smoke and dust at their backs was simply a game to it.

She pulled him on, punching more doors open to show more executive offices. Arm around his shoulder, Kelly brought them to a stop at a junction. Ahead, one corridor passed a couple of meeting rooms, from which the fresh, morning light shone to the floor, and another corridor jutting off to their left. Nothing down there but a dead end and a lone door.

Screeching mindless joy, Kelly pulled on Simon. He tensed, rooting himself to the spot. For a second, her grip came away from his neck and a lifetime of fears and doubts crowded in on him, eager to offer their assurance that trust and hope were pointless for someone like him.

"It's a dead end," he shouted.

"The roof." She stabbed a finger towards the door.

Ten feet behind, the pulsing smoke filled their corridor. It came at a rush, as if propelled by a great wind.

If she's wrong, then you're dead.

Simon nodded. Kelly's arm slammed down on his neck, pulled him close, and they pitched forward. Their eyes straining, and their bodies battered. Kelly spat blood. They staggered on, and the smoke claimed her blood a few seconds later.

They came to the door together, the nondescript metal a faded grey, the bar in its centre like the one covering the fire exit which had proved useless. Simon thought he might weep like a child.

Kelly brought her hands to the bar.

Seven feet away, the cloud sped down on them. Six. Five.

Simon slammed both his gore-streaked hands on Kelly's and heard her call out her sister's name in a hurt, desperate gasp.

Four feet. Three.

They shoved on the bar with everything they had.

Chapter Fifty-Five

Darkness.

That was first. Then cold.

"Are we dead?" Kelly said.

"Don't ask me." Simon focused his energy on keeping hold of Kelly rather than raising his voice. Doing so was out of the question in any case. So was running from the door at their backs. All he could manage was staying upright and holding on to what little food they'd had in over a day.

Against his body, Kelly shivered. He'd been too consumed by the previous few minutes to feel the cold, and the chill closed in fast as Kelly shook again. Simon did the same and tried to hug himself without giving up his hold on Kelly's slim shoulders. The harsh air caught in his throat, making him want to cough, and he had a flash of a memory: being a kid no older than ten and walking to school in the middle of a sharp winter. Everything bright and pure white on all sides, and the morning too cold.

"Where are we?" Kelly whispered.

Her answer came from behind. An ugly sound of scraping nails ran down metal. They both let out weak shouts and jumped forward. The scraping continued. It was like a dozen knives being dragged across a stone floor, and that couldn't be right because there was nothing out in the corridor but dense smoke.

You think that matters? Simon asked himself bitterly. Whatever they'd left behind after their mad jump through the heavy door, it was no more than a few feet away, and if it found a way in, it'd be all over them in a second.

Shaking in the frozen air, Kelly fumbled in her jeans pocket and managed to slide her lighter free. It slipped out of her damp hold and hit the ground with a soft tap.

"Shit," she spat, fighting off hot tears. All the exhaustion of her broken body and broken heart said to lie down, close her eyes, and let Greenham Place do its dark work. Kelly breathed through her mouth, which helped to lessen the fire in her nose. "My lighter. I dropped it."

"Okay. Down. Together."

They crouched, their free hands tracing over a ground that felt like ice. The jagged scrapes on the door ceased for a moment, and then a massive crash struck the entrance. Simon's cry met Kelly's yell. The thud hit the door again, some terrible thing pounding its rage and demanding entry.

"What the fuck is that?" Kelly cried.

Her fingers brushed metal, passing over it almost quick enough for her not to realise she'd found the lighter. Laughing her triumph and not hearing the mad note living in the sound, she yanked it from the floor and jerked upright. Simon came with her; the moisture coating her fingers made flicking the lighter on almost impossible. Boiling with frustration, Kelly tried again. A tiny flame flickered into life for a few seconds, sending writhing shadows over the floor for a few feet and stretching them towards the wall on their left. An instant before the lighter went out, they saw the clear floor, pipework covering the walls with valves and taps, then the light limning what looked like a pole, rising up to the ceiling. Thick darkness crashed down and brought a new sound.

The slide of a lone footstep.

Without thought, Kelly moved to flick the lighter again and Simon stilled her.

"Don't," he breathed. "It'll see us."

Out in the corridor, a volley of mad laughter rang out. Another crash struck the door. Simon shoved his face to the side of Kelly's head and found her ear.

"Move to the wall on our left. The pole. I think it's a ladder," he whispered.

Another step hissed in the dark. Whatever was with them, it was happy to take its time. That knowledge was no comfort.

Gripping each other in a death grip, Simon and Kelly crossed to the left wall, both reaching blindly. They hit a cold surface at the same time, their fingers splaying across the surface.

"Where is it?" Kelly whispered.

Another hiss of a sliding step sounded from the other side of the room.

"Where the fuck—"

Kelly found a jutting pole, then one stretching horizontally to a third pole. A vertical pole. A ladder.

"Up," Simon whispered. A terrible sense of fatalism descended on him, as if he stood on the top of a tall building, peering over the edge, full of the mad desire to jump. With a laugh threatening to bubble over, he realised that image was pretty much the truth of their situation.

Simon's hand shook in hers. "Go," he said. "I'm right behind you."

For the first time in what felt like hours, Kelly dropped the man's hand, then grasped the rungs. She pulled herself up, expecting the roof to smack into the top of her skull at any second. Below, Simon grabbed the frozen metal of the ladder and clambered up two rungs. The skin of his palms and fingers stuck to the ladder for a second, stinging as he pulled free. Kelly ascended further and froze when a voice with no humanity oozed through the inky darkness.

I'm here for you.

Voices, tones, and inflections all living together and turning the four words into something no more human than a dog's bark.

Coming for you.

Inside the shrieking mess of her head, Kelly named the speakers: Carl, her mother, and Alex. The three joined to judge her for her mistakes and to punish her for her stupidity and selfishness. They'd reach an arm formed of two women and one man, of snapped bones, of flesh eaten by cancer, and of pulsing muscles; they'd reach for her, yank her off the ladder, and throw her into the mouth of the nightmare thing that called Greenham Place its home. That *was*

Greenham Place. And down there, she'd be chewed into an eternity of pain just like Dao, Alex, and Rod.

"Move," Simon whispered.

The first blow on the door in a few moments crashed through the little room. In the moment after its echo faded, Kelly registered the new sound of bending metal. Two realisations smashed down at the same time: the door was buckling, and the thing outside was simply playing with them. The door was nothing to it. Their fear was everything. Their fear was its meal.

"Go," Simon roared.

Hand off the rung; hand lifted; hand on the next rung, moving without thought as she had on the stairs before—

Kelly cut the thought off, the memory of her mother's shadow and the pouring blood belonging in a life outside the room. Up, that was all that mattered, not the stink of blood or the feet shuffling closer. The voices of three people turned into a single tone, calling for her to stop, stop, stop—

Kelly's head hit the hatch. The thud sent a lightning bolt of hurt through her skull, then down. Ignoring it, she shoved a hand up, hit metal and pushed.

The hatch didn't give at all.

"Shift it," Simon hissed.

"I can't. It doesn't open."

Kelly pushed as hard as she could. The hatch could have been welded closed. A terrified sob escaped her mouth; she couldn't keep it inside.

"What is it?" Simon whispered.

"It's locked."

One more sneaky step, one more soft mutter in the dark. And the thing outside coming closer, taking its time because it knew they were trapped and the door would explode whenever the fuck the thing wanted it to. Its giant mouth would tear a hole in the wall and maybe they'd have a moment to see it fully before its teeth closed over them and all would go black. If they were lucky.

"Use the fucking lighter!" Simon yelled.

Kelly flicked it and shoved the dancing flame towards the hatch. It turned the metal into a faded grey and sent shadows across the ceiling. Maybe one of those shadows looked like a bundle of twitching arms; she didn't want to know for sure. Kelly ran the light over the hatch, seeing nothing but a flat surface, nothing to get hold of or push or pull and—

There.

Three simple bolts shoved across the hatch, locking it. A mad laugh bubbled to the surface. Kelly swallowed it a second before it emerged. If she laughed now, she might never stop.

We've gone through all this shit, and the only things stopping us from the roof were these fucking locks, she thought tiredly. And wasn't that just perfect for this place? The final joke from Greenham Place on them. The final nasty joke.

Kelly thumbed the first bolt. It slid free, grating as it moved.

At her feet, Simon shrieked. Kelly looked down.

A hand had emerged from the gloom. Black and white skin lived together, the colours squirming over one another instead of turning the forearm grey. The skinny bone of an old man's wrist met the thick muscles of a younger man's well-tended muscles. As more of the arm came into view, Kelly saw the elbow, black and obviously female, turn over to reveal a scant bicep and then a woman's shoulder.

Her mother, Alex's dad, and Carl all together, all one obscene body here for her. And when the light from above reached the thing's joined faces, her head would explode, and all this horror would be finished.

NO, I WON'T SEE IT I WON'T I WON'T.

Yelling, Simon punched into the gloom, and then pulled back. The arm become something inhuman rose. Fingers twisted and shoved at Simon's face. He howled as nails tore his skin.

"Open it, Kelly. Open the fucking hatch."

The arm, its fingers splattered with gore, closed in on his face again. Roaring, Simon threw another punch. The arm pulled away into the dark.

Her soaking fingers almost useless, Kelly fumbled with the next bolt, missed her grip and reached again. Simon cried her name. She shrieked a noise completely removed from speech and smacked the second bolt across.

You screw up this last one, and you're both dead.

Fingers belonging to someone else, Kelly shoved a thumb on the bolt and pushed. It slid free without a sound.

Crying, Kelly hammered a fist at the hatch. With shocking ease, it flew up, revealing an utterly smooth sky of unmarked blue.

Kelly lurched upwards, trying to yell for Simon to follow her, to not look back. She shot free of the hatch, hit a small ledge, and tipped herself over it. For a few seconds, up became down, down collapsed to the sides; then she struck rock hard ground, scraping skin from her forearms, grazing her forehead on cold gravel.

Still on the ladder and doing all he could not to think about the fire burning through his cheek, Simon kicked out with all his fading strength. The toe of his shoe caught the face of the grinning demon, mashing its lips over teeth and breaking one free. The thing spat it to the floor and reached again. Howling, Simon threw a punch as hard as he could. His fist sank into a hot surface and plunged deeper. In a millisecond, he realised what had happened and his repulsion was a white explosion in the centre of his head.

He'd punched into the thing's face and *his hand was inside its head.*

Simon yanked his gore-splattered hand free as the horror twisted and bit down. Teeth like rocks snapped on the middle knuckle of Simon's index finger. Bone and skin shredded with terrible ease, and his hand was a detonation. All the fire in the world lived at the end of his arm.

There were no shrieks. He didn't have the breath for them. Yanking his hand back as the stump of his finger squirted blood, and his insides capered and gibbered at the awful, sickening feel of being inside the thing's head. Simon whirled back to the ladder.

The monster came for him.

On the far side of the little room, a shape flew from the door. Simon caught the briefest image of a woman shooting over the floor, her mouth open in a scream of pure fury. The shape collided with the abomination that had bitten his finger off and tried to tear his face away as the door to the corridor flew open. Simon understood that he'd been right when he told Kelly this wasn't his mother's ghost. This thing only wore his mother's face. It took her shape, but Nicola Law was not here. She rotted in the ground while something from outside the world dressed in her shape as the horror from below the building wore whatever shamed and hurt them.

The thoughts sped by, sensations more than words because there was no time for a reaction. The woman had been keeping the door jammed. Without her, he was exposed to the mouth in the smoke and dust of the ruined building. And that smoke was streaming straight for him. And the mouth in the smoke was opening for him.

Holding his ruined hand to his chest and tasting the blood streaming from his cheek, Simon lunged upwards to the sweet blue of the sky.

Chapter Fifty-Six

He emerged as if being born.

Kelly grabbed Simon under his arms and yanked. He tipped, momentum speeding his movement. His legs kicked at the murky light inside the hatchway before he tipped with Kelly and sent them both down.

A hand pulled at the top of the ladder. In the clear daylight, the awful mashup of skin colours and differing muscle tone came straight from a bad dream. Three bodies turned into one; three people come to punish her for everything she had got wrong in her entire life.

They raced for the hatch together. They found the lid and swung it as the black air reached the opening.

Metal crushed the dancing fingers, snapping a couple from the hand. The broken digits fell to the roof, blood pattering down with them. Red smeared the edge of the hatch, staining the metal. From inside the small room, pounding fists struck the other side of the hatch. Kelly backed away as Simon shoved the outside bolts into place, then fell against her. He sobbed as the agony in his finger and face bellowed at him.

"Oh, Jesus, Simon." Kelly reached for him. He pulled back, shaking his head as the pounding struck the hatch. The fire in his head and hand vanished. Even the racket coming from below was shut away, trapped with his suffering on the other side of the world. Side-by-side, they saw the sky and roofs of high buildings, all quiet in the morning sun.

Willington spread in all directions. Streets grew to roads; the roads marched towards a parkway. Acres of smooth green surrounded the grey parkway, and pockets of woodland dotted the fields. Above, the blue reached down to the horizon, meeting land in the far distance. And two suns filled the ceiling of the world.

Hanging above the cathedral, the white-yellow ball of the sun shone. Straight ahead and high over where the fields made their way towards the surrounding countryside, a second sun glared its white light.

"That's it, isn't it?" Kelly wanted to cry. She couldn't. "The explosion. The bomb. We're dead and that's why."

She pointed to the second sun, expecting a billion degrees of heat to turn them to ash at any moment. Nothing but the silent, cool air came.

"We're not dead," Simon replied.

In reply, a storm of blows hit the hatch and the damage done to Simon's face and finger returned, the pain beyond savage. The lid shook, the bolt holding for the moment. Simon listened to the shouts below the attack on the hatch. The woman's voice, telling him his mother was so sorry, telling him she knew she'd been a monster.

Inside, grief and rage yelled at him and he shut them down, too exhausted and in too much pain to fight anymore.

"You need to run for that."

While his ruined finger continued to spit blood down his shirt, he nodded towards the burning white light of the explosion.

Chapter Fifty-Seven

She stared at him as if he'd abruptly started speaking a foreign language. Except there was no time to think. All they had was time to *do*.

"That." He pointed to the light, sitting like a fat king over its land. "Listen to me. We're not dead. We never were, and this place can *fuck off.*"

Another savage roar, and what might have been a mocking laugh, came back. Somewhere close by, windows exploded. Simon heard shards of glass tinkle as they rained to the floor and cut the air on their long journey down to the street. Another explosion sent chunks of brick flying from the sides of Greenham Place. The roof pitched, threatening to spill them, threatening to cave in and drop them down, down, down into the mouth of the beast.

Drop them as if they were falling down a slope.

"Run for it, Kelly. It's fine. You go."

"What?"

"I can stop it. We can't burn it, but I can stop it. You run for that light. It's the way out of here. It always was. It's the fire. It's the explosion, but it's the way out." He was babbling and couldn't stop. No time to consider words or reason. Only time to get her away from the roars coming closer and closer with every second.

"It's a door. It's the way out. You have to get to it," he yelled.

"How? Fly?"

Kelly. We want to see you. We have to talk about Alex and what you did.

Simon refused to turn at the ugly shout that came from a man he'd never met.

"You have to jump," Simon said.

She stared at him and he tried to smile. He failed.

"You jump for it," he muttered.

"We jump," she replied, and he shook his head. Again, the wounded eye and finger lived far away—if only for a few seconds. In that relief, he was able to think beyond everything that hurt.

"No. All this, it's not really here. I don't think we are. Not really. Everything's stopped, right? Everything's waiting. So, whether that's a bomb about to go off or a way out, it'll start everything when it either goes off or closes. And you need to be inside it when it does."

The banging on the hatch increased in fury and volume. While the ladder below it was only big enough for one person at a time to come up, it didn't change a thing. God knows how many fists were hammering on it in the dark.

Kelly. We're going to kill you. We're going to take you with us, take you to your mother so you can see what's happened to her. You can see what the cancer has done to her. What it's always doing to her.

"Fuck you," she whispered, and pulled Simon by the shoulder. He shook her loose.

"Listen to me. You run for it and you jump. I'll deal with this place."

"No, Simon—"

"Just take a run for it and jump. I can make this go away." Simon began to cry, and his voice wavered like a child's. "It's nothing, right? And that's what I've got. Nothing. I'll give it my nothing."

He shoved her. She backed up, feet kicking through the pebbles. They faced the awful light burning in the blue. It was half the distance it had been. A winking white shone through an opening door with something on the other side.

It was impossible to make out. More light, maybe. Blinding light.

Kelly spun around to Simon. He was already nearing the hatch, smart shoes kicking through the pebbles coating the surface of the roof, the hem of his suit jacket flying from his sides.

"Simon."

He didn't look back. "Oh, Jesus. I don't want to die."

The banging reached a crescendo and a metallic clang rang out. The hatch was open.

Simon's yell was mad and full of tears.

"I've got nothing, and that's just fine."

Chapter Fifty-Eight

Simon collapsed beside the hatch, pebbles digging into his palms and wrists. A hand found pipework. He pulled himself up and turned to see Kelly, clearly torn between running and coming for him. He tried to wave at her, to signal she should run. Doing so was out of the question. All he could do was bleed and try to stop crying while the barrage of raging voices yelled from the room below, calling him a cunt, a waste of life, and a failure to every single person he'd known. And once they got out to the roof, they'd tear him into pieces.

You there? he asked the air.

If the creature dressed and shaped as his mother was close, it remained silent. Maybe it'd never been there and this whole plan was a disaster.

No. No. Fucking no a million times.

"No," Simon whispered, managing a trembling smile.

The fury of the attack on the hatch increased massively. It was like being in the middle of a gunfight, and that was okay because it meant the things below couldn't smash through his protection.

"Simon," Kelly screamed, from either ten or a hundred feet away. The sweat dripping into his eyes made it impossible to tell.

"Go," he muttered, and readied himself for what was coming.

"Nothing's coming," he said, managing an honest, real laugh for the first time in maybe weeks.

Torn in two by her choice, Kelly stood with her body at the edge of the roof and her face turned back towards Simon. Slouched on the floor of the roof, bleeding from a dozen places, he looked almost dead.

The man's body jerked and before his head fell against his chest. Kelly saw him smiling.

Go. He is with me. I will keep him safe.

Kelly caught the faint outline of an image— something or someone bent double over the hatch, body pressing against it, face turned towards her, and the mouth a perfect display of strain. Nothing human belonged to that face. She was looking at something that dwarfed humanity.

It sent a wordless command—*GO*—and there was no possible argument Kelly could give. It would be like arguing against—*run child run for your life*

She ran: legs pumping, arms tucked against her sides. It seemed to Kelly she ran through water and it seemed to Simon he looked through it. Things slowed enough for him to take in the bracing air, the discomfort of the cold vent at his back and the light in the sky growing brighter, turning into a single star glowing in the morning sky.

He drew breath and let his words fly. *"I've got nothing and that's just fine."*

On all sides, pressure pushed at the air. There was no need to try to see whatever was causing the pressure. It didn't matter. Whether he looked or not, he wouldn't be able to see them, because he had nothing, and nothing was what he would give to the building. A big nothing.

Simon smiled.

The roof at his splayed feet dropped away, stone, brick and glass falling inwards. It formed a slide that dropped into a massive tunnel. The now familiar stink of air from all the way down blew up into his face.

Still smiling, Simon inhaled. The stench filled his nose and mouth. He took another breath.

Above and on both sides, the pressure increased. It was like being inside a bubble, secure from the outside world while dozens of hands punched and hammered at the layer between him and them. Hands raging because they couldn't get to him.

Dead hands, he thought, and found he didn't really care. If the dead people from the ground floor had found their way up, or if the ghosts of Rod, Dao, and Alex were here—eager to tear him free from his bubble—then so be it.

Simon shifted as more of the roof gave way, not hearing the crash of raining pipework and snapping metal. Near its edge, Kelly was still running, her small feet kicking through pebbles and sending them high as she neared the end of the roof and the light. Black pulsed in the corners of his vision; a monstrous face filled the air to his right and there was nothing human left in it. All he saw was a broken mess, smashed into a bloody pulp by its speeding impact into the ground.

It fell away and something pushed in towards his head. Then at his sides. Then grew darker.

Kill you, Simon. Eat you. Burn you.

They were almost through his bubble.

Simon laughed, fear of being swallowed by the monster lost, if only for a moment. It felt like blood drowned every inch of his face and body. He bathed in it and took in its rich scent with every gasping breath.

He gazed down into the tunnel. While he couldn't be sure, it looked as something right at the bottom might be on its way up, eager to meet him finally. All the years of his life with nothing to show for it. All that time spent wasted on surface things and now here he was, the tips of his shoes half an inch from the edge of the tunnel and the smooth ride all the way down.

It would take a long time to get there. A very long time. But then, Simon figured he had some time to kill. Time to wonder if regret really had a point.

I don't forgive you, Mum. I wish I did but I don't. But I know...

He knew what? Why she'd done those things to him? No. Never that. Diseased or not, damaged inside or not, nothing justified those nights when he'd been a kid. But maybe he didn't need to think about that now. Maybe that could stay here in the bright chill of the light from the two suns. Maybe that time could cook in the fire and be taken away from the world, from him.

Maybe.

He took one last look at Kelly, a second away from the edge and her jump. He took a tight hold of the memory of her dry kiss and the salty aroma of her sweat, feeling as if the kiss was happening this very second. And, with a bit of luck, he could hold on to the touch of Kelly's lips and the tang of her sweat for a time much longer than this lone second.

With a bit of luck.

Simon dropped into the ever-opening mouth.

Chapter Fifty-Nine

Kelly existed in two states side by side. Her body raced on, feet powering through millions of pebbles, kicking them to the side. Her mouth became a snarl of strain and effort; her loose hair flew beside her head and the air parted at her racing assault. At the same time, she was a petrified mouse, cowering in a hole while a storm crashed above. That storm had a voice: hellish, full of disgust, and judgement. It closed in while she tried to cover her eyes and ears. It shrieked its disgust, its hate, and turned her into a sobbing child.

In front and zooming closer, the white ball grew to fill the world. Seeing it was agony in her eyes; looking away was impossible. It cooked her vision and sank shining fire into her head. Still, Kelly ran, not looking back. She ran, crying out her apology. She ran, yelling her sister's name to the blinding radiance covering every inch of the world.

She ran and everything from her feet to the storm in the centre of her face was a sickening ache.

A single thought chased itself around her head in a senseless blur.

I don't want to die don't want to die don't want to die.

Behind, a creature that might have looked like a lizard sped after her: its mouth a cavern, a stench from outside the world gusting from its throat. Its wings flapped once, launching the thing twenty feet over the roof in an instant before it barrelled down on Kelly, its shadow blotting out the light from the two suns.

The stain swallowed the top of Greenham Place, turned day to night, and turned the struggling warmth of the day into a glacial freeze of a planet lost in the far reaches of the galaxy. Or the underside of the earth, where entities dozed in their uneasy sleep and dreamed their dreams of food in the world of sunlight.

Shadow raced for Kelly's back and a screech of triumph shook the empty world.

Kelly reached the edge of the roof.

Oh, God, Alex. I'm sorry but I don't want to die

White light bloomed.

The silence turned her to ash and seared that ash into nothing as it had done to the county and city and its people in less than a second.

Kelly's nothing fell forever through a searing light, aware of every beam, every mote and fire. She was no flesh, no skin or bone; she was burned a thousand times and she was all the screaming in the world thrown from one throat and out of one mouth.

She was the sun.

She was the centre of the sun. She was all the fire.

And she was forever.

Chapter Sixty

Soft light.

Warmth.

Coming down like a floating feather.

Green spreading, growing, becoming clearer, more detailed. A billion blades of grass, waving gently in a soft breeze. A narrow pathway emerging from a copse of tall trees to snake its way through the green.

Cool, refreshing wind.

Everything—light, the ease of the air, green of the grass growing more distinct—merged into one sense and that sense was sight.

Kelly fell to the ground, striking it as if the earth was a bed. For a time that could have been a few seconds or hours. She kept her eyes closed, thinking of nothing, letting no images or memories come in too close because those memories were all the grief she would ever know.

More seconds and minutes drifted by. More time of no thought, and that was fine. That was what she could handle; she—

Open your eyes, Kel.

No. She would not.

Yes, you will. Right now.

No. Never.

Open your eyes and stand up.

Yes. She needed to do both. Even if the terrible white filling the world remained, she had to stand and face it.

Kelly rose, legs shaking, breath full of the salty tang of her own blood and the rotten stink of drying sweat. She spat red flecks and felt her ruined nose as gently as she could manage. It was a broken chunk of rock and, while it hurt, she could take that pain. Take it. Own it.

What was next? Her eyes? Opening them? Yeah. That sounded like a plan.

Kelly opened her eyes.

She stood on a massive field. Woodland grew about a quarter of a mile away. The land rolled and dipped in places; the crowded trees stood on a higher section of grass. She scanned the roof of the wood before looking higher. Several clouds, light and fluffy, floated in the thick blue. The day wasn't as warm as she'd first thought. As it'd been for the last couple of weeks when the threat of winter whispered it was coming closer with each passing day.

"Alex."

Kelly shivered at the sound of her own voice. The name had come before she'd realised she'd thought it. Now it was out, and she couldn't take it back.

"You here, Ali?"

Of course she wasn't. Alex was dead, and that was purely down to her own selfish, stupid self and her even more stupid actions.

A few tears fell. Kelly let them come, too exhausted to fight. She'd made it out; Alex hadn't. The others hadn't, either. Their fears had won.

Except for Simon. The guy—awkward and irritating at first—had beaten his fear and, in doing so, had saved her. He'd taken the thing desperate to ruin them and he'd given her another chance. They all had, in their own way. And that thing pretending to be his mother… that thing from somewhere as awful as the monster controlling the building.

That thing come too late to save Alex. And all she could do now was try and live with that, just as she had to live with what she'd done.

Without much thought, Kelly walked. She stayed with the grass, ignoring the pathway. Her route took her towards the sun, the warmth matching her step for step. Despite her ruined nose and dry throat, she talked to her sister as she moved.

"I'm so sorry, Alex. You wouldn't believe how sorry. I fucked it all up. I ruined it all and I can't do a thing to change that. I can't fix a thing. All I can do is say sorry. All I can do is say it over and over."

Without realising she was going to do so, Kelly stopped and tilted her head to peer at the sky. One sun. No white ball full of fire and no white light caught in the breath before its roar obliterated everything.

"Simon. You there?"

He was not. Simon remained on the other side of the white. If there was anything kind in the world, then maybe his actions had undone the torture and horrors of Greenham Place. Maybe hoping the others were free from it wasn't too much to ask.

Kelly wept. She had no idea if her hope was pointless, like wishing for the events of her eighteenth birthday to be changed. All she could do was ask the world to let the others go. They hadn't deserved the shit of Greenham Place. Not one little bit.

Not bothering to wipe her eyes, Kelly walked on. After another few minutes, she stopped. Further over the grass, a building site stood. New houses were beside buildings formed only from a frame. A high wire fence shielded the development from the open land. Dozens of diggers, vans, and earth movers covered the road that cut its way through the area.

She was looking at the early stages of a new development of homes for families, a place where kids could play in the surrounding countryside, where they could explore woods and people could walk their dogs alongside a man-made lake. An area ready for a fresh start.

It hit Kelly with a weak punch.

She had to be at least forty or fifty miles from Willington. This was the outskirts of one of the county's smaller towns.

This was RAF Lakenheath.

This was not RAF Lakenheath. Not anymore. The world of that base and that Willington was back on the other side of the forever white, and maybe that was okay. Maybe that was the best place for it.

You are not Kelly Brown. Not here. Be someone else. Be anyone you want to be.

Yes, she could do that. She could start again. And if she met a woman with a couple of kids, a woman who might look a bit like her and who is a person who deserved a good life, she would be that woman's friend.

She would start again.

"Alex," Kelly whispered to the quiet.

Not here. Alex was not here, but someone was. All Kelly had to do was find her.

Her heart thudded painfully and again she could take that hurt.

Own it because it was all for her. Alex, not here. Maybe… maybe…

Maybe, if the world was kind, she'd be friends with a woman she did not yet know. Or three men who had never met each other. Or her. Whoever she was on this side of the explosion.

Weeping, the sun at her side and blood drying all over her clothing and face, Kelly staggered towards the new development and the new morning.

About Your Author

Luke Walker has been writing dark fiction for most of his life after getting hold of paperbacks belonging to his dad and brother and reading Poe, King, Herbert and Lovecraft when he was far too young. His books include the horrors The Unredeemed, Hometown and The Mirror Of The Nameless as well as the dark fantasy Dead Sun. Several of his short stories have been published online and in magazines and books.

When not writing, he can found watching bad films or reading good books. He has novels and short stories to be published soon and is currently working on new fiction.

Luke welcomes comments at his blog which can be read at www.lukewalkerwriter.com and his Twitter page is @lukewalkerbooks. Sign up to his newsletter at www.tinyletter.com/LukeWalkerWriter.

He is forty-one and lives in England with his wife.

Other HellBound Books Titles
Available at:
www.hellboundbookspublishing.com

The Unredeemed

Four hundred years ago, Benjamin Harwood butchered whoever he saw fit to kill, knowing that sacrificing his murder victims to a demon would keep him safe from eternal punishment.

But now, their agreement has been torn in half and the demon is coming for Harwood's soul, coming to set him to burn.

Preparing for war, Harwood gathers the worst of the worst, the monsters and murderers he calls friends.

With this group of damned killers, Harwood must return to the crimes of his past and seek help from his most recent prey: a teenage girl whose family he destroyed, a girl with more reason to loathe him than anyone in his life or death.

Only then he can try for a redemption that may be impossible or face a universe of suffering.

But Harwood doesn't know there is a hole in the floor of the world. And something much worse than the dead is down there…

Blood in The Woods

Based upon true events...

For Jody, growing up in the late eighties and early nineties in the small Louisiana town of Hammond with his best friend Jack was filled with wonderful childhood memories.

Time spent playing in the woods, shooting pellet guns, blowing up mailboxes, fighting at school and upon the dawning of interest in the fairer sex, their carefree lives typical of children with few responsibilities and no worries beyond the next pop-quiz or getting to second base. As they grow older together and experience the joys and pains of life, love, family and friendship, they uncover a grim secret that their home town has kept, and through little more than an innocent, idle curiosity, Jody and Jack stumble upon something horrific in the woods and their lives quickly take a most sinister and dangerous turn as they find themselves hunted by an unspeakable evil...

Them

Ray Sanders returns home from Florida to bury his mother.

Soon, the supernatural evidence behind his mother's demise begins to surface in the form of dreams and mysterious happenings.

During all of the madness, Sanders must face his destiny and vanquish the generations-old evil that has plagued his family since the 1800's...

In 1854, Louis Sanders, with the help of Elias Atkins, dug a well to provide water to the family farm. What they did not anticipate was the water to be infested with Odomulites - ancient sins. These malevolent beings - were trapped in our world on their way to the spirit world - formed a pact of protection with both Sanders and Atkins; the families would serve as guardians of the Odomulite nests and in return, a blind eye would be cast when the Odomulites took host bodies to inhabit and feed upon. It was this pact, which in 2016 would propel Sanders and Julie Fontaine - a young woman with a special connection to the Spirit World - into the heart of the last active nest to rid the town of its insidious Odomulite population.

Southern House

"Move over Slenderman, there's a whole new reason to be afraid of the dark!"

There are some places that lie where the barrier between worlds is thin and growing thinner. These corridors are as old as the Earth itself, hidden in dark and forgotten places, waiting to be found. There is a being who stalks these places and travels between those worlds. He was given the name Mr. Shift by generations of children and madmen. Just as Hickory Grimble hits rock bottom, he inherits his grandparents' farm and believes his luck is changing. He soon finds he inherited more than money and land. Haunted by his own inner demons, now he has new problems. He begins to see strange creatures on the dark, sprawling acreage, animals that have no business living in middle Tennessee. He also discovers a decrepit, abandoned house in the forest that never seems to be in the same place twice. Balanced on a razor's edge between, addiction and fate, Hick is now face to face with an ancient evil that has returned once more to claim more of the town's children.

Worship Me

Something is listening to the prayers of St. Paul's United Church, but it's not the god they asked for; it's something much, much older.

A quiet Sunday service turns into a living hell when this ancient entity descends upon the house of worship and claims the congregation for its own.
The terrified churchgoers must now prove their loyalty to their new god by giving it one of their children or in two days time it will return and destroy them all.

As fear rips the congregation apart, it becomes clear that if they're to survive this untold horror, the faithful must become the faithless and enter into a battle against God itself.

But as time runs out, they discover that true monsters come not from heaven or hell...
...they come from within.

These Walls Don't Talk, They Scream

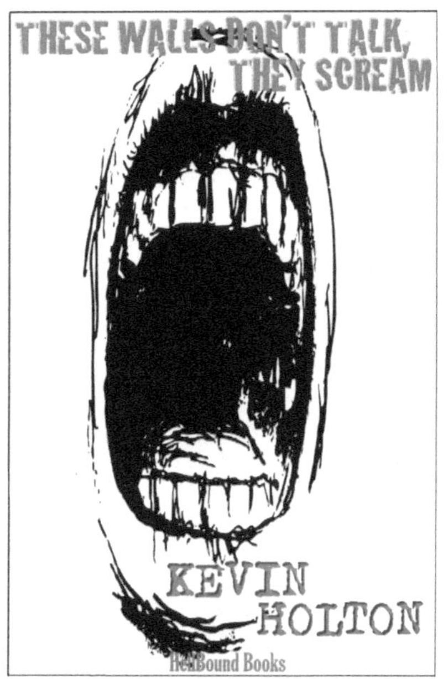

When three-year-old Charlotte witnessed her mother's death and was left alone with the body, she began hearing the voice of a person living in the walls of her house.

This voice comforted her as best it could, guiding her to call 9-1-1. Twenty five years later, Charlotte has returned with her own family to reconnect with this presence.

The recent death of her son leaves her distracted and mourning, though, so she doesn't realize her daughter can hear this entity too.

The Children of Hydesville

When the malevolent entity that Maggie and Katie Fox unleashed in Hydesville in 1848 returns in 2018, it must be stopped - at all costs. Manhattanites Derek David and his wife Edith receive an invitation to visit the Keilgarden Colony, a secluded community located five hours north of the city in the village of Hydesville. Dedicated to nurturing children with psychic abilities, the colony was built in 1948 on land that includes the cottage where Maggie and Katie Fox first heard the ghostly rappings in 1848 - which started the Spiritualist movement.

But what begins as a late-summer respite swiftly turns into a confusing and terrifying ordeal as Derek and Edith experience increasingly bizarre and disturbing events, which drives Derek to set fire to the Fox house.

Months later, New York Times reporter Sheila Irving and her boyfriend, Kevin Jackson, visit Hydesville to investigate Derek's motivation. If those gathered in the village succumb to the powerful entity that controls the area, they will partake in the creation of union children - psychically gifted offspring whose malevolent powers will reach far beyond the confines of the small township.

Schlock! Horror!

An anthology of short stories based upon/inspired by and in loving homage to all of those great gorefest movies and books of the 1980's - that golden age when horror well and truly came kicking, screaming and spraying blood, gore & body parts out from the shadows... It was the decade that brought us everything in the cinema and on VHS from the Italian 'nasties' to *Elm Street, The Lost Boys, Hellraiser, The Thing, Day of the Dead, Reanimator, Return of the Living Dead, My Bloody Valentine, Henry: Portrait of a Serial Killer, Cannibal Holocaust*....and superlative directors such as David Cronenburg, John Waters, Roger Corman and - of course - Clive Barker.

All of this was, naturally, reflected in the books we devoured - Guy N Smith, Clive Barker's *Books of Blood*, James Herbert, Jack Ketchum, Gary Brandner and Richard Laymon, to name but a mere handful.

This 80's themed/inspired tales of terror is compiled by one Mr. **Bret McCormick**, himself a writer, producer and director of many a schlock classic, including *Bio-Tech Warrior, Time Tracers, The Abomination, Ozone: The Attack of the Redneck Mutants* and the inimitable *Repligator*.

A HellBound Books LLC Publication

http://www.hellboundbookspublishing.com

Printed in the United States of America